Temperature's Rising

Temperature's Rising

Karen Kelley

BRAVA

KENSINGTON PUBLISHING CORP.
http://www.kensingtonbooks.com

BRAVA BOOKS are published by

Kensington Publishing Corp.
850 Third Avenue
New York, NY 10022

All Kensington titles, imprints and distributed lines are available at special quantity discounts for bulk purchases for sales promotion, premiums, fundraising, educational or institutional use.

Special book excerpts or customized printings can also be created to fit specific needs. For details, write or phone the office of the Kensington Special Sales Manager: Kensington Publishing Corp., 850 Third Avenue, New York, NY 10022. Attn. Special Sales Department. Phone: 1-800-221-2647.

Brava and the B logo Reg. U.S. Pat. & TM Off.

ISBN 0-7582-1170-8

First Kensington Trade Paperback Printing: October 2005
10 9 8 7 6 5 4 3 2 1

Printed in the United States of America

This book is dedicated to my son-in-law, Special Agent Skip Wheeler. I admire your courage and strength. The word "can't" isn't part of your vocabulary. You are a true hero.

To my father-in-law, Charles Kelley, who says If you want it bad enough then don't let anything hold you back.

To Mary Duncan, longtime friend and writing buddy. My life is so much richer because of you.

To Angie Kappel, friend and fan. Thanks for showing up at my book signings!

Chapter 1

Jessica Nelson was out to impress only one person today. It was going to be a damn good impression. She wouldn't settle for anything less.

She adjusted her rearview mirror and caught a glimpse of her reflection. One eyebrow cocked upward. She could easily see herself as the poster girl for female real estate agents across the country. *I am woman, hear me roar!*

John Bitters *would* make an offer for the property and she'd prove to her family once and for all she could make it in a job outside law enforcement, the fire department, and the blasted medical field. She'd turned in her badge . . . and made the right decision.

Her hands tightened on the steering wheel. Yes, it *was* the right decision.

"You are a female," she told herself with conviction. "No more uniforms. No more guns. No more being *Jess*, one of the guys." She drew in a deep breath—just like the spiritualist had taught her on the discounted CD she'd found in a bookstore bin. "Yom-da-da-da-da-da."

This was her day to shine.

POP! Psssssstttttttt! Thump—thump—thump—thump . . .

She flinched. Or maybe not.

Damn! Not today. She slapped her turn signal on and limped her car into a vacant parking lot. No, not today of all days. She eased her foot down on the brake and when the car jerked to a stop, shifted into Park. Great, she thought as she glanced around. The streets were practically deserted on this side of town, and she knew why: broken windows, bottles, and graffiti decorated the buildings. If she called a service station it would be at least an hour before anyone showed up.

One glance at her watch and she began twisting the top button on her blouse. She was supposed to meet John in ten minutes. She had everything timed so she wouldn't appear overeager to sell him the property. Now, she was going to be late.

Deep breaths. Calm. She closed her eyes. "Yom-da-da-da . . ."

Oh, screw it. She'd just change the damn tire, and if she was late, she'd apologize. It wasn't as if she hadn't changed a tire before. Maybe growing up with mostly male cousins and a brother hadn't been *that* horrible. She'd come away with a few useful talents.

She opened the door, grabbed her keys out of the ignition, and hit the button that popped the trunk. Good thing she had a spare—even if it was the doughnut. The smaller tire would get her to her appointment, then to a service station.

She cringed as she strode past the flat tire. They were practically new.

Once she was at the back of the car, she raised the trunk and leaned inside, flipping aside the gray carpet so she could get to the spare. You'd think the manufacturer would . . .

"Hey, baby. I like what you're showing me so far, but I think you can do better than that."

She stilled.

"The lady looks sweet, Frankie. Maybe she wants to party with us."

Her father would tell her it was her own fault. She'd taken a shortcut to get to the property, right through the seediest part of town.

"Come on, baby, show us what you got."

She shrugged. If that's what he wanted. She slid her hand

to the right, lifting the lid off the small, wooden box that she always kept in the trunk of whatever car she owned at the time. It was a gift from Daddy on her sixteenth birthday eleven years ago, along with the 9mm.

"Maybe she don't hear so good." His voice hardened. "We want to see more, *baby*."

The gun felt good in her hand—almost like an old friend. She turned, pointing the barrel at them. "And just what exactly do you want to see, boys? The bullets? I have a full clip. I can show you a hell of a lot more than you expected to see."

They paled.

Ah, Jessica, shame on you. They couldn't be more than seventeen, and wearing baggy pants that showed more than half their dingy underwear. They didn't look like gang members. At least, they didn't wear the colors. She sighed. But if they wanted to play with the big boys—or in her case, girl, then they had to take the consequences.

They raised their hands and backed away. "Hey, lady, we didn't mean nothin'." His laugh was more like a high-pitched squeak.

"Yeah, lady. We were just jokin' around."

She twirled the gun once, not an easy feat with a loaded 9mm, bent her knees, and waved the gun back and forth between them, making the face that always scared the hell out of her cousins when they were growing up. It was a cross between sucking on a lemon and baring her teeth all at the same time. "I just got out of a mental institution. Maybe I *would* like to play. What say, boys?" She began to twitch her right eye, then her shoulder. "Are you up for a little Russian roulette? But I get to hold the gun."

"Shit!" They turned and took off so fast she'd be surprised if they hadn't broken some kind of speed record.

She shook her head. "Kids." Apparently they didn't want to play, after all. She laughed. Her gaze fell on her watch. Damn! She had to be at the property in five minutes. She replaced her gun, and brought out the jack.

By the time she'd loosened the lug nuts she was hot and sweaty. It was worth the few seconds it took to toss her jacket into the backseat. *Better.* Cooler, if nothing else. She glanced at her watch: one minute before her meeting.

"Hurry, hurry, hurry." She tugged on the punctured tire. It came off with a whoosh. *Rip!* She landed on her butt with a splat.

The tearing sound couldn't have been her skirt. Not good. Her pulse quickened.

"Yom-da-da-da-da." Deep breaths. She could almost hear the spiritualist's soothing voice, like gentle rain on a tin roof, *"Relax the mind, then the body."*

Assess the situation, she told herself. With one eye closed, she glanced down. She jerked her head up. *Don't hyperventilate!* It wasn't *that* bad. The slit in the side of her skirt was only . . . only a few inches higher. She twisted her button, wanting to scream. No, she wouldn't scream.

She was a big girl—having a really bad fucking day!

Okay, she could get through this. Gathering her wits, and her dignity, she stood. All was not lost . . . if she hurried. She grabbed the smaller tire and slapped it on, throwing all her one hundred and twenty pounds into tightening the lug bolts.

Ten minutes later, she put the bad tire in the trunk, and pulled out of the parking lot. Her gaze moved to the dash clock. If nothing else slowed her down she might not miss her appointment. Any normal person would wait a few minutes.

She glanced in the rearview mirror and flinched. So much for looking professional. Ten minutes in a bathroom would do wonders for her appearance, but she just couldn't spare the time. She wiped her hand across the smudge on her cheek. Her lipstick was gone, and she'd lost the clip that had held her hair in its tidy little French twist. She could live with loose hair. She just wasn't sure about the run in her hose. Okay, more like the Boston Marathon.

After all this, John better be waiting.

The closer she got to the downtown property, the slower

traffic became as people rushed home from work. The minutes ticked by until finally, she pulled behind the property and parked her car.

Jessica rushed around to the front of the building, smoothing her hands down the sides of her skirt. She was only twenty-five minutes late. Maybe John was still waiting.

The sidewalk was empty. No one waited.

Damn! Damn! And double damn! She strode up and down the sidewalk, twisting the top button on her blouse and frowning.

I've probably lost the sale.

This couldn't possibly be happening to her . . . Okay, so maybe she didn't have the best luck in the world. But today?

She drew in a deep breath to calm her jangled nerves and inhaled the acidic taste of fumes from the rush-hour traffic. Her eyes were already starting to water from the noxious odor.

Her gaze skimmed the commercial district of White Plains, or at least what she could see of it. Not one blue car zoomed past. Every color in the rainbow except blue.

Come on, John, show up!

The ink wasn't even dry on her real estate license. This would really impress her boss, and her family was already taking bets she'd return to the force within six months. Her pride wouldn't let it happen, but if John didn't show in the next ten minutes, she'd be forced to grovel and hope he'd reschedule. She'd wanted this sale to go smoothly. Stupid flat tire . . .

As she strode up the sidewalk, she caught her reflection in the plate-glass window. Her belly flip-flopped. She slowly walked closer. Oh, this was really bad. She furiously twisted her button in the opposite direction. If the slit were any higher, she'd be arrested.

Good thing her father was the police chief.

She almost laughed, but remembered her predicament and sobered. This was no time for hysteria.

Okay, think. Troy had told her that his brother John would meet her at the property around five-thirty. She glanced at her watch. *After six.* Had he already been here and left?

Exhaling a sigh of regret, she walked to the small parking area behind the building where she'd left her car and unlocked the door. Maybe Troy would know something.

Grabbing her cell phone, she dropped her keys inside her purse and made herself comfortable on the seat, then punched in Troy's number.

Nothing.

Dead.

Great. What was this—Friday the thirteenth? As she stood, she tossed the cell phone in the seat and slammed the door.

It only took her a couple of seconds to realize the door was locked and her keys were in her purse, which had slid to the floorboard when she sat down.

Take a deep breath, she told herself. "Yom da-da-da-fucking-da!"

She strode back to the street front, trying to regain her composure with each step she took. *Think positive.*

Maybe John Bitters hadn't arrived yet. He'd probably show up in a few minutes, they'd laugh about her absolutely horrendous day, she'd sell the property and make a big commission. She'd prove to her family she could do her job and do it well. She rubbed her fingers over the smooth surface of the button, twisting the other way as she sought composure, peace, and tranquility. Anything that would calm her freakin' nerves!

Deep breaths. She inhaled, and coughed. No, bad idea. Her throat was already getting scratchy and her eyes were watering from inhaling fumes.

Think about something peaceful. Like where she would vacation when she got her first big check. A cruise, maybe. In fact, her commission would probably be at least . . .

The imitation pearl button came loose in her hand. Her gaze dropped to her white blouse and the amount of cleavage that showed. At the rate she was going, the damn cruise ship would blow up if she were aboard.

Her boobs were practically spilling out. She looked like a slut. Oh lord, she didn't want to look like a slut.

When she'd gotten dressed this morning, she'd looked like a professional real estate agent: crisp, black skirt; a white blouse with little imitation pearl buttons; heels; and a tailored black jacket. She'd even combed her hair into a sleek twist. Damn, she'd looked good. And now her clothes were ripped and dirty.

The longer she stared at her reflection in the window, the worse it became. She finally dragged her gaze away, no longer able to look at her reflection, and walked back to the curb. No two ways about it, she looked like a slut. If John Bitters did arrive, she'd be the last person he'd want to buy property from. He'd probably run away as fast . . .

A blue Oldsmobile pulled to the curb.

Oh, crap! Troy had told her that his brother drove a blue car. She thought he'd said Lincoln, though. Whatever. She scrubbed her hands across her watery eyes, brushed her hair behind her ears, and pasted a smile on her face. At least she hadn't entirely blown the sale . . . yet. He turned the engine off, opened his door, and stepped out.

Tall and dark. He fit the description she'd been given. She smiled. Friendly, that's how she wanted to appear. Like they'd known each other for a while, rather than just meeting for the first time. Real Estate 101— Be their best friend.

"John?" She inwardly winced. She'd inhaled so many fumes that her voice was raspy. No time to worry about that now. *Shake it off. You're a professional.* She walked closer, smile widening.

The man hesitated before he walked around the front of his car toward the sidewalk where she stood. Jessica gave him a quick once-over. Then went back for seconds. Troy certainly hadn't mentioned scrumptious, sexy, and downright delicious. Not that he would think of his brother like that.

Her gaze blazed a trail past wide shoulders and across a broad chest covered by a maroon polo shirt before her glance slid downward.

Liquid heat coursed through her veins. There was just something about a man who wore his jeans low on his hips. It was almost as if he were telling the world he didn't really give a damn, and telling women he could fulfill their every desire.

His jeans pulled taut across nicely developed muscles as a booted foot stepped to the sidewalk. Drawing in a ragged breath, she forced her gaze back to his face, and the knowing look in his eyes.

Oops. Caught staring.

She mentally shrugged. As sexy as he was, he should be used to appreciative looks from women.

"How much?" His roughly textured words scraped across her skin, leaving a heated flush in its wake.

Her thighs trembled. "You don't waste any time, do you?"

"We both know what I want."

"Wouldn't you like to see it first?" Did he turn a little red? She mentally shook her head. It was probably just the way the sun had hit his face.

He cleared his throat. "Why not get the trivial details out of the way? Then we can . . . concentrate on other things."

His rich, southern drawl wrapped around her, causing a small earthquake inside her body. Three leisurely steps and he stood in front of her. Slowly, his gaze slid over her, lingering, touching, caressing.

At least six feet four inches of raw male magnetism invaded her space. She inhaled and caught the scent of his musky aftershave. Much nicer than car fumes.

Pull yourself together. Business before pleasure. Yeah, right, at this rate she'd give him the damn property and take the payment out in trade. Okay, deep breath. Jeez, what brand of aftershave was that? *Pheromones for Men?* She couldn't think with him this close. Turning away, she walked a short distance down the sidewalk to clear her muddled brain.

Think about the property.

The building was nice. Not too large. Taxes were low. Only single-story, but it would make a great travel agency, which is what Troy said his brother wanted.

White stone pillars gave the small, commercial building a more prestigious appearance. She bit her bottom lip. Some of the ceiling tiles needed to be changed—water damage, but the owner had replaced the roof. A couple of the interior walls had rather large, gaping holes, though. In fact, the inside of the building needed a major overhaul. Personally, she thought the asking price a little steep, but the facts remained: it was in a prime location, the Texas town was growing, and this district had the fastest rate of improvement.

Only one teensy-tiny problem.

The eyesore across the street. Triple X's flashed on the marquee of what used to be an old movie theater. If that wasn't bad enough, three scantily clad ladies had arrived a few minutes ago to stand on the corner. She grimaced. That wasn't good.

At least there were only three this evening. Two blondes, and she wasn't positive, but the third hooker's hair color looked deep purple. The one in question raised her hand and waved.

As unobtrusively as possible, Jessica motioned for them to leave. One cast her a grin and flashed a little leg. Great. She could see her sale gurgling as it choked its way down the drain.

Oh lord, he was probably staring at them right now. Maybe she could redirect his attention away from the *women of the night*, and focus it on the property once again.

She wheeled around.

His gaze riveted on her chest.

Well, her boobs practically thrown in his face had certainly drawn his attention.

Her hand automatically fluttered toward the next button before she stopped the nervous habit from making her more exposed. She pointedly cleared her throat. He didn't seem in any hurry to raise his head or appear a bit embarrassed at being caught staring.

"Two hundred," she stated, ignoring the little flare of desire that swept through her, and concentrated on the matter at hand. She wanted this sale. And actually, two hundred thousand wasn't a *bad* asking price for the land and building. She bit her bottom lip and waited for his reply.

Damn, he was cute. Why did he have to be such a distraction? Maybe they could get together after the deal was final. She inwardly smiled as naughty thoughts filled her head. She could easily picture them naked in bed, bodies pressed against each other. She sighed, wondering what he thought of her.

Conor Richmond thought the woman in front of him looked a little desperate. He wondered why she worked the streets. He figured her more for a high-priced call girl than a street hooker.

New in town, maybe? Like him?

Except she wanted to start a business. And the way she looked, it wouldn't take her long to have a whole string of Johns begging for her favors and willing to shell out more than a couple of hundred dollars. If she cleaned up a little, that is, and bought some decent clothes. Her hose were ripped so bad she'd do better without them, and her skirt looked like she'd dug it out of the Salvation Army trash bin.

What had driven her to this way of life? Drugs? Her eyes were a little red-rimmed. She *could* be a user, although he didn't see any track marks running up her arms.

But underneath the smudge of dirt on her face and the worn clothes, he saw a sensuous woman, and he had a hell of a time keeping his gaze from straying. The amount of cleavage showing beckoned him to bury his face in her lush curves.

The view only got better. Her long, silky legs drew his attention even if her hose were shredded. They were the kind of legs made to wrap around a man. Pulling him deeper and deeper inside her hot body. Yeah, she was made for sex. The kind that got down and dirty.

A carload of boys driving by whistled and honked their horn. She looked momentarily distracted, then tossed a saucy grin in their direction as they laughed and sped down the street.

The smile transformed her face. Meant to pull an unsuspecting male into her web. He wasn't immune to her charms any more than the next poor sucker would be. But he wasn't her next customer, either. Sometimes he hated his job.

"Don't you think two hundred's a little steep?" he asked.

She wet her lips, her gaze returning to his. A temptress. Conor inwardly groaned.

"Not for what you'll get."

The way she said the words, kind of husky, made him wish just for a few hours he could pretend he wasn't a cop. Made him wish he hadn't seen her standing on the sidewalk. And made him wish that for a moment he hadn't thought she looked out of place and vulnerable.

Man, had he misjudged. She was a pro, all right. Her sultry eyes promised sinful delights. His gaze was drawn to her low-cut blouse when her hand moved toward the buttons . . . just as the gesture was meant to do.

His vision clouded as he remembered the way she'd walked down the sidewalk. Hell, how could he forget! Hips swaying seductively, and the way she'd slowly turned back around so he could see what he'd be giving up if she chose to keep going. He'd burned all the way down to his boots. No, she knew exactly what she did to him.

"And what will I get for my money?" he asked, wanting her to spell it out.

Her eyes widened innocently. "Why, everything, of course."

Sliding his hand into his pocket, he emerged with a roll of

crisp, green bills. Thumbing them, he drew two out and handed them to her. She took the money—looking a little confused, he thought—but decided it was part of her act. He pocketed the rest.

"A down payment?" she asked, staring at the bills.

Figured. She knew she had him by the balls. Why not twist a little harder? Get as much of his cash as she could.

"Is that okay?" He stepped forward. So near, her scent washed over him, bathing him with erotic fantasies. She might look like she'd been sleeping in the streets, but she smelled oh-so-sweet. She raised her head. Her lips so close. So kissable. He ached to pull her into his arms and see if her mouth was as hot as it looked.

"I . . . suppose."

Too bad.

In one swift motion, he reached behind him, drew the handcuffs from the leather case hooked to his belt, and snapped them shut over her wrists.

A damn shame he couldn't have met her in another place. He had a gut feeling they would've been good together.

"Lady, you're under arrest for solicitation."

Chapter 2

"What the hell are you doing?" Jessica demanded, glancing down at her wrists, handcuffed in front of her.

"I'm a cop . . . Officer Conor Richmond. You have the right to remain silent . . ."

Damn, *not* John, Troy's brother. Oh hell, he'd probably thought she'd been looking for a *John*. She frowned. "I'm familiar with the Miranda Warning."

"I just bet you are." He finished it anyway.

Smart-ass.

Her father had mentioned a new officer when she'd had lunch with him last Sunday. In fact, all he'd talked about was how he'd like them to meet. The name Conor Richmond sounded embarrassingly familiar.

He tugged her toward his car. The three women across the street started yelling obscenities and laughing. Great, an audience. Her brow creased. They might come in handy if she needed their help, though.

"I'm not going anywhere with you, Buster." She dug in her heels. "Just because you claim to be a cop, it doesn't make you one. You're out of uniform, and I've never seen you before." She wanted to see some identification.

He reached in his back pocket and pulled out a thin, brown wallet. Flipping it open, he flashed a badge and ID.

"Here's your proof."

She read the bold print under his picture. Officer Conor Richmond. The license looked legit. Okay, so this *was* the new man on the force.

When he looked at her, her pulse skipped a beat. She sighed deeply. His gaze strayed to her chest again. Her nipples tightened in response.

Too bad she'd sworn never to get involved with a cop. If she didn't want to be one, then she damn well didn't want to have a relationship with one, either. But it might've been nice having him pressed against her. Feeling the ripple of each sinewy muscle beneath her hands as she explored his body.

Apparently, he wasn't immune to her, either. In fact, he reminded her of a little boy with his nose pressed against the glass of a candy store window. He suddenly shifted his feet and cleared his throat.

"It won't work." He met her gaze. "And just because you've been arrested a few times doesn't mean you know all the officers. This *is* my first week, though."

She didn't mention she'd figured that one out. Her father had extolled the new officer's qualities until she'd eventually tuned him out. She frowned. He'd blatantly hinted Officer Richmond happened to be single. Her father hadn't described him, though.

Not the sexy green eyes or the thick black hair or the way a woman would ache to run her hands over his firm, muscled body.

She cleared her mind when she realized the direction her thoughts had strayed. Her father had only mentioned his name. Maybe he should have listed the officer's other qualities as well?

No, no, no! She wasn't about to get involved with a cop.

"What won't work?" she wanted to know as she refocused her attention.

"Trying to seduce me."

Oh really! His ego was slightly inflated.

The situation was too funny. She'd love to see his expression when he hauled her in front of her father with handcuffs . . .

No, that would be cruel. She quickly dismissed the thought scampering across her brain, but it popped right back up.

A quirky sense of humor ran in her family, so it wasn't her fault that all sorts of possibilities were going through her mind. You might even call it an inherited trait. Totally out of her control. And right now she really couldn't help herself, and besides, she did need a ride since her car was locked.

Lowering her voice, she said, "Is that what I'm attempting to do?" She slid her tongue slowly over her upper lip. "Seduce you?"

His mouth parted slightly and he swallowed. The air sizzled between them as his gaze swept over her, raw and hungry. It started at her shoulders and moved downward, touching her breasts and causing her nipples to ache.

Slowly his gaze lowered. She caught her breath when it lingered on her hips, before moving downward. Her legs trembled with the need to feel him pressed between them.

The radio in the front seat crackled with static.

She expelled her breath in a whoosh and shifted from one foot to the other. Furiously, she began twisting the second button on her blouse. When the cuffs jangled, she jerked her hands down. Damn habit!

Okay, this game had gone on long enough. Time to end it. "You've made a mistake. In fact, you couldn't be more wrong. My name is Jessica Ne . . ."

"You can tell it all to the chief."

Stubborn man! She opened her mouth, then snapped it shut. Fine, she hadn't talked to her father since last Sunday, so she'd be able to kill two birds with one stone. He was always saying she didn't visit him at the office enough.

Reaching through the open window on the passenger side, Conor grabbed the microphone off the seat. "One-fifty-six will be in route with a ten-ninety-five in custody."

He looked over his shoulder. She followed his gaze, but the other three women had quickly departed.

"Your friends got lucky this time," he told her.

"They're not my friends."

"Don't try to deny it. I saw you wave at them."

She didn't try to explain she'd been attempting to wave them away so they wouldn't lower the property values. He probably wouldn't believe her anyway.

The radio crackled. "Received one-fifty-six." He dropped the mike in the seat and opened the back door.

Jessica hesitated. He must have thought she'd do something foolish, like try to run, because he took a firmer grip on her arm.

"Do you want to go to the station the easy way, or the hard?"

The officer was starting to annoy her. She batted her lashes and in her sexiest voice said, "Oh, the easy way, of course. I'd hate to think I'd made anything hard on you."

His brow creased into tiny lines.

"If you think you're being cute, think again. Maybe you don't realize just how much trouble you're in."

"This isn't my first trip to the police station." Jessica tossed her blond hair over her shoulder, winked, and eased down onto the light blue vinyl seat.

"Why do you do it?" he asked, his tone suddenly serious as he leaned forward.

She turned. Their faces were only inches apart. His lips were set in a grim line. This charade needed to end here and now.

"Listen, this isn't what you think . . ." she began, only to be interrupted.

"I won't change my mind."

If that's the way he wanted it. At least no one could say she hadn't tried to warn him. She shrugged. "A girl has to make a living somehow." She was almost certain she'd regret that remark.

With a look of disgust, Conor slammed the door. She tried to stop the grin from spreading across her face, but couldn't. Maybe if she hadn't known what to expect. If she'd been just a little frightened, things might have been different. But, Jessica had a good idea what would transpire once they arrived at the station.

A niggle of guilt tickled her spine, but she ignored it. She hadn't instigated any of this. What happened would serve him right for not letting her explain the situation. She glanced down at her clothes. Okay, so maybe some of it was her fault, but she certainly hadn't awakened this morning and decided to end her day looking slutty and getting arrested.

He opened the door on the driver's side and climbed behind the wheel. The car purred to life when he turned the key. After looking to make sure it was clear, he eased into traffic.

"You know, there's no reason for you to continue in this line of work."

Jessica met his gaze in the rearview mirror. He had the deepest, darkest green eyes she'd ever seen. They grabbed her, making it hard to look away. Not that she tried.

"I bet there's a lot of things you'd be qualified for," he continued, making a left at the stoplight.

"You mean—*me?*" She quirked an eyebrow.

"Sure." He turned his attention back to the road and took the entrance to the freeway, increasing his speed as he merged with the flow of traffic.

She'd seen the expression on his face. Like he was preparing himself to explain the *real* facts of life. She'd only heard it all a zillion times from her father ever since she'd reached high-school age: the importance of being a productive citizen.

Year after year, the same tired speech, even though she was twenty-seven years old. Why did all cops want to save the world? Officer Richmond didn't appear any different.

And real estate was a good, honest profession, even if it wasn't the job her father wanted for her. She'd tried it his way, but it hadn't worked out.

They passed the mall and garden center. Well, it would be over soon. They were almost to the station.

Maybe she really should attempt to explain one more time that she wasn't a hooker. He was new in town. What would it hurt to cut him a little slack?

Ah, what the heck? If she did convince him that her profession was perfectly legal, the fun would end before it ever really started. And she wanted to see Conor's expression when he discovered who she was. Her father had a great sense of humor so he'd get a good laugh out of it.

"I bet there are a lot of jobs you'd be good at," he continued. "And all legal. You could be a waitress or care for the elderly."

And here she'd thought her college degree showed. She frowned and glanced downward, turning her foot to the side. Maybe it was her three-inch black heels? In her profession, sensible loafers would work better, but she had a fetish for shoes—heels being on the top of her list. They made her feel like a lady, even if they were murder on her feet and it'd taken a month of practicing to walk in the blasted things.

He looked like he expected her to comment on his brilliant idea. She knew her sarcasm would be lost on him. "Or what about a high-powered real estate agent who sells expensive properties and makes a bundle on commissions?" A little stretch of the truth. She hadn't made a bundle of money yet. The sale of the commercial property would've been her first major deal.

"Well . . . yeah." Slowing, he exited on Rifle Road. "But you'd probably have to go back to school. The main thing is the life you're leading can get you killed."

"Ha! And yours won't?"

"That's different."

When she opened her mouth to argue, he sent her a quelling look. She clamped her lips together.

He turned his signal light on and pulled into the parking lot in front of the red brick police station. She noted that most of the day shift had left. There were only five patrol cars and around ten personal vehicles. Jessica knew who owned three of the cars.

Officer Richmond didn't speak again until he'd pulled to a stop and helped her out. "I really hate doing this, but it's my job. Someday you might even thank me."

Yeah, but he'd kill her. "Listen, Officer Richmond, I've been trying to explain something to you. I really don't think you want to do this. It will hurt you a lot more than me . . ."

"Don't make this harder than it already is."

Her gaze lowered naughtily. It didn't appear to be, but she could change that if given a moment alone with him.

His grip tightened on her elbow as he led her down the hedge-lined sidewalk and up a short flight of steps. After opening the double glass doors, he nudged her shoulder so she'd go inside.

"Okay, it's your funeral," she muttered, stepping into the cool interior of the building. Her heels clicked across the black-and-white tiled floor.

The dispatcher, seated behind a smudged glass window, casually raised her head. The widening of her eyes was the only indication that everything wasn't quite right.

Mike Winslow stepped from one of the closed rooms. He barely spared them a glance as he looked at the report in his hand.

"Hi, Jess. Conor," he absently mumbled.

Mike suddenly stumbled, his head jerking up.

"Hello," she answered between clenched teeth. The look she sent in his direction had him snapping his mouth shut and continuing on without saying a word.

"You know Mike?" Conor asked with obvious surprise.

"We used to sleep together." Okay, she'd probably pay for that remark, too, but she couldn't help it. Her father always said she had a mischievous streak a mile wide. It wasn't really a lie. She and Mike *had* slept together. Of course, she'd left out the fact she'd been three, Mike four, and they were second cousins.

"Do you also know he's married?"

"Oh, yeah." She should. They'd gotten married February fourteenth and she'd been one of the bridesmaids. Ugh! His wife had chosen the ugliest red bridesmaids' dresses and huge red straw hats adorned with red feathers. Her colors had been red and redder. The church had looked like the St. Valentine Day Massacre, but the only thing that truly mattered was Mike's happiness. She would've worn a dress made of burlap if it made her cousin and new cousin-in-law happy.

But Officer Richmond didn't look pleased by her admission she'd slept with Mike. His lips thinned as they turned a corner and started down a long, narrow hallway wide enough for only two and a half people. Offices opened on either side, but most of the doors were locked, the men and women having left for the day.

They were taking the shortcut.

Jessica caught her breath when her Aunt Gloria rounded the corner with a stack of papers in her hands.

Her soft brown hair was neatly combed away from her face, and she wore a blue print dress that looked new. Jessica liked the way it brought out the color of her eyes.

Her aunt glanced up, down, then her head jerked up again. Her gaze strayed to the missing button on Jessica's blouse. "I told you playing with buttons would get you in trouble some day."

Jessica pleaded with her eyes for her aunt not to say anything.

"What?" Conor asked.

Her aunt countered with her own question. "What'd she do?"

"Soliciting." His voice was gruff, almost like he hated being the bearer of bad news.

Aunt Gloria's lips twitched. "You know, if you'd wanted a man there are other ways to go about it."

Jessica crossed her eyes, wanting her aunt to pick up the game. She shouldn't have worried. Aunt Gloria was a Nelson, after all.

With an impish gleam, the older woman shifted the papers to her other arm. "I bet the chief will want to talk to her. This isn't her first trip to the station."

"So she told me. You'd think she'd pick a different profession. I was taking her to lock-up, though."

"No, I'm sure the chief will want to see this prisoner personally. Follow me." She turned.

"You don't have to come with us. I remember where his office is," Conor informed her.

"Don't mind a bit." She continued down the hall, bumped the door to her office open with her hip, set the papers down on an already crowded desk, and sauntered to the chief's door.

She rapped her knuckles on the opaque glass and without waiting for an answer, opened the door. "The new officer brought you a criminal, Chief."

"Do what?" He'd begun to stand when they entered. "What the . . ." His salt-and-pepper eyebrows drew together, forming a single line.

Jessica pulled away from the officer and strolled over to him. "Well, hello, sugar. Seems like forever since I saw you, but we both know it was only last Sunday, don't we?" She winked at Conor. Then kissed her father on the cheek.

Chapter 3

The way the hooker leaned close to the chief made Conor want to throw up. This job had appealed to him because of the family-like atmosphere. Boy, had he been fooled!

He glanced around the office. Hell, the chief even had ivy growing along the windowsill. He'd assumed the pictures on his desk were family, even though he hadn't seen the faces. A man like that didn't keep a mistress young enough to be his daughter, even if he was widowed.

But if this hooker had corrupted his boss, and Mike, then the whole blasted precinct was probably crooked. He grimaced. Not that he could really blame them. Her body begged for a man to pull her close, tangle his hands in the soft waves of her blond hair, lower his mouth to her lips and taste the sensuous pleasures she had to offer.

"What's the matter, Officer Richmond? Cat got your tongue?"

Her throaty purr brought him out of his stupor. He planted his hands on his hips and glared at her while murderous thoughts ran through his head.

That's why she hadn't looked worried about being run in. Hell, she probably hopped from one officer's bed to the next. She'd been laughing at him all the way to the station.

"Okay," the chief began, holding the handcuffs by the center chain and raising them. "Anyone care to explain these?"

Taking a key from his desk drawer, he unlocked the cuffs and tossed them toward Conor.

He deftly caught them. This job had been nice while it lasted. He replaced his cuffs and waited for the axe to fall. It didn't take long.

"He arrested me." Honey dripped from her words.

His cheeks puffed out. "For what?"

Any minute he expected the chief to explode. Well, he didn't have anything to lose now. "I thought that would be obvious," he commented dryly.

"Solicitation," Gloria supplied in a matter-of-fact tone.

"A woman of the streets," the hooker elaborated.

"Solici . . . Woman of the . . ." He coughed and sputtered.

Gloria hurried to the water dispenser by the door and filled a cup.

"Here, drink this." She handed him the cold liquid.

He swallowed the water and crumpled the cup. "Now, let me get this straight." Thoughtfully, he looked at each person in the room before tossing the cup into the wastebasket beside his desk. It hit the rim and fell inside.

"Two points," the two women spoke in unison.

He frowned at them, and they immediately became interested in their shoes. Something didn't fit, but he couldn't put his finger on what it was about the situation that didn't quite click.

"You arrested her for soliciting?" the chief asked, drawing Conor's attention.

"Yes, sir." He wouldn't deny it.

When the chief began to laugh, Conor couldn't take any more. If he wanted to fire him, that was fine, but he wouldn't let the man throw a street hooker in his face, no matter how great she looked. He spun around. It wouldn't take him long to empty his locker.

"What's the matter, Officer Richmond?"

Her heels hadn't made a sound on the deep brown carpet,

but his nostrils twitched when he caught the scent of her sensuous fragrance. It held enough mystery and allure that all he could think about was turning around and pulling her into his arms. So maybe he didn't blame the chief for falling under her spell.

"Is it getting a little warm in here?"

His hand stilled on the doorknob. Yeah, with her body this close, it did feel too damn hot in the room.

"That's enough of the games, Jess. You two go play somewhere else. I've got work to do."

Go play! Conor slowly turned and stared at the older man. Was he sharing his hooker? This had to be the most bizarre . . .

"Oh, Dad, you're no fun anymore. And he did arrest me for solicitation. Aren't you going to defend my honor?"

"Dad?" Conor choked.

They glanced in his direction. The same smoky-blue eyes twinkled back at him. Why hadn't he noticed all three sets of eyes were the same shade? His stomach rumbled uncomfortably.

The chair behind the chief's desk creaked when he took his seat. "If I defended your honor every time you got into trouble I wouldn't have time to arrest the real criminals."

Jessica gave a very unladylike snort. "I happened to be waiting to show the property on North Forty-second when supercop decided I was selling more than real estate."

Conor flinched.

"This rash of burglaries is going to be the death of me as it is," the chief said, shuffling through some papers on his desk. "Besides, we all know you can take care of yourself." His gaze met Conor's. "Didn't you just get off duty this afternoon, Officer Richmond?"

"Yes, sir."

"Then go home and get some rest." His gaze fell on Jessica. "Apologize to our new officer."

"Me? What did I do?"

The chief's gaze swept over his daughter and then back to the papers on his desk.

"You've lost the top button on your blouse. How many times have I told you to quit twisting the blasted things?" He carefully placed his pen on the desk, his expression full of pain when it landed on Conor. "Do you know every day she lived at home I had to sew buttons on her clothes?"

"I beg your pardon, brother," his sister interjected. "I sewed on my fair share."

"We both did," he conceded, then cleared his throat and frowned, turning his attention on his daughter. "That skirt is too short, besides being ripped, and your heels too high. It's a wonder I didn't have to go to the hospital because you broke your neck. What did you do this time? Looks like you've been wrestling in the dirt. And . . ."

"Never mind. I get the picture." It might not be a bad idea if she changed the subject. "Suspects? Are you about to close in on the perps behind the burglaries?"

She had to admit, at least to herself, she *was* curious. With elections looming in their moderately sized Texas town, the mayor was anxious to put a stop to the break-ins, and in the process, securing his reelection. People were getting antsy. He'd already started applying the screws to the police department. The pressure her father was under had begun to show in the tired lines on his face. She wished there was something she could do. A wave of guilt washed over her. Maybe if she'd kept her job as a cop, she could've been more help. No, she wouldn't let herself think like that; she'd made the right decision.

"I don't believe it would be a good idea to discuss the case with a civilian," Conor spoke up.

Her gaze jerked toward him. He smiled at her, but it didn't quite reach his eyes.

The only thing he hadn't done was pat her on top of the head. Talk about holding a grudge.

He had a lot to learn if he thought she was just a civilian, though. Her teething ring had been a pair of handcuffs, and instead of Nancy Drew mysteries, she'd actually pored over old cases with her father. She probably had more knowledge about the workings of a police department in her little finger than he had in his entire body!

Slowly, she smoothed her palms down the sides of her black skirt and squared her shoulders. Even in heels she didn't come close to his height. He was well over six feet. But nothing would suit her better than to wipe that condescending smile off his face.

She tossed her blond hair over her shoulder with a flick of her head. "I happen to be a policewoman, duly licensed in the state of Texas." She didn't know what she expected—an apology, maybe, for his sudden supercilious attitude? What she got was a slow, heated look that started at the top of her head and burned down to her toes. It couldn't have lasted more than a few seconds, but long enough that her breath caught in her throat and her body tingled.

"I'd heard something to that effect." His words implied that she was anything *but* an officer of the law.

Her hands curled into fists. She opened her mouth, then snapped it shut. No, she wouldn't tell him what she was thinking. Taking a deep, calming breath, she turned to her father and aunt.

"Since you're busy, I'll talk to you later about what's going on. Besides, Al should be here any second. He's taking me to dinner." As if her words had conjured him up, there was a knock. She marched forward and flung the door open, wanting to leave as soon as possible.

"Not interrupting a family get-together, am I?" Al smiled broadly as he pushed his way inside the crowded office. His glance lingered on her before he looked up. "Maybe we should stop by your apartment before we go to dinner."

His gentle reprimand set her teeth on edge. Being critical was a major flaw with Al, but he had good qualities, too, although the scales were tipping toward the dumping point more each time she went out with him.

But he did have nice attributes. Pale blond hair, manicured nails, and he always wore an immaculate suit. He looked like he'd just stepped from the cover of a magazine, and most of the time he made her feel like the lady she desperately wanted to be.

Maybe her insecurities stemmed from the fact that she played with cars and toy guns as a child rather than dolls and dress-up. That was all changing, though.

Her earlier irritation began to vanish—until she noticed Conor had the same sour-stomach expression her father always wore when she even mentioned Al's name.

"More than ready," she cast a scathing look in Conor's direction before returning her attention back to her father. "I'll call you later. 'Bye, Auntie."

Conor watched Jessica sweep from the room. So this was the chief's daughter everyone had mentioned. Cute. But a cop? After what happened earlier, maybe it was a good thing she got out when she did. He couldn't quite see her handling a gun, let alone taking down a perp.

Besides, if a cop couldn't control her emotions, she shouldn't be in this line of work. He wasn't sure why she'd gotten irritated with him when her father had mentioned the burglaries, but he'd known the moment her hackles started to rise.

It wasn't like he'd said something out of the way. She should know it was against policy to talk about an ongoing case with someone on the outside. Women. He'd never understand how their minds worked.

"I don't particularly like that young man," the chief said, drawing his attention. "He's too . . . pretty."

"Humph." Gloria Nelson glared at her brother. "You don't like anyone who doesn't have a badge, stethoscope, or fire hose."

"You mean to stand there and tell me you actually think that boy is good enough for our Jess?"

Gloria smoothed a stray wisp of hair behind her ear. "It doesn't matter what *we* think. Jessica's the one who's going out with him." Without another word, she turned on her heel and left the room, firmly closing the door behind her.

"Women," the chief snorted. "You can't make them see what's right in front of their noses." He cleared his throat. "So, what'd you think of my daughter?"

The older man's piercing gaze swiveled toward him. Conor shifted from one foot to the other. It felt almost like he was wearing a suit and tie—and it was all he could do to keep from running a finger between the collar and his neck. Why hadn't he left when he'd had the chance?

"Nice," he said hesitantly.

"Nice, hell! Looks just like her momma did at that age. Same stubborn streak, too."

Conor might have argued which side of the family her headstrong nature came from, but the chief didn't give him a chance. Not that he would have mentioned the fact. He happened to like his job.

"She's twenty-seven. Time she got married. The least she could do is give me a few more grandchildren before I kick the bucket. Gabe and Marsha's two are growin' up fast. What about you? Any plans for the future?"

One eyebrow raised. "Don't you think your daughter and I should exchange more than a couple of sentences before we get married?"

"That's not what I meant," the chief snorted. Grabbing the snow globe paperweight on his desk, he began turning it over and over. Tiny white flakes soon obscured the cowboy and horse on the inside.

Conor's mouth stopped just shy of a grin. "I don't have any plans right now. Single life suits me." He could tick off a number of reasons. Namely, he had a penchant for impossible relationships. Women either wanted him to give up law en-forcement, or there was something wrong with them. The last one had been a kleptomaniac.

His stomach rumbled uncomfortably. Damn, he should've realized she had a problem sooner. Like every time they left a restaurant and her purse rattled and clanked. How was he to know she'd pilfered the silverware?

"No steady girl, huh?" The chief's hand stilled. The snow swirled around on the inside of the globe. Carefully, he set it back on his desk.

"No," Conor cautiously answered.

The chief didn't look up until the snow had once more set-tled to the bottom. As soon as he did, Conor saw the unmistak-able glimmer in his eyes. The sooner he put a stop to any matchmaking ideas, the better off he'd be.

He'd taken this transfer because it would give him a better chance for advancement. But he wasn't looking to become an official part of the Nelson clan. The badge was the only wife he needed.

"I've always made it a policy not to date the boss's daugh-ter." A small lie, but it should do the trick. No one could say he wasn't a fast thinker.

"Yeah, Jess has dumb rules, too. Says she doesn't date cops. Have a seat, son."

That was a relief. Getting involved with the chief's daugh-ter didn't sit well with him, anyway. Conor sat in the chair across from him, wondering how the conversation had jumped track from the suspects to his own social life. There must be something awfully wrong with his daughter to make him want to unload her so fast.

And what'd she have against dating a cop?

Not that he would date her, but he had to admit he wasn't unaffected by her looks. He'd always been a sucker for blond hair and mysterious, smoky blue eyes. It wouldn't be much of a strain to his imagination envisioning her nude body pressed intimately against his.

What was he thinking? From what he'd gathered since coming to work in White Plains a week ago, Jessica Nelson would never be the type for a casual affair. To hear her cousin tell it, she was as pure as new snow.

Not that it mattered one way or the other; he wouldn't break his policy of not getting emotionally involved with anyone. Much safer that way.

He didn't want another woman asking him to take a safe desk job, then getting pissed when he refused. Being a cop on the streets was his life. It would be easier for him to stop breathing than give it up.

Mentally, he hung a NO TRESPASSING sign around Jessica's neck. It was time he turned the game back to his side of the court and stopped thinking about the chief's daughter.

"About those suspects, sir?"

The chief looked unwilling to change the conversation, but after a brief hesitation, reached across his desk and picked up a folder. "The Meredith family is on the top of my list right now."

Conor let out a deep breath, glad he'd temporarily given up the quest for his daughter's hand.

"There's three of them," he continued. "The father's name is Winston and his two sons are Barry and George. They've recently moved back to the area. Just about the time the robberies started. Right now they're our prime suspects."

"Why them?"

"Kelvin Adams spotted Winston in Wal-Mart and called to let me know our old friend was back in town. Kelvin's retired now, but he used to be the chief here."

"Maybe Winston has gone straight."

He shook his head. "Not a chance. Winston's got a rap sheet that stretches all the way from El Paso to Houston." A thoughtful frown wrinkled his brow. "Something tells me they're not working alone, though. He never did in the past. He's a follower . . . not a leader. Besides, things are too orchestrated."

He tossed the folder across his desk. Conor leaned forward and picked it up, flipping through the pages. "What do you mean?"

"Winston's not stupid, but he's also not smart enough to plan these burglaries. He's getting inside information when the victims are going to be away from home—the layout of the houses. That sort of thing."

Conor turned the next sheet of paper and paused, staring at the picture of a flashy young man.

"The youngest son, George," he supplied. "He's thirty and recently married." The chief stood and came around the desk.

"Is this guy for real?" George looked like something out of a bad Mafia film. The side-view picture showed slicked back hair pulled into a thin ponytail, pale skin, and a cocky expression.

"He's a piece of work, isn't he? I arrested him a few times when I was still working a beat. He was just a kid back then. Fourteen or fifteen. Not too bright. I remember once George tried to break into a house through the doggy door. He took off all his clothes and greased himself down. Used half a can of Crisco. George made it halfway through before getting stuck. I'd love to have seen the expressions on the homeowners' faces when they returned that evening."

"Talk about a full moon." Conor chuckled.

"That's George." The chief laughed. "About the time he turned eighteen he began telling everyone he was Italian. A social worker once told me his mother was American, though. She dumped him on his father's doorstep when he was about six. As far as I know, she's never contacted him." He perched on a corner of his desk, crossing his arms in front of him.

Conor flipped to the next picture. "And this one, I suppose, is his brother."

The chief nodded. "Barry. He's thirty-six. The oldest. As mean as his old man. He's already had a stint in the joint. Stole a car before he turned fifteen. After that, he'd hit liquor stores. Convenience stores. Penny-ante stuff until now. Gut feeling tells me he's graduated."

The older brother had the same wiry build as George, but that's where the similarity ended. His beady eyes held a calculating gleam.

He went to the next picture. "The father?"

"Dear old Dad. Meaner than a two-headed rattlesnake and built like a bulldozer. Only thing, the elevator doesn't go all the way to the top. You wouldn't want to turn your back on that one."

Conor closed the file. "I assume you have a plan?"

"We're sending in a surveillance team. They'll act as a newly married couple, something in common with George and his bride."

"Surveillance?" His eyebrows rose.

"I'd thought about giving the assignment to Marty and Angie. It won't be the first time they've pretended to be married. There's a house next door to the Merediths that's unoccupied and up for sale. We'll have them go through all the motions of renting and moving in. But you know . . ." The chief scratched his chin thoughtfully. "This would be just the right assignment for you instead of Marty. In fact, you might even call it fate."

Conor looked gratefully toward the chief, but his smile faltered when he saw the speculative gleam in the corner of the older man's eyes. An uneasy premonition stole over him. The chief said it might be fate, but something told Conor he'd better move forward cautiously.

Now he was being paranoid. He shook the feeling off. Sure, he'd guessed the chief would like to hook him up with Jessica, but what could he actually do? Handcuff him to her? That wouldn't happen. At least, not in Conor's lifetime.

Chapter 4

Jessica pulled her red Mustang convertible into her father's driveway. Something about coming home made her all soft and satisfied on the inside.

It didn't matter how often she visited. She'd grown up in this house, played with her brother's toy trucks and plastic guns under the big oak tree, and shot hoops with her cousins and brother in the driveway.

The basketball net had deteriorated ages ago, but they still played every holiday. It didn't seem to matter to anyone that there was nothing left but a bare metal hoop.

Her brother was pretty decent . . . most of the time, but her cousins had been rascals. Rotten to the core. They still pulled pranks on her to this day. So far they hadn't been able to top the stuff she'd pulled on them. She grinned. Of course, she always told them she was too pure and innocent to do anything wrong. God, she loved revenge warfare. Especially since most times she came out the winner.

She got out of the car, strolling past the pink and purple petunias that bloomed in the flower beds running the length of the sidewalk, noticing that her father had added another basket of trailing ivy to the porch.

That made four ivies, two ferns, and one spiked plant that he'd given her a cutting from, saying no one could kill that kind of plant. She had. Her thumb ran more toward purple than green. But her father loved growing them and had a pretty good knack for it. She shook her head. Someday his plants were going to be so thick you couldn't get to the house.

She smiled.

Her father met her at the door . . . frowning.

"Don't young people dress for dinner anymore? What was all that talk about wanting to be a lady?"

Ouch.

She glanced down and felt the heat rising to her face. Loose, black button-down shirt and black tights.

He had her there.

She'd chosen the outfit because it was comfortable. But he was right. She didn't look much like the lady she'd told him she wanted to be. This was her day off, though.

"What's wrong with what I'm wearing?" She jutted her chin forward. "It's just the two of us, right? When you called and invited me to dinner you didn't mention anyone else."

He ushered her in with one hand and shoved the door closed with the other.

"Well, you never know when someone might drop by."

Her steps faltered. If her father were in court, the judge would throw the book at him just from the look on his face. It screamed: *I'm guilty*! She'd seen that look at least a hundred times, and it usually involved a man.

What was her matchmaking father plotting?

She surveyed the room as if she expected single men to start popping out from the woodwork, but everything looked the same.

The deep green drapes in the living room had been pulled back and the sheer panels exposed, letting the evening light cascade into the room. The furniture had been cleaned and dusted, giving the house a light, lemony smell.

Her father had even filled the candy dish with caramels. Hmmm. And magazines on the coffee table . . . she stepped closer. *New Bride? June Bride? Wedding Bells? Baby Makes Three!* Good lord!

She'd walked right into a trap. Her eyes narrowed. "Okay, Dad. What's up? Why aren't you at the office working on the burglary case?" The last time she'd spoken with him, that's all he'd talked about.

"Sometimes it helps me think better if I get away from the office."

He was right. It was a joke at the station that her father had solved a hell of a lot of cases with a dust cloth in his hand.

His bushy eyebrows rose almost to his hairline. "Besides, can't I invite my daughter to dinner? I've missed you."

"Missed me? I saw you Monday when supercop arrested me. I talked to you on the phone Tuesday, and this is just Friday." She paused, her gaze skimming over him. Odd magazines? Not remembering when he'd last seen her?

Maybe it wasn't a setup?

It could be something entirely different. Fear swept over her. No one ever wanted to believe their parents were creeping up on . . . old age, but her father wasn't getting any younger.

She hesitated before she asked the question uppermost in her mind. "You're not getting forgetful, are you?"

Something between a growl and a cough sputtered from him. "Of course I'm not getting forgetful. I'm not that old." His tone softened. "It's just that you're my little girl. I enjoy your company."

She sighed with relief. "I enjoy yours, too." Wrapping her arms around his middle, she hugged him close, breathing in the familiar smell of peppermint. Her father always kept a jar close by, saying the candy was good for an upset stomach. She knew better. He had an incurable sweet tooth.

A sigh escaped. In the future she'd have to remember how sensitive he was about his age.

The doorbell chimed.

Her father jumped as if he'd been shot.

"Oh." He coughed, then cleared his throat and tried again. "Now I wonder who that could be?"

She just bet he did.

"Why don't you open the door and find out?" She stepped back, folding her arms in front of her as suspicion coursed through her veins. His air of innocence didn't fool her for one minute. Damn, she'd been hoodwinked! Her father was a master at the game and she a lowly novice.

"Sometimes I wonder where my mind has gone," he mumbled as he strolled to the door and opened it. "Officer Richmond—what a pleasant surprise."

She looked from her father to Conor. Great! Mr. Testosterone himself. He seemed startled she was there, but quickly recovered and turned his attention back to her father.

"I have those papers you wanted, Chief." He hesitated. "You did ask me to drop them by after work, didn't you?"

"Yes, of course. I've been so busy today I guess it slipped my mind."

Jessica just bet it had. Couldn't her father see the man wasn't interested in her? He'd been ticked off when he discovered who she was, then treated her like a child. He could care less about her.

I wonder why? She frowned.

The last time she'd looked in the mirror she hadn't noticed any warts. She squared her shoulders. Not that it mattered what he thought about her appearance.

She dragged her attention back to the two men when Conor handed her father a thick, brown envelope.

"Ms. Nelson." He nodded toward her.

Oh my, now wasn't he polite?

"If there's nothing else you needed, then I'll see you Monday."

"Nonsense! I won't hear of you leaving since you drove all this way. Come in and visit for a while. I always like to get to know my new officers."

Her father dragged the younger man inside and shoved the door closed. Jessica wondered if he thought Conor might try to escape. She should be so lucky. He wasn't her type at all. The man had absolutely no sense of humor. He was as dry as a West Texas dust storm.

Absently, her gaze wandered over him. He dressed nicely, though. The deep brown sports coat fit his broad shoulders rather well. Her gaze slowly slid over the cream-colored shirt and down his tan slacks. She envisioned herself wallowing in a decadence of layered chocolate. Damn, she had to quit thinking about Conor like he was . . . like he was a piece of candy and she was about to gobble him up.

She knew what her problem was—she'd been dating Al too long. They hadn't slept together. There was just something about him that held her back, kept her from making a commitment.

And when she dreamed at night, it wasn't Al who filled her dreams. Her lover was faceless, but he had an incredible body and slow-moving hands that swept her off to a world filled with erotic pleasure. Sweat always drenched her body when she woke up, and left her yearning for her fantasy lover.

She sighed.

When she caught her father's raised eyebrows, she realized she'd begun twisting her button. Sheesh! A daughter didn't have impure thoughts about a man—especially a virtual stranger—when her father was in the room. She had to get hold of herself . . . and her vivid imagination. She could have impure thoughts when she was alone.

"Make yourselves comfortable in the living room. I'll get us something to drink. Soda okay?"

Conor hesitated.

"I did want to go over a few things concerning the burglaries."

"Soda is fine," Conor conceded.

"I think I smell a rat," Jessica muttered as she watched her father disappear toward the kitchen. "I'd bet my last dollar he's matchmaking. If you want to sneak out while you have the chance . . ." Her words trailed off when she caught his blatant stare.

He looked as if he'd never seen her before. A deep, penetrating look that sent waves of heat over her. The walls began closing in, making it hard to breathe. She could almost feel his hands touching, caressing her body.

When he met her gaze, the spell he'd weaved over her magically vanished, leaving her feeling as if she were a candle that had been left out in the sun too long.

If just looking at her could cause a meltdown, she wondered what having sex with Conor would be like. Lord, she'd love to find out.

Not that she intended to. She certainly didn't want to become infatuated with the new cop, even if he did look pretty damn good. She was just sexually deprived right now, and Conor made her think about the kind of sex that left her sweaty and satisfied. She hadn't gotten sweaty or been satisfied in a very long time.

He continued to stare.

"What?" she finally asked, wondering if she had a smudge of dirt on her face.

He shook his head. "Nothing. I guess you just seem different from the other day."

She cocked an eyebrow. "Cleaner?"

He grinned, and her world tilted.

"You look really nice," he told her.

As much as she tried to deny it, his words sent shivers of delight over her. She didn't know why his opinion mattered. It shouldn't, but it did, for some odd reason.

Ridiculous.

The first time he'd thought she was a down-on-her-luck hooker. Now, with no makeup and her hair pulled back into a ponytail, he was probably thinking she never fixed herself up. Not that she cared. After all, she was comfortable.

Absently, she smoothed her hand over her hair and straightened her shirt.

"Here we go." Her father rejoined them, interrupting her thoughts. He shoved canned sodas into their hands. "Jess, are you planning on keeping our guest in the hall all day?"

"Listen, Dad, maybe it would be better if you and the officer . . ."

"Conor."

She glanced toward him. "What?"

"Just Conor."

She frowned. Too personal, but it would be rude to call him anything else now. *Conor.* She did like the name. It had a nice ring to it. Great, next thing she knew she'd be dragging out old yearbooks and scrawling his name across the inside cover.

"Maybe it would be a good idea if we had supper some other night," she told her father. The less she was around Conor, the better.

"Nonsense, come in and sit down."

She hesitated. Why did she even try? She couldn't win against her dad. When he got an idea in his head, he was like a starving dog with a juicy bone. She'd have a heart-to-heart talk with him later.

After casting a warning look in his direction, she headed toward her favorite chair as Conor sat on the sofa.

"Honey, do you mind if I sit there? That old sofa is so worn out it hurts my back." He slipped into the cushioned seat before she had a chance to do anything.

"Dad! Don't you think you're being a little obv . . ."

Ring!

"I'll get that!" Her father vaulted out of the chair, racing to the other room. He didn't appear to have a bit of back trouble.

Before she could even sit on the sofa, he returned.

"I'm sorry, but I have to go to the station. Nothing important, but something I need to take care of. Jess, my car's been acting funny. Do you mind if I borrow yours?" His words tumbled out and ran together.

"I can take you." Conor stood, but that was as far as he got.

"Oh no, Jess doesn't mind if I drive her car. I'm not sure how long I'll be, but if you don't mind waiting, I should be back in less than an hour. Food's on the stove." He glanced her way. "Make sure Conor eats."

Before she knew what was happening, her father snatched her keys out of her hand and scurried out the door.

"But . . . but . . ." That conniving old coot! He'd managed . . .

The sound of her convertible purring to life caught her attention. Oh, good lord! He was driving her car again.

"Don't touch anything!" She made a dash for the door and flung it open. Her father waved over his head and zoomed out of sight.

She looked at Conor, who'd come up behind her. His eyes sparkled. Where was the *all-business cop?* Now he decided to show amusement? And at her expense? She wasn't laughing.

"I don't think being ramrodded is at all funny. And the last time he took my car he thought he'd turned the radio on. Do you know how much a new top for a convertible costs?"

He laughed, but quickly stifled his humor when she glared at him.

"Sorry, my family is the same way about borrowing things."

"No family could compare to mine. Growing up around my relatives was total chaos. Aunts, uncles, and cousins flowing in and out of the house like a pipe that'd sprung a leak."

Knowing he had a family and hadn't just magically hatched from a rotten egg made him more . . . human. *He's still a cop,* a persistent little voice whispered in her ear. And one who seemed to doubt her knowledge about law enforcement. She still resented his pat-on-the-head attitude.

She'd always thought she made a decent cop. It just wasn't the profession she wanted for the rest of her life.

Apparently, supercop had his doubts she'd ever worked the streets. In uniform, that is. A frown furrowed her brow. She wondered why he was apparently unable to visualize her taking down a perp.

Conor could picture Jessica in the middle of a big family. What he couldn't visualize was her in a uniform. Especially after what her cousin Mike had told him about her. Hell, the way he'd talked, she could walk through the door of a nunnery without a smidgen of guilt. She was so pure she almost had a halo around her head.

And right now, he felt more at home than he had in a long time. He was afraid he'd stepped into dangerous territory where she was concerned, because his thoughts were anything but pure.

It was all he could do to swallow past the bile that rose inside his throat. Jessica probably never even thought about sex. If she did, then not the down and dirty kind. She would be the type of woman who'd want the lights off to preserve her modesty.

Damn, and he'd arrested her for soliciting. He'd misinterpreted everything that happened that day. And he was supposed to be such a good cop. Suddenly, he felt like a rookie.

She hadn't seemed pure and innocent, though, he rationalized. But all the pieces were starting to fit. Why she was no longer a cop. Why she dated a wuss like Al.

Hell, no wonder she'd turned in her badge. The harsh reality of a cop's life had probably been too much for her. He had no explanation why she was dating Al, though. Maybe the guy hadn't made a pass yet. He looked like the kind of man women considered safe. He probably still lived at home with his mother.

Was he any better, though? Or maybe he'd done her more harm. Conor had no idea how he could screw everything up in such a short time. He was a real jerk.

He'd stepped into Jessica's little world and fucked it up royally. She'd been a babe in the woods. A fawn hesitantly moving from the safety of the trees. Then *bam!* The brutal hunter showed up and hauled her off to jail. He'd never felt so low in all his life as he did right now.

"Have you eaten?" she asked, breaking into his thoughts.

He looked at her for a long moment. She seemed uncomfortable around him. She furiously twisted her top button around and around. Surely she wasn't afraid of him. No, he didn't think that was it, but he wouldn't make her suffer his company any longer.

"I think it's time I left."

Her tongue came out and licked her upper lip. He almost groaned. Didn't she realize what she was doing to him? Stupid question. Of course she didn't.

"Dad was right. You came all this way, so you might as well stay and have dinner. Besides, didn't Dad say he wanted to go over a few things with you concerning the burglaries?"

"You shouldn't have to wait on me, though."

"I'm not." She suddenly tossed a saucy grin in his direction.

His heart skipped a beat. God, she was so damned beautiful it made him ache just looking at her. She might be the wholesome girl next door, but the signals she sent out told an entirely different story, whether she meant them to or not.

"Everyone does his share around here," she told him. "Come on, if my nose is right, he made stew. That's about the only thing Dad can cook really well. It'll serve him right if we eat every last bite."

Okay, he'd stay for a while. If her father didn't return soon he'd make up some kind of excuse and leave, but damned if he didn't find himself wanting to hang around a little longer.

Motioning for him to follow, she led the way down the hall, through the dining room and into the kitchen. She had the sweetest sway in her step. His gaze was glued to the way her hips went from side to side, an easy, natural walk, but on her it looked damned sexy.

The kitchen was yellow and white . . . cozy. And it smelled great. It surprised him the chief was so much of a homebody. Or maybe it didn't when he thought about it. The chief seemed to be a good parent, even if a little meddlesome.

Jessica raised the lid and looked inside the pot. "I love Pop's stew. He uses chunks of the best beef money can buy, then adds carrots and potatoes and simmers it all in its own juices. I'm still not sure how he makes the brown gravy it cooks in. He told me as soon as I marry he'll give me the recipe. It might be worth getting married just so I can get it." She looked up with a smile on her face.

Conor took a deep breath. His stomach rumbled, but it wasn't from the need to eat . . . at least, not food.

She pointed toward the cabinet. "Grab some bowls and I'll get spoons."

Anything that would take his attention off Jessica. He removed two ceramic bowls from the shelf and closed the cabinet. As he set them on the table, his gaze fell on the refrigerator. An assortment of childish drawings were scattered over the white surface, held on by a set of heart magnets, a bumblebee, and one glittery butterfly. Longing filled him.

"Conor?"

He looked at her. "I'm sorry, what did you say?"

"I asked if you'd like to sit." She laughed lightly. "You seemed so far away. What were you thinking about?" She placed a large bowl filled with stew in the middle of the red-checkered tablecloth and waited.

"The pictures." He nodded toward them. "Cute stuff. My sister's two kids have papers stuck all over the fridge, too."

"Where do they live?"

"All over. Her husband is Air Force. Right now, McGuire Air Force Base in New Jersey."

"Long way from Texas," she said, going to the pantry and grabbing a box of crackers.

"Too far. Especially since my parents moved to Florida."

He didn't like the feeling of not knowing exactly where he belonged. He missed the few family gatherings they'd all shared.

His parents had been more cemented in the business world when he and his sister were growing up, but did attempt an occasional holiday function of sorts when they weren't out of town on one of their numerous trips. They just weren't the home-and-hearth type of family, but he knew they loved both their kids and that did count for something.

He nodded toward the refrigerator, drawing himself out of the past. "So, who are the artists?"

"My brother Gabe's two kids." She sat in one of the chairs at the table and motioned for him to take the one across from her. "Dad has always encouraged their creative side."

He straddled the chair while she dipped them each a bowl of the steaming stew. The rich aroma wafted up to his nose and he couldn't do anything except breathe in the wonderful smell. He realized it had been a while since he'd eaten.

After straightening her napkin, she picked up the conversation. "I think Dad saved everything Gabe and I ever drew. Somewhere in the attic is a trunk stuffed with stick-figure drawings."

He took a bite of the stew. Damn, she was right. Her father could cook. "Not bad." He scooped another bite.

Her pride in her father's cooking was evident on her face. "Dad's half-Irish. He always tells us he couldn't mess it up if he wanted. He also says that's why our family are cops, medics, and firefighters."

"Except you."

"Except me," she murmured.

Her eyes were fascinating—smoky-blue, kind of dark and mysterious, all at the same time. As soon as he realized where his thoughts were wandering, he returned his attention to his food. He didn't want to think about her eyes or how they drew him in.

There was one question he'd like to ask, though. "Why don't you date cops?"

The spoon stopped midway to her mouth and her forehead wrinkled. "How did you know I don't date cops?"

"Your father told me."

"Ah, of course. My father has been telling my secrets . . . again." She set her spoon down and brushed some loose tendrils of hair behind her ear. "Why date a cop if I don't want to be one? I want a normal relationship. Cops aren't normal."

He frowned. "I beg your pardon?"

She chuckled. "I didn't mean you weren't normal. I don't know what you are. I meant the hours you keep. For example, if you moved your jacket back a fraction, I bet I'd see a pager hooked on your belt."

He immediately reached down. She didn't even try to hide her knowing smile.

"Told you so. My dad, brother, cousins . . . even my aunt, for goodness' sake, couldn't survive without the PD, the fire department, or ambulance. You all live for that adrenaline rush."

"Not everyone is like that," he argued.

"If you heard shots right now, I bet you'd be the first to investigate. And what about when you're called out at midnight? Believe me, I won't be showing a house in the middle of the night."

He took another bite and chewed thoughtfully. "Is that why you gave up being a cop?"

Instead of answering him, she countered with a question of her own. "Don't you get tired of living on the edge? You never know if the dispatcher received the correct information. Or if the call will be a hoax, or if your life might be in danger. And what about when you only have seconds to make a decision? Do you ever worry if it's the right one?"

"But that's the exciting part. Not knowing exactly what to

expect. Every call will be different because people are different." He set his spoon to the side of his bowl and leaned back in his chair. "And as far as making the right decision, that's part of it. A chance you have to take."

"Not me." She shook her head. "I don't have to. Being a real estate agent may not be nine to five, but it's certainly more normal than the hours you keep, and I don't hold anyone's fate in my hands."

Her answer was pat. Almost like she'd memorized it, and maybe she had. He felt like there was more to her story, but he wouldn't question her. She might just want to see if the grass was greener on the other side. Hell, he couldn't fault her for that. Like he told himself before—she wasn't meant to be a cop.

Something in the air seemed to shift between them. Like she realized they were actually carrying on a conversation, and he didn't think she liked him that much. And why should she? Not after he'd arrested her. At the very least, she seemed edgy around him.

Suddenly, though, it seemed like she was closing herself off from him. He wasn't sure he liked the feeling, but one thing was certain—she was definitely safe.

No matter how bad her father wanted to see his little girl married to a cop, and he'd already guessed as much, she refused to date one. She'd said so herself. And even though she was damn easy on the eyes, he didn't have to worry about becoming involved with her. He could relax.

"You were right." He stared at her, liking the way her eyes widened just slightly when she looked at him.

"About what?" she asked.

For a moment he forgot everything except the expectant look on her face; then he remembered what he'd wanted to tell her. "The stew. It was good."

She suddenly laughed. His senses absorbed the light and beauty of the sound. The dying notes wrapped around him, bringing an unfamiliar longing that settled in the center of his chest. He held his breath, not wanting the moment to escape.

"I'm glad you liked Dad's cooking."

The spell broke and Conor exhaled. What the hell had just happened? One minute he had everything under control, and in the next, he was lost in the sound of her laughter, and wishing he could get to know her better.

Abruptly, he stood, reaching for her bowl. "Here, I'll take the dishes to the sink."

"I can do that."

She sprang from her chair, grabbing her bowl, but instead of ceramic, her hand closed over his. The room grew quiet. Her fingers were soft and warm. His insides quaked.

Her pupils dilated, and she leaned just a fraction toward him. The urge to pull her into his arms and taste the sweetness of her mouth was almost unbearable. Conor didn't think she'd put up much resistance.

Hell, why not? One kiss wouldn't hurt. He set the bowls on the table and pulled her into his arms, lowering his mouth to hers.

Damn, she tasted sweet . . . and hot. She snuggled closer to his body. Softness and heat wrapped around him. He tangled his fingers in her hair, wanting her closer still. Tremors swept over his body. He slid his hand down her back, then around to cup the fullness of her breast. He could feel the nipple tighten when he barely brushed across it.

She moaned. He stilled, ending the kiss, moving his hand away. Damn, what the hell was he doing? He knew the answer, though. He was seducing the chief's daughter in the chief's kitchen.

Had he really thought Jessica was safe?

He had to end what he felt before it got out of control. All he needed was the chief to walk in on him and Jessica having a go at it on the kitchen floor. There was only one way to kill anything that might be starting between them.

He drew in a deep breath as he stepped away, picking up the bowls off the table. "You know, it might be a good thing you didn't pursue law enforcement."

She jerked her hand away from his. "Why do you say that?"

"You're soft."

Her shoulders stiffened. It was for the best, he told himself, even as an empty feeling began to swallow him.

"Soft." She put some distance between them, then planted her hands on her hips.

Damn, she looked sweet, even though right at this moment she reminded him of a cute little kitten spitting and hissing at him.

He cleared his throat. "In a nice way, I mean. You'd never have made a good cop. You're lacking that hard edge, the gut instincts it takes to be good at the job. I suspected as much when I found out you were an ex-cop. I mean, not even an ex-cop would let herself get arrested for soliciting. No, selling property suits you much better."

Her eyes sparked. "I'm so glad you approve of my job choice, Officer Richmond," she ground out between her teeth. "If you'd been around sooner, you could have saved me the trouble of going through the academy. And, if I remember correctly, you were the one who jumped to conclusions. I was selling property, not my body. I only let you take me in because I needed a ride."

"There are other ways to get a ride than being arrested. All you had to do was ask. And from what I've heard, it was your decision to quit law enforcement. Right? You're not upset with something I said, are you?"

"Upset? Upset! Why would I be upset?"

"I didn't think so," he lied. "I need to run some errands, so tell your father I enjoyed his cooking and the company. If he wants to discuss the burglaries, he can contact me at home in a couple of hours." He set their bowls in the sink.

"I'll be sure and tell my father exactly how much I *enjoyed* visiting with you, too." She followed as he strode toward the front door. He could almost feel the daggers landing in his back.

Shuuuuuu . . . thunk!

He hesitated at the front door, then turned. Damn. Her expression could've been carved from stone, but she still made a pretty sexy statue.

Jessica De Milo, except she had the arms to caress him . . . or slap the shit out of him if he didn't get the hell out of her life.

It was a damn shame they couldn't have met at a different time or place. Some things weren't meant to be. He certainly wouldn't be the one to corrupt her. He had *some* ethics, but he did hate leaving her with a bad impression of him.

He opened his mouth, but no words came. What could he say? That he didn't mean what he said?

No, he'd done the right thing. Long-term relationships never seemed to work out for him, and being the boss's daughter, Jessica spelled trouble with a capital T. It was only one step up from being a preacher's daughter.

"See you around." He opened the door. Then why did he feel lower than a sunken ship?

"I doubt it. I don't get to the station that often." Her words were clipped.

Conor took a deep breath as he stepped outside. All the way to his car he told himself he *had* done the right thing. Sometimes doing the right thing sure felt wrong, though.

Chapter 5

The front door opened and Jessica's father hurried inside. "Has Conor left?"

She uncrossed her legs and tapped her toe as she scowled at her obviously unrepentant father. "You're three hours late, and you didn't fool me one iota."

He closed the door and tossed her the keys to her Mustang. She deftly caught them.

"How'd it go?" He hurried to the sofa, rubbing his hands together. "I knew you two would hit it off right from the start."

Maybe her father needed to call Dr. Parker and make an appointment to have a CT scan of his brain. It definitely wasn't functioning right. "The first time I saw Officer Richmond, he arrested me! How did you get an attraction from that encounter?"

His forehead puckered. "That's irrelevant. He saw you on the corner and stopped. Never discount the role fate plays in your life."

Fate? She could think of a dozen other words, and *fate* wasn't one of them.

And her father wasn't showing one bit of remorse. He acted like an engagement announcement was just around the corner. She couldn't believe he harbored such notions. On second thought, this was her father—the matchmaker.

Well, she was about to burst his bubble. "If I never see Conor Richmond again, it'll be too soon. The man is full of himself." And darn it, why did he have to be such a great kisser? A spark of electricity had jumped between them. At least, that's what it had seemed like to her. Electricity and fire and . . . Damn, he was doing it to her again.

Being attracted to him ticked her off almost as much as Conor did. He'd said she was soft. Where had he gotten that impression? She was thoughtful for a moment. Unless her cousins had been scamming him. Very possible.

Once they'd told a rookie that she had three boobs. When curiosity got the better of him and he'd asked to see her chest, she'd punched him in the nose.

They were always pulling some kind of prank. She grinned inwardly. Of course, she was just as devious. Like the time she'd put pretzels on every desk—the really salty kind—then made sure there was water in the coolers so they would drink plenty of it.

Devious? Oh yeah, she'd put an OUT OF ORDER sign on the men's restroom at work, after Saran-wrapping the toilet seats in the ladies' room.

She'd stayed in her Aunt Gloria's office, with the door partially open. They'd grinned and high-fived when the yelling began. Sometimes she amazed herself. Her smile slipped.

They still hadn't retaliated.

Her father's frown deepened as he sat across from her, drawing her attention. "What'd Conor do to make you mad?"

Her irritation rose to the surface. "He . . . he . . . ."

What exactly had he done? For starters, Conor had told her selling property suited her, but hadn't she said those very same words to her father?

She tapped her toe. "It doesn't matter. We mix about as well as water and oil, so you can forget about any matchmaking schemes. I plan to stay far away from Officer Richmond."

Her father was silent, and she wondered if she might have hurt his feelings. She hadn't meant to come down quite so hard. After all, he only wanted the best for her. She peeked at him from the corner of her eye. He didn't look that distraught. He could be hiding his pain, though. She *was* his only daughter, after all, and she'd always been Daddy's little girl.

"You may be right," he finally said.

She breathed a sigh of relief. Maybe she'd *needed* to be a little firm. It was just so damn hard when it was her father. He'd always been there for her. But still, he had to stop butting into her love life. She was a mature woman, perfectly able to pick who she dated.

"How would you like to help me out, though?"

"Help you?" Her eyes narrowed. For all that she loved him, she didn't quite trust her father not to pull another stunt. She studied him for a moment. He looked innocent enough as he continued to steadily meet her gaze.

"Help you do what?" she asked.

"I need a realtor to show the house next to the burglary suspects. It's listed through your company, and since you're still a reserve and have a badge, it'd be perfect for you without getting too involved."

Back in the field? Her heart began to race. A drop of familiar adrenaline trickled into her bloodstream and quickened her pulse. *Take a deep breath*, she told herself. That life was behind her. Her father only wanted her to show a house, not arrest the criminals.

She could do that and stay uninvolved with law enforcement. The best of both worlds, kind of. She'd even get to wear a dress. A flutter of excitement skipped up and down her spine. She quickly tamped it down. She'd only be pretending to show a house. Nothing more. The only reason she was remotely considering it was because her father needed her help, but could she really trust him?

"You're sure that's all I'd be doing?" She wanted her father to spell it out, just to be on the safe side. He wasn't about to trap her into rejoining the department.

"Scout's honor." He held up his fingers.

"I thought you told me and Gabe they kicked you out of Scouts because you didn't follow the rules."

"Old habit." He cleared his throat and hurried on. "The burglars are getting gutsy." Her father leaned forward in his chair, resting his arms on his knees. "They robbed Mrs. Huntley's home the day before yesterday—in broad daylight. She was having a garden party in the backyard. They waltzed in and stole everything out of the front rooms—even the area rugs."

"How? Surely someone saw them."

He shook his head. "Apparently not, or if they did, they paid them no mind. All the extra help claimed they were either in the kitchen putting together trays of food or in the garden, serving. The only one up front was the housekeeper. She's half blind, got one foot in the grave, and couldn't identify anyone if she'd wanted to. The only reason Mrs. Huntley keeps her around is because the housekeeper is older than she is."

"Even so, wouldn't the housekeeper have suspected something?"

"Apparently not. The burglars told her they were there to remove the stuff for cleaning and she believed them. When a thundercloud threatened to rain on their get-together, Mrs. Huntley invited her guests inside, and—"

"—and discovered a tornado had already swept through."

"—and sucked everything up." He studied her. "So, are you in?"

She began twisting her top button. *Calm down*, she told herself. It wasn't like she wanted to return to law enforcement.

But it might relieve her boredom. She hadn't sold a blasted house since the Randolph home. Even the real estate deal with Troy's brother, John, had fallen through. John had decided to open his travel agency in another town. Troy had profusely apologized after his brother missed their appointment the other evening.

Still, she eyed her father and his innocent expression. It could be another ploy on his part. He didn't *look* like he had anything up his sleeve.

"It would be just this one time, and I'd only be doing it to help you out." She wanted him to be perfectly aware of that fact so he wouldn't get any foolish notions in his head.

"Of course. I just need to get the mayor off my back."

There was a sudden, sour taste in her mouth. Her father and the mayor went back a long way—as far as grade school, in fact—and they never had liked each other.

"I don't trust him," she said. "I think he's on the take. The only reason he's worried about the burglaries is because he's up for reelection."

Her father grunted. "You and me both. It seems like an awful lot of his cronies are getting some juicy city contracts, too. Problem is, he has a squeaky-clean record. If he is crooked, he'll slip up sooner or later. They always do."

She hoped it would be sooner rather than later. At least she could help her father in the meantime. But this would be the absolute last time she worked as a cop.

"Okay, then as long as we understand each other, I'll show the house. Do I need to say anything to my boss? It isn't as if the police department will actually be buying the place, right?" she asked as she stood.

"The department will be leasing the house. That way the *newlyweds* will be able to move in immediately. I've already called your boss and explained the situation. I'll just let him know you'll be the one showing the place." He came to his feet. The smile on his face wavered. "Oh, there's just one other thing." His gaze fixed on the keys she lightly swung back and forth.

She was afraid he was about to tell her something she didn't really want to hear.

"About your car . . ."

*   *   *

Jessica gripped the steering wheel. Her initial excitement had waned. She should've just told her father no, that she didn't want to get involved. She'd only kept her reserve status in case there was a national disaster or something.

The light changed. She let off the brake and stepped on the gas, passing by one of the city's three parks and a high school. At least the house was in a decent part of town. She'd make a quick run-through of the property and be done.

Her father wanted everything carried out in the most normal way possible. At least she knew Marty and Angie. She assumed they would be the surveillance team posing as a married couple. Her father hadn't really said, but they were usually his first choice.

And her father was right about her being the one to show the property. Since he was setting up the surveillance, he might as well have someone on both sides. Her father was certainly thorough.

Jessica slowed as she pulled into the driveway. Her gaze flittered to the house next door, then quickly back. She shouldn't be obvious. She'd act casual. Like a realtor.

Duh!

She turned the ignition off and climbed out of her car. Her gaze strayed to the medium-size dent in the fender. She bit her bottom lip. Her pride and joy . . . injured. Something about her car was bad luck for her father. Some lady had pulled out in front of him and dinged the fender. The Mustang was going in the shop tomorrow.

As she hurried to the front door, her gaze was once more drawn toward the suspects' house. It looked peaceful enough. A well-manicured front lawn. An almost-new red Lincoln in the driveway. Obviously, they weren't hurting financially, but nowadays if you had a few credit cards, anyone could be upper-middle class. Or, in their case, if you were stealing from other people.

A boy of about twelve rode by on his bike, and she noticed a little girl sat on the porch down the street playing with a doll. Just a typical residential neighborhood.

Except for the criminals, of course.

She fumbled in her purse for the key. After casting one more look over her shoulder, she let herself inside. Marty and Angie should arrive at any time. Leaving the door open, she entered the foyer.

The house was nice, although the smallest one on the block. It wasn't as spectacular as some of her company's listings, but she liked the bold, straight lines. The two-bedroom was just right for a newlywed couple.

A short staircase led to the second floor. The mahogany banister gleamed. She knew from the specs there'd be a large master suite, a smaller bedroom, a bathroom upstairs, a half bath downstairs, and a small balcony on the upper floor.

She strolled to the empty living room, stopping in front of the fireplace. As she ran her fingers across the smooth surface of the mantel, she heard someone bound up the front steps and into the hall. Jessica turned, surprise stopping her smile from completely forming.

"Conor?"

"Jessica?"

She closed her eyes. Yom-da-da-da-da. When she opened her eyes, Conor was still there.

"I'm supposed to be meeting Marty and Angie. What are you doing here?" She willed her heart to slow its frantic beat as she drank in the sight of him. What was it about this man that tugged at her senses and irritated the hell out of her, all at the same time?

"Your father gave me the case. I'll be posing as Angie's husband. And you?"

She drew in a deep breath to steady her warring emotions and concentrated on getting this mess straight. "Dad thought it'd be more realistic if I showed the house."

Damn, her father scammed her again. He hadn't told her that Conor was on the case. She'd assumed Marty and Angie would be posing as the married couple.

His game wouldn't work. She'd show the house and be out in the blink of an eye. She wouldn't let Conor rattle her this time. Yeah, right. The man had already rattled her just by walking in the front door.

Conor Richmond was the best thing she'd ever seen . . . and she wanted him. Even though her brain was telling her to run away as fast as she could, her body responded like a sexually starved female on Viagra for women. But then, her gut instinct told her that he'd be a fantastic lover.

Would one night spent lying in his arms be so bad? She certainly didn't want to have any kind of relationship or anything remotely long-term.

No, she wouldn't break her own vow not to get involved with a cop. Besides, he probably wasn't interested in having sex with her. Hell, he'd practically run away after only one kiss.

Odd how that bothered her. Right now, his expression showed more irritation than anything else. She wondered why he was so disinterested.

Conor grimaced as he tried to rein in his emotions. Jessica had taken him by surprise. His glance swept over her. Damn, she looked sexy as hell and, from the looks of it, fidgety. She was furiously twisting the top button of her peach-colored blouse.

Think innocence! He'd spoken with Mike one more time, just to make sure he'd understood her cousin. Mike had confirmed that Jessica was practically nun material. Damn it, her kiss hadn't felt innocent, but her cousin had no reason to lie. He definitely had no room in his life for someone who was inexperienced.

The way she twisted her button, he didn't think she'd hang around long. Apparently, she had no taste for burglars. What the hell was she doing here anyway?

"You're posing as a pawnshop owner?" she asked.

"How'd you know my cover?" He held up a hand, guessing the answer. "Never mind. Your father, right?"

"Dad thought I should know a little about the prospective buyers."

"Surely the chief could've sent someone else. You shouldn't be here. What was your father thinking?" How could he put his daughter in danger like this? Mike had spilled the beans about how shy and timid Jessica was. She should never have joined the police force.

"I beg your pardon," she said, her hands braced on her hips as she glared at him. "I'm perfectly capable of taking care of myself. For your information, I'm still a licensed police officer. I'm also in real estate. If anyone checks, it'll be legit. And I'm pretty damn good at doing both." She scanned the living room before turning her gaze back to him. "I could have you salivating to buy this house. I'm very good."

He just bet she was—nun material or not. She looked ready to take on half the police force, and any bad guy that got in her way. How the hell could he concentrate on the suspects with her around? Jessica tempted him to do more than just look, even if she didn't realize it.

He wanted her gone.

"This isn't a game," he warned. "Those are real criminals next door and they're very dangerous, so I suggest you get that cute little fanny of yours back in your car. Angie and I can look at the place by ourselves."

"Oh, is that right? I'm sorry to disappoint you, but you don't have any say in the matter."

Conor admired her spunk, but he still wanted her somewhere far away from him. In two steps he closed the distance between them. "Don't try to play with the big boys, Jessica. You're out of your league."

Anger flared in her eyes, but just as suddenly it disappeared. Her gaze softened as she looked at him through partially lowered lids.

"So tell me, who's more dangerous, you or the people next door?" Her tongue darted out to lick her lips.

His gaze slid over her. From the top of her golden halo of hair, down past the open neck of her shirt and to those incredibly long legs. Her words were a challenge if ever he'd heard one.

What the hell was he thinking about? *Back off, Conor!* Casual affairs were his M.O. Skimming the surface—no pain, no regrets, no woman telling him he needed a safe desk job.

Jessica would be more than a casual fling. She had that look about her. The one that said she wanted a real good time, but he was certain it meant, *as long as a ring followed.* He wasn't about to let her experiment with him. No, she could test her sexual wings on some other poor sucker.

Still, he couldn't seem to stop himself from cupping her chin, drawing her even closer, until he tasted the cinnamon of her breath as it fanned across his face. He didn't mind so much giving her a lesson in kissing. It might even scare her off.

"Maybe you're the most dangerous." He trailed his fingers down the side of her jaw, feeling the smoothness before lowering his mouth. He inhaled the sigh that escaped her lips as his lips brushed across hers before fully tasting the sweetness she had to offer.

For someone supposedly so innocent, she kissed damn good. God, she was hot. She pressed her body closer, her soft curves melding with his hardness. Just how well did Mike know his cousin?

Her body language told him an entirely different story, the kind that said she was an open book and wanted to be read. Blood began to pound through his veins and his belly knotted with the effort it took to keep his emotions in check as her tongue stroked against his. God, she tasted good. He wanted to strip her clothes from her body and caress every inch of her naked skin.

Conor was so lost in the kiss he didn't realize anyone had

entered the room until he heard a throat clear. It vaguely registered inside his brain that Angie had finally arrived. As much
as he wanted to continue, Conor pulled away.

"You don't have the best timing in the world . . ." he
began, turning around. His words faltered when he realized
it wasn't Angie at all, but the next-door neighbor.

George.

The wiry man stood in the doorway that led to the living
room. He'd seen everything. Damn! How could he be so stupid? Not in the house five minutes, and he'd blown his cover.
The chief had trusted him with this assignment. He could
visualize his job slowly being sucked down the drain.

Or maybe not. His brain kicked into overdrive.

"I thought you were the woman who's going to show us
the house," he told George, and squeezed Jessica's arm, hoping she'd go along with him.

"Excus-a. I am-a sorry to startle you." He clicked his heels
and bowed. "I am-a Georgio, the neighbor from-a next
door."

George spoke with the worst imitation of an Italian accent
Conor had ever heard. It went well with his maroon, pol-
ished cotton suit and black patent-leather shoes. And the guy
had so many gold chains draped around his neck it would be
fatal if he fell into the deep end of a swimming pool.

When the other man's gaze slithered over Jessica, though,
he realized what it was about George that made his skin
crawl. He didn't like the way George looked at her, like he
was starving and she was his next meal.

"When I see the lady, well, I just-a thought I would check and
make-a sure everything was okay." When George smoothed
the side of his slicked-back hair, his gold-nugget ring caught
on his hoop earring. He sucked in half the air in the room
and carefully tugged his ring free, then smiled as if nothing
out of the ordinary had happened.

Gritting his teeth, Conor smiled back. "That's nice of you
to watch out for other people's property." He turned and

faced Jessica. "See, honey? I told you this looked like a great neighborhood."

Her expression said she thought he'd lost his mind. Great, she wasn't going along with the change in plans. He waited for her to stalk out of the house and run to her father. As it was, the chief would probably kill him for involving his daughter this much. Then he'd fire his butt.

Suddenly, she smiled smugly, as though she was telling him if not for her, he'd have blown the whole assignment. He wanted to strangle her, right after he kissed her one more time. Damn, she'd been sweet snuggled against him, all feminine and soft. She'd fit perfectly in his arms.

She sashayed around him. "You're right. I love the house," she said. "The bookcases are just what I've always wanted. It will be a great place to lease."

Conor breathed a sigh of relief. He'd figure some way to get her out of the picture as soon as possible.

"Let me be the first-a to welcome you to the neighborhood." George's smile broadened as his gaze leisurely raked over Jessica. "My door will-a always be open for you." He brought his fingers to his lips and kissed the tips. "*Bella, bella.*"

Yeah, his bedroom door! Okay, he'd had enough. Conor stepped forward. Job or no job, he wasn't about to let this creep . . .

Jessica hurried across the green carpet with an outstretched hand. "It's nice to know we'll have such considerate neighbors. I'm sure we'll be great friends. And what did you say your name was?"

"Georgio," he answered, taking Jessica's hand.

"How wonderful to know there'll be another man around in case Conor's at work. He owns a pawnshop and sometimes gets calls at all hours of the night. A woman can't be too careful these days."

George bent over her fingers. Before his lips could touch her skin, she slid her hand from his and ambled to the window. George stumbled forward. Jessica turned, the light catching the gold streaks in her hair. Conor sucked in a breath, no more immune to her than George.

"Call. Anytime-a. Day or night!" George's voice cracked.

"We haven't even spoken with the realtor yet, so the lease isn't final." Conor glared at the suspect. "I'm not sure we even want the house." He didn't like the way the other man ogled Jessica. Like a starving rat looking at a chunk of cheese.

"I will-a be happy to . . ."

Well, the cat was home! Grabbing George's arm, Conor slapped him on the back. "That's real nice of you."

George coughed and sputtered as he tried to catch his breath.

How could the department not catch these guys? The man was an imbecile. Surely the other two weren't that much brighter. There *had* to be someone else calling the shots. Telling them when and who to hit. But then, the chief had said Winston and Barry weren't stupid. Maybe George had fallen off a truck and hit his head when he was little.

The rustle of material and the click of high heels drew his attention toward the doorway. Angie stepped into the room. Conor returned her direct gaze.

"Good morning. I see you beat me here. I thought you might. That's why I gave your wife the key," Angie stated.

Apparently she'd heard enough to realize the situation had changed.

"I see you are-a busy. I will-a go, but please—" George's gaze lingered on Jessica "—feel-a free to call me if you need help-a with anything—*arrivederci*." Snapping his heels together, George strutted from the house.

"Is that guy for real?" Angie whispered as the front door closed. "I thought I was going to have to put my sunglasses back on. The guy damn near blinded me with all the gold he was wearing. And what's with that suit? An Armani knock-off?"

"About as original as his accent," Jessica supplied.

Both women laughed. Conor frowned.

"And his shirt! Good lord, it looked like he'd walked into a paint store right before it exploded." Jessica covered her mouth in an attempt to stifle her laughter.

"How'd the tables get turned?" Angie asked.

Jessica sputtered and coughed.

Conor felt his face heat.

"Oh-ho, so that's the way the wind blows." She pushed the strap of her black purse higher on her shoulder and raised an eyebrow in Conor's direction. "And to think I put on a dress just for you. So, what do we do now?"

"I'll just have to continue on, minus the wife."

Jessica's eyebrows rose. "Are you planning on murdering me?"

The way she'd flirted with George, he could very easily kill her. Her father would never give him a promotion if he bumped her off, though. "We'll have a fight, and you can run home. It happens every day."

She moved away from the window, tapping her fingernail against her teeth. "No, George will spill the beans about the burglaries. Give me a few minutes alone with him and . . ."

"Not on your life. We'll have a fight and you'll leave."

"Now, just a minute." Hands on hips, she stepped in front of him. "I thought you wanted to catch these guys. George responded to me."

"He was responding to the fact you have breasts and sexy legs."

"Hey." Angie stepped forward. "I resent that remark. He didn't even look twice at me."

How in the hell had he got in the line of fire of both women? Jessica was bad enough. He walked across the room to give himself a little space to think.

After a few deep breaths, he faced them once more, his thoughts in order. "That's not what I meant. The fact hasn't changed that Jessica is no longer a police officer. Catching these burglars is not worth putting a civilian's life in danger. She can't stay."

"I beg your pardon." Jessica glared at him.

"She can take care of herself," Angie informed him in an offhand manner.

"Angie is right." Jessica squared her shoulders and glared at him.

"You left the force because you couldn't hack it. You damn well don't belong here."

"I left because I wanted to!"

"Yeah, right!"

Her lips drew to a fine line. "I don't want to be stuck pretending to be supercop's wife any more than you want me here. So, call it a fight or whatever. I don't really care. I'm out of here." He was right—she didn't belong in the middle of an investigation. That part of her life was over. And she damn well didn't want to hang around him.

"It's not quite that easy." Angie spoke before Jessica could take more than two steps toward the door. "The stakes have been raised."

"What do you mean?" they both asked in unison.

"There's been a new development. I heard about it right before I left the precinct to come over here. That's why I was a little late. We have to nail these guys or the chief will be busted back to the streets. Or worse."

Chapter 6

Since there wasn't any furniture, Conor led Jessica to the stairway and made her sit. She'd scared the hell out of him when her face turned pasty white.

"My father a street cop?" she mumbled. "That can't happen. He worked hard to make chief. The disgrace will kill him. And how's he going to keep up with the younger men?"

"What happened?" Conor turned to Angie.

"The mayor's house was robbed this morning," she explained. "The burglars made off with about thirty thousand dollars of his wife's jewelry. Oh, and a tape he had in the safe. Sentimental value. Said his mother was on it. The last video he has of her. He's pretty upset."

"Surely they don't think it's these numbskulls?" Conor asked with disbelief.

"Apparently so," Angie continued. "Everything fits with their M.O.—grab and run, leaving a stuffed raccoon behind with a scrawled note saying the masked bandit has struck again. This time they also left behind an oil stain in the alleyway of the mayor's house, but that's not all."

"There's more?" Jessica asked. "What'd they do? Drop by the judge's house, too?"

"Almost as bad." Angie shook her head. "The mayor was at a big fund-raiser breakfast, giving a speech about how he was working closely with law enforcement officials to catch the criminals, when he was notified about the break-in. I heard his face turned red and he blurted out: *I was robbed*? I don't think it did a lot to boost the people's confidence—or his contributions."

"This is the second burglary they've pulled in broad daylight. They're bound to get caught sooner or later," Conor said.

"They almost did this time." Angie sat beside Jessica on the step, slipped off one high heel and absently massaged her foot. "Their truck broke down. They left everything behind except the contents of the safe. The truck was stolen, but we're checking for prints."

Jessica shook her head in denial. "Dad can't be held responsible."

"He already has been." Angie looked apologetic. "The mayor's been caught with his pants down. He wants the suspects in jail, or else." She slipped her shoe back on.

"Dad's doing everything humanly possible to catch these jerks. Even the mayor knows Dad has to get enough evidence to make an arrest or take the chance of losing a conviction."

Conor noted that Jessica's color had returned—a little too much. Her face was going beyond pink. More like red fury. He took a cautious step back when she sprang from the steps. She stomped into the living room, going directly to the window and glaring at the house next door.

"They won't get away with this. No one is going to hurt my father. I'll make sure of that." She clenched and unclenched her fists.

Conor followed her into the other room, knowing she had to get all the anger out of her system. He was almost certain she'd calm down any minute now.

Abruptly, Jessica whirled around, a determined set to her jaw. "We have to stop them."

Conor stilled. "There's no *we* about it. This isn't your fight. You stopped being a police officer when you turned in your badge and gun."

"Being a cop isn't a badge, it's a state of mind. I'm not leaving."

Damn it! Jessica was a civilian. Even if she did think she could help her father, she had no business getting involved with a surveillance operation, especially since George had made contact with them. It was too dangerous.

"She's right, Conor. They won't suspect anything as long as Jess is in the picture. If she leaves, they might not be quite so trusting."

He shook his head. "I don't like it. And I don't think the chief will be happy, either. He said there might be more people involved. Someone giving them orders." He paused, thinking about the problem, before coming up with only one reasonable solution. "No, the situation could get sticky, and I don't want her caught in the middle."

"If Dad hadn't thought I could take care of myself, he wouldn't have encouraged me to become a police officer."

It was as if she defied him to dispute the fact. What was she thinking? Judging from the stubborn look in her eye, he didn't think she'd listen to reason. He had to give it a shot, though. "You said you weren't meant to be a cop," he said softly.

Her eyes narrowed. "I said I didn't *want* to be a cop. My choice. There's a difference."

He gritted his teeth. Stay calm, he told himself. Losing his temper would only make matters worse. Even with her training, she wasn't experienced enough for a stakeout. He knew she'd only been a street cop, but from what Mike had told him, she'd been given the easiest assignments.

What had he said about her? That she was as delicate as a rose petal. Looking at her, Conor knew Mike was telling the truth. Jessica was the picture of purity—even if her kisses told another story. A twinge of guilt rippled down his spine. He felt like the great corrupter.

Right now, she had to see he was right and the best possible solution, the only solution, was that she let him do his job. He took a deep, relaxing breath and continued. "How can I protect you *and* catch the bad guys?"

Her eyes narrowed to slits. "Excuse me? When I need a man to protect me, that'll be the day I run out and buy a Betty Crocker cookbook and tie on an apron."

Stubborn, ornery, mule-headed . . . He opened his mouth, but Angie quickly spoke up.

"Listen, before the next world war breaks out, why don't you give it a try? Just for a few days. You have to at least move in before you have a fight. If not, you'll blow your cover and the chief will lose his job."

He wanted to continue his argument, but damn it, Angie was right. As much as he hated to admit it, after the kiss George witnessed, he'd be awfully skeptical if Jessica took off. He closed his eyes and counted to five. It didn't help. He knew without a doubt she'd only get in his way.

But was there another reason he didn't want her around?

He clamped his lips together. If he were honest with himself, Conor knew why he didn't want Jessica in the same house with him. She was too tempting. He raked a hand through his hair, torn between the emotional upheaval she caused every time she was within touching distance and not wanting to blow the surveillance. Angie was right—if Jessica stormed out, the suspects would be suspicious of their new neighbor.

"Okay—" he reluctantly gave in "—but only for a few days." He watched for any sign that she might be unwilling to go along with the arrangement.

"Agreed."

That was too easy. She looked almost submissive. He hesitated, wondering exactly what she was plotting. He'd been around too many criminals not to spot a ruse. He didn't buy that wide-eyed innocent look for a minute.

Unless he was misreading her again. The conversation he'd had with Mike flashed across his mind.

"Oh, no, Jess did most of the paper filing, looking up information—that sort of stuff. Occasionally we'd let her patrol the streets, but only if we knew she'd be protected from the harsher elements. Why, she's just a sweet, innocent kid."

So maybe he was misjudging her. She could actually be pure as silk, but she damn well didn't kiss like a virgin. But just in case Jessica balked at leaving, Conor had a few surprises up his sleeve. And he'd use every tactic in his arsenal if she even thought about hanging around longer than necessary. It would be for her own good.

Jessica forced her gaze not to waver from Conor's. She wasn't about to go anywhere. "I swear I'll leave as soon as possible." Which would be as soon as they had enough evidence for a conviction.

"Good, I'm glad you can at least recognize the danger you'd be in if you stayed," he said. "I'm going to look around. Stay inside. I don't want you wandering away from the house."

She and Angie watched him leave the room.

"You can uncross your fingers now," Angie spoke dryly.

Jessica grinned. "I haven't crossed my fingers since I was ten. Now I just flat-out lie—when I have to, that is."

Angie looked above the rim of her glasses. "I knew you weren't about to let your father lose his job without a darn good fight. Loyalty means a lot in your family."

"Yeah, it does," Jessica quietly replied.

She glanced up when Conor strode back into the room.

"They look like the typical middle-class family," he stated. "Picnic table and grill behind their house."

"I think you two have everything under control," Angie informed them. Adjusting her purse once more, she prepared to leave. "I'll give the chief a rundown on the situation when I get back to the station."

Jessica tried to listen to what Angie was saying, but she could only think about brushing back a lock of Conor's hair that had fallen forward. He might be obstinate and stubborn as hell, *and a cop*, but it didn't stop him from being damn scrumptious.

" 'Bye, Angie," she absently told the other woman, vaguely registering the closing of the door as Angie left. Her thoughts were too centered on Conor.

"Have you thought about the sleeping arrangements?" he asked.

"Hmmm?"

His slow grin sent a rush of heat swirling through her.

"There's only one master bedroom," he drawled.

"I don't plan on playing mistress to your master, so don't get any ideas."

"We're newlyweds. Remember? We're supposed to have ideas."

Now what was his game? Did he think he'd frighten her off because they'd be alone? Her eyes narrowed. His strategy wouldn't work. She wouldn't let his charm affect her senses.

He sauntered toward her, stopping only inches away. The woodsy scent of his cologne wafted to her nose, swirling around her as his body heat snuggled closer. She took a deep breath. Not a good idea. Visions of what they could do in the master bedroom played around inside her head.

Conor would sweep her into his arms and carry her upstairs. It didn't matter that there wasn't a bed. It was the thought that counted, and anyone who could imitate Rhett Butler was okay in her book. That was a man with charisma, and a hell of a lot of sex appeal.

Her gaze met his, crumbling her resolve to remain immune to his magnetism. Why did she have to think about a stupid old movie? She lowered her head, unable to meet his burning gaze, not when this hungry need swept over her, obliterating everything else. But with one finger he gently raised her chin, not allowing her to escape.

Such dark eyes. Dark with passion. Jessica knew without a

doubt that he wanted her. Instead of scaring her, the thought sent a thrill of desire through her. She wondered if this was the way Scarlett had felt.

"You're playing with fire, Jessica." His hand slid around to the back of her neck and began to gently massage. "Leave while you still can. I don't play for keeps. You're the type of woman who does."

She shook her head, trying to clear it of his softly spoken warning. When she stepped out of his reach, Conor let her go. She turned on her heel and marched toward the door. After a couple of deep breaths, she faced him.

Conor wasn't Rhett Butler and she certainly wasn't Scarlett. So what was it about this man that sent her into a tizzy with just a touch or a whisper? In the future, she'd be more careful around him. Somehow.

"Just because I like what I see doesn't mean I'm going to sleep with you. I'm attracted to a lot of men. I certainly don't go to bed with them. Whether you play for keeps or not matters little to me."

The distance between them helped her regain control of her emotions. No man had ever gotten the best of her. She'd be damned if she'd let it happen now. "I'll be staying for a few days. Get used to it."

Ignoring her body when it begged her to stay, she hurried from the house and climbed into her car. *Oh yeah, you're real cool.* Her hand shook so badly she could barely get the key in the ignition.

As she backed out of the driveway, she glanced one last time at the structure she'd be calling home for no telling how long. She had a lot to do before she set up house with Conor. Gather some clothes. Buy some pajamas. Something with feet and buttons all the way to the neck. That might just keep her out of trouble. And lots of smelly night cream.

But even if she could get Conor to wear all that, could she resist him?

*   *   *

Jessica twisted her button. Lord, she didn't want to move in with Conor. At least, not in a platonic sense. No, not sexually, either! Did she?

Yom-da-da-da-da.

Deep breaths.

Think calming thoughts.

She glanced across the street. Hadn't worked. She still felt like she was strung too tight and might pop any second.

It was all his fault. "I don't see why we have to arrive in the same car," Jessica muttered, keeping to the far side of the passenger seat.

She'd been sitting a little closer, but with every breath she took, inhaling his musky cologne, naughty thoughts began to intrude into her mind. She didn't want to have naughty thoughts involving Conor.

"I thought you said your car was in the shop," Conor commented.

"It is." They had a taxi service in White Plains she could've used, though.

"A taxi would've looked a little strange, don't you think?"

Great, now he could read her mind. She squirmed in her seat. That was scary. Especially when she found her thoughts wandering more and more to the kisses they'd shared and the way his lips had felt against hers—firm, demanding. And the way his strong arms had pulled her close.

A delicious shiver wove its way over her body. She wanted more. Why deny it? But then, she wanted a lot of things in life, but that didn't mean she'd succumb to temptation.

She really, really needed to stay focused. "Calling a cab didn't even occur to me." She'd probably go to hell for lying, too.

"It looks better for newlyweds to arrive together."

He was right, of course. Not that she'd admit any such thing.

"By the way, what'd you tell your boyfriend?"

She frowned. "Boyfriend?"

"The guy who picked you up that day in your father's office."

"Al?" She'd never really thought of Al as her boyfriend. "He's a friend. We date occasionally, but nothing serious. I sold him a property not far from town. I didn't tell him anything. We don't keep tabs on each other." Besides, Al had said he was going on a business trip for a few days.

"Good, I'd hate to ruin your love life."

Yeah, she just bet he would.

"Home sweet home." Conor pulled into the driveway.

The moving truck that had followed with their furniture pulled to the curb. Her father had arranged everything right down to crossing all the t's and dotting the i's.

He'd seemed particularly happy about the whole situation. After explaining several times they weren't really newlyweds, and having him brush aside her words, she'd given up. Let him think what he would. Her father didn't realize she and Conor were on opposite ends of the spectrum. Maybe old age *was* setting in. She'd have a talk with Gabe after the bad guys were caught. See if he'd noticed anything.

Conor shut off the engine and climbed out, then leaned back inside. "Dear, are you planning on staying in the car all day?"

Now he was trying his hand at humor. And there was a decidedly mischievous twinkle in his eyes. Living next door to the suspects didn't bother her nearly as much as the fact she'd be calling Conor husband for at least the next few days.

But she wouldn't let him get the best of her. Smiling sweetly, she gazed adoringly into his face. "It's much more preferable than spending time with you, *darling*."

Frowning, he darted a look over his shoulder. When he turned back around, she'd already scooted out her side and walked to the back of the car, waiting for him to unlock the trunk. Which he did, but before she could grab her suitcase, he brushed her hand aside. Grunting, he hauled her large bag out of the back. It was three times the size of his.

"What the hell did you pack in here, anyway?"

Protection, she thought to herself. A smile curved the corners of her mouth. She glanced up with feigned innocence. "Just a few toiletries."

"The toilet *and* the bathroom sink," he grumbled under his breath as he lugged their suitcases toward the house, but she caught what he'd said and her grin widened.

Conor would be a distraction, but she could get around that as long as she kept reminding herself why she was here. For her father's sake, she had to ignore the strange little tremors that erupted inside her every time he came near. Or that he'd managed to make her body hunger for more than just one kiss.

Her father had been chief too long to lose his job now. After her mother died, he'd poured everything into his job and two children. She'd been four and Gabe eight. Family and work had become his life. And if he'd never really forgotten her mother's death, at least he'd made peace. No matter what Conor said or did, she would help her father.

She pulled her thoughts back to the present, glancing at the men unloading the furniture. Undercover officers. Two of her cousins. She stared as if she hadn't seen them before. Funny, she'd never noticed how handsome Jimmy and Lucas were. And both single. Lucas glanced her way and winked. A real heartthrob. Who did she know . . . Jeez! She was as bad as the rest of her matchmaking family. Neither Lucas nor Jimmy needed her help finding a wife.

"We might as well do this right." Conor emerged from the house, her suitcase having been placed inside.

"Do what right?" She pulled her attention away from her cousins.

"This."

He scooped her up before she could protest. Her arms automatically went around his neck, putting her in even closer contact with his hard body. She wondered if the sudden dizziness washing over her was from being lifted up or being in his arms.

She was so close she could see flecks of gold in his green eyes—the way they dilated when he met her gaze, so close their noses almost touched, so close she inhaled the minty freshness of his breath. A few inches and she'd be able to taste his lips, feel the heat as his tongue ravaged her mouth. She drew in a shuddering breath.

"Put me down," she whispered frantically. It wasn't natural for her to feel this surge of desire when he touched her. Not when she didn't even like the man.

"The curtain next door moved. We're being watched," Conor said, his breath tickling her ear with each word he spoke. She leaned closer. Then realized what he'd said. He cradled her in his arms because someone watched, not because he wanted her there.

Her cousins' snickers effectively grounded her the rest of the way. She knew exactly what the topic of conversation would be at the next family gathering. Didn't Conor know his actions were only making her life miserable?

Yes, he probably did. He'd made no secret about not wanting her there. And *she* hadn't seen any movement at the window. Her eyes narrowed. Was this his game? Scare her off with blatant flirting?

"We're newlyweds, remember," he stated as if he sensed her disbelief. "Isn't this customary?"

She studied his look of innocence for a long minute. Okay, so maybe her imagination had gone into overdrive, and she was reading too much into his actions.

He strolled inside as if she weighed no more than a box of cartridges. She noticed he didn't seem to be in any hurry to let go.

"You smell nice, by the way." His voice turned husky. "That scent suits you."

His words sent a shiver of longing over her, and when he released her, he did it in a way that pressed her body intimately against his. She longed for more . . . to caress with her hands, to test each sinewy muscle beneath her fingers.

A noise from outside brought her back to her senses. She stepped out of his reach, legs trembling. Damn it, he was doing it again.

"If you think you're going to run me off, think again." She'd meant her words to be harsh, but they sounded more breathy than anything.

He probably thought she was pathetic. That she'd even enjoyed being carried inside. Okay, she might have liked the strong feel of his arms wrapped around her, and the way he'd cuddled her close to his hard muscles, but she wouldn't give in to the temptation of Conor Richmond.

Grunting and groaning from the doorway drew her attention.

What was her cousins' problem? Lucas grumbled to himself as he struggled with his end of the mattress. He scrunched and mashed while Jimmy shoved from outside, trying to make it fit through the doorway. Good grief, couldn't they carry in a stupid mattress?

It burst through and popped back into shape. Her eyes widened. This was taking things too far. Had Conor been instrumental in this? His tactics hadn't worked a minute ago and they wouldn't work now. When she glared at him, he only raised his eyebrows. Her cousins' laughter didn't help matters.

"There isn't a darn thing funny about this. Of all the juvenile stunts! A heart-shaped mattress? I would've thought you had a little more imagination."

Conor shook his head. "Hey, this wasn't my idea. Blame someone else for the sense of humor."

"I'm not laughing," she ground out, her gaze swinging to her cousins.

They held up their hands at the same time, then grabbed for the falling mattress. "Not us. We swear, cuz." Lucas grinned from ear to ear, then nodded toward her. "Don't twist your button off, squirt."

She frowned and clasped her hands together in front of her. Damn nervous habit.

If not them, and not Conor, then who? Her father could've sent the mattress. No, surely not. She glared at the monstrosity dominating the hall. Angie? No . . . well . . . maybe. She glanced at Conor again.

He shrugged. "Don't look at me. I don't have any idea."

She shook her head. This was ridiculous. The whole situation was ridiculous. This was a stakeout, not a love nest.

As her cousins dragged the mammoth mattress upstairs, she turned on Conor. "It doesn't matter who sent it. The only thing that'll happen in that bed is sleep," she whispered furiously.

"Positive?" He casually leaned against the wall, crossing his arms.

She scowled. "Positive."

So that was the game he played. A game of seduction so he could run her off. Humph. Like she would fall for that trick. It did make her wonder just how far he would take it.

Tantalizing images played across her mind. Conor tugging a black T-shirt over his head, skin oiled down and glistening in the muted light, but not so muted she couldn't see every bulging muscle.

Her mouth went dry as the image grew stronger.

He'd fling the shirt away and slowly undo his tight jeans. First the top button, then he'd slide the zipper down, hook his fingers in the waistband and begin pushing his jeans over his hips.

"You okay?" Conor asked.

The vision vanished. She blinked several times. He was fully dressed. She'd hoped for a moment . . . It didn't matter.

They would just see who could turn up the heat until the other cried uncle.

She, after all, was a Nelson, and Nelsons didn't play fair.

"I'm perfectly fine . . . thank you very much." She squared her shoulders and looked him straight in the eye. He wasn't about to run her off.

Chapter 7

Someone had a warped sense of humor. Jessica helped with unpacking boxes and putting away stuff, and with each box she died just a little more. There was a small box of cinnamon-scented candles and glass holders to place the votives in. That wasn't so bad. It was the way they were decorated. Little golden cupids with little bows and arrows, all in the shape of little hearts.

They were disgustingly cute.

Then her cousins had lugged in a plush love seat that could only be meant for snuggling. They didn't even dare look her way when they added heart pillows.

And really! A white, faux bearskin rug? She could see herself and Conor wrapped in each other's arms in front of a roaring fire with the temperature outside pushing ninety degrees. It wouldn't be the sweat of passion rolling down their faces.

She leaned against the banister as her gaze moved toward the rug. The bear's mouth was locked open, teeth bared. Her vision blurred and for just a moment she could imagine Conor lying naked on the white fur, leaning back on his elbow with one knee bent. His skin sleek and tanned. Her gaze moved slowly over him, her mouth going dry. He wouldn't even try to hide all his . . . glorious . . . uh . . . attributes.

A bead of sweat slid down her face and into the vee of her blouse, tickling her breasts as it slipped between them.

She drew in a shaky breath, realizing her hands were caressing the knob of the newel post.

"Oh, now that's sick," she told herself.

When she looked back up, the vision had vanished. Disappointment flooded her. She even took a step toward the stupid rug, as if that would make her wanton image materialize once again.

Damn, it didn't. Even so, it took a few more minutes to cool down.

Her eyes narrowed. Whoever set them up had put a lot of thought into their planning, but it wouldn't work. She'd resist. It was the only choice she had. She stiffened her spine and returned to unpacking boxes.

It didn't take long to empty the truck, since the bigger appliances came with the house. Other than what they'd already unloaded, there were a couple of armchairs, a dresser for the bedroom, table and chairs for the kitchen, and some boxes of dishes, along with other odds and ends. Before she knew it, Lucas and Jimmy were gone.

They were alone.

Just the two of them.

She and Conor.

Jessica covertly glanced in Conor's direction. Instead of making a smart remark about some of the stuff they'd unloaded, he turned and strode toward the kitchen, calling over his shoulder, "I'm starved. Do you think they might have stocked the refrigerator?"

Food? At a time like this? How could he think about his stomach? She braced her hands on her hips, staring at his retreating back. They'd be practically living as man and wife for who knows how long, and all he could think about was eating? She certainly had other things on her mind.

She squeezed her eyes shut as the rug and a nude Conor invaded her thoughts. No, not that. She wasn't thinking about sex. The burglars—that's what had skipped across her mind.

Right, and if a frog had wings he wouldn't bump his butt when he hopped.

Laughter came from the kitchen, drawing her attention. She hadn't thought Conor the type of man who laughed. He'd been too serious the day he'd arrested her. So what did he find so damn funny all of a sudden? It certainly wasn't a heart-shaped refrigerator. She'd seen the kitchen.

Proceeding cautiously, she eased down the hall and through the open doorway. Her gaze swept the room. The kitchen was large with a long row of white cabinets. A wooden table and four matching chairs were by a window looking out into the backyard. Most of the house next door was also visible.

In the center of the room was an island with a chopping block and small chrome sink. Above that, one of the guys had hung copper pans.

Shivers ran up and down her arms. It felt too warm and cozy, too . . . homey, but it looked just as it had earlier. At least, nothing seemed out of place.

The stove was to her left, then a span of counter. At the end of the counter was the refrigerator. Conor leaned against the open door with a smirky grin on his face. The kind of smile that said she wouldn't like what he was looking at any more than she had liked the love seat built for two or the bearskin rug. Okay, maybe she hadn't minded *looking* at the bearskin rug—drooling, salivating, slobbering . . .

So what had he found that could be so funny? She met his gaze. Laughter twinkled in his eyes. She had to admit, she rather liked this lighter side of him. As long as she didn't have to shove his grin down his throat. She edged closer and leaned around him, peering inside.

"I see they sent the staples," she commented dryly. "Champagne, oysters, chocolate, and strawberries." If she ever found out who did this . . .

A frown wrinkled her brow as her suspicion grew. She reached past Conor and picked up one of the foil-wrapped chocolates, unwrapped it, and bit into the candy, taking half into her mouth.

Wonderful. She closed her eyes for a moment of heavenly delight as she took pleasure in the burst of raspberry flavor that shot out. When Conor's hand circled her wrist, her eyes flew open. Slowly he brought the rest of the candy toward him. Their gazes locked.

Some of the creamy, soft center had dribbled down the side of her finger. His tongue licked, scooping the gooey, rich candy into his mouth. He closed his eyes as if savoring the taste.

A slow, aching need started in her belly, trembled down her legs, and curled her toes.

He opened his eyes, then brought her hand to his mouth again—and stole the rest of the candy.

"That—" she cleared her throat "—was mine."

"But since we're going to be living together, we'll have to learn to compromise . . . and to share."

"I don't like sharing."

He leaned closer. So close she could smell the raspberry on his breath. She had an incredible urge to taste him. She already enjoyed kissing him, but mix the flavor of chocolate and raspberries and man . . . you couldn't ask for more than that, except maybe if you threw in a heart-shaped bed draped in silk sheets.

Without thinking, she leaned a little closer, so close she could almost feel the heat of his lips against hers. His fingers lightly stroked hers, causing the embers inside her to glow.

He groaned, effectively bringing her to her senses. She tugged her hand free. He was doing it again. His whole personality changed when he tried his seduction routine. He went from cop to flirt in the blink of an eye before she could put her guard up.

That was her problem. He was more tempting than any

man she'd ever been around. If he kept this up, she had a feeling the days were going to be exquisite torture. Hell, they hadn't been together but a few hours and she wanted to drizzle him in chocolate and slowly lick his entire body. Chocolate-covered hunk.

Note to self: start new diet. One that doesn't include chocolate of any kind.

"I could teach you how much fun sharing can be," he drawled. "We could share the shower—save on hot water. I could wash your back. I've been told I'm pretty good at washing backs . . . and other body areas."

Ohhhh, so not fair. Conor was good. Really good. Two could play this game. "And maybe while I'm here I'll teach *you* a few things," she told him in a throaty whisper, not about to let him know how much he affected her.

His frown told her she'd won this round. Funny, but she didn't much feel like a winner.

Conor looked sorely disappointed that she hadn't run from the house to get away from his animal magnetism. That gave her some measure of satisfaction.

But then, he didn't realize how close she was to jumping his bones, not running away. She'd have to keep her guard up at all times around him now that she knew his game. Oh yes, Conor thought he could seduce her right out of the house.

Over his shoulder he said, "Come on."

She let the smallest of smiles curve her lips upward. He only wanted to scare her. She wouldn't run home to her safe apartment just because he flirted with her.

What was he up to now, though? "Where are we going?" she asked before moving an inch.

Stopping, he faced her, and with the sexiest grin she'd ever seen, said, "Although sweet and tasty, I can't live on what's in the fridge. We need to stock up on groceries and linens. Unless you want to sleep bare."

"Bare?" she croaked, her muscles turning to the consistency of jelly. Darn—now, instead of on the bearskin rug, she pictured him in the same position, no clothes and on the heart-shaped bed. Her thighs trembled. This time he'd crook his finger as he beckoned her to join him.

"Yeah, on a bare mattress," he said.

He probably knew exactly where her mind would go— right in the gutter when he'd mentioned sleeping bare. Conor wasn't giving up, and he wasn't playing fair.

The way he looked at her, his gaze slowly traveling over her body, told her the food in the refrigerator and a sheetless bed weren't all he envisioned. She only hoped the arsenal she'd packed in her suitcase would be enough to ensure her survival over the length of time it took to gather enough evidence to get a conviction on the burglars.

And speaking of which, would it be wise to leave? "What about the suspects?"

"Since George made contact, we can't stay home all the time. That would look strange, even for newlyweds, but if they see us coming and going, they shouldn't get suspicious. Someone in an unmarked car will patrol while we're away. They'll probably still be there when we get back."

That's what she was afraid of. The suspects had better hurry and make a mistake so she could be done with this stakeout and go home.

"You coming?"

She certainly hoped not, but she was very close to doing just that every time he looked at her. She rolled her eyes. *Get your mind out of the gutter, Jessica.*

Conor was right about not staying home all the time. It would look odd. Maybe food would take her mind off all the sexy images she was having. And they did need to eat.

Apparently her father wasn't too worried about his job. She scowled. If he was, he wouldn't have set up this surveillance like he had. Heart-shaped bed! Didn't he have more imagination than that?

But the Godiva Chocolate. She had to admit that was a good idea, and a dead giveaway. Only her father would have purchased the specialty candy. He always gave her a box on her birthday, at Christmas, and on special occasions . . . like when she'd made it through the academy. How appropriate for him to send it now—her first surveillance. If he was trying to tell her he liked Conor, giving his stamp of approval, she hated to disappoint him, because she still wasn't getting involved with a cop.

She trailed behind Conor, thinking what a shame. He had the sexiest walk she'd ever seen on a man. A slow, easy gait. And those hip-riding jeans. She drew in a deep, shuddering breath. They were enough to take her breath away. As she passed by the thermostat, she bumped the central air down a notch. Maybe it would be cold enough when they returned to keep her passion under control. She looked one more time at his butt.

Or maybe not.

"We want heart-shaped sheets," Conor told the saleswoman.

Jessica wondered how he could ask that with a straight face. Hell, she couldn't even say it without spitting.

Earth to Jessica. What was her problem? Was she getting spacey? No, her problem was she didn't want to be in this store. It was embarrassing. Not only were there female mannequins wearing skimpy, lacy nighties, but there were male mannequins, too. They'd actually put a black leather thong on one, and from the bulge it looked anatomically correct. What man would be caught dead wearing a black leather thong?

Her gaze moved back to the mannequin's face. It winked at her! She blinked several times. No, mannequins didn't wink. She frowned. It looked a lot like Conor, too. Great, now she was imagining things. Lack of sleep, that's all it could be. Knowing they'd be moving in together had kept her up most of the night.

"You okay?" Conor asked.

She jerked her attention away from the man of plastic and narrowed her eyes on Conor. He thought the situation was hilarious.

"It's just a little crowded in here." She wasn't about to give him the satisfaction of knowing she was uncomfortable being in the store with him.

Didn't anyone use the Internet to shop? Or order from a catalog? She found it much easier doing that than actually shopping for something as ridiculous as heart-shaped sheets.

She bought all her sexy lingerie off the Internet . . . along with deliciously sexy toys that she certainly didn't want to think about with Conor standing near her. Or what she could do with a certain stimulating device. She was self-conscious enough as it was.

Hell, she wanted to crawl underneath the counter just listening to Conor. Anyone would think he came into this store every day. She looked at him from the corner of her eye. Maybe he did. It was always the dark, quiet ones who surprised people the most.

He glanced her way, looking as innocent as a newborn babe. She attempted a smile, but knew he saw through her act. She couldn't help it; she didn't like the way the other customers were eavesdropping.

The gum-smacking saleswoman never missed a beat as she looked over her shoulder. "Hey, Myrtle," she bellowed. "We got any heart-shaped sheets?"

Those customers who hadn't been paying attention now turned to look at them. Expressions ranged from leering to snickering.

"Heart-shaped pillows?" the older woman yelled back.

Apparently Myrtle was a little hard of hearing.

"No! Heart-shaped sheets!" she called out again.

"What color do they want?" Myrtle bellowed.

"It doesn't matter! Do you have them or not?" Jessica asked with exasperation.

Conor's shoulders shook with mirth. Had she really

thought he didn't have a sense of humor? Apparently, when it came to her, he found a lot to laugh about. Great—when she thought about him she pictured the two of them rolling around in bed together; he apparently only saw someone who inspired him to laughter.

Myrtle waddled over, lifting her glasses that hung on a chain around her neck and placing them on her nose. She grunted as she bent down in front of one of the cabinets under a counter and slid the door open. "Here's some pretty red ones." She pulled the package out as she straightened. "They're those silky kind that feel so good against your skin when you're lying naked in the bed."

Oh lord, T*M*I. She really hadn't needed to visualize the grandmotherly salesclerk lying naked in bed. She grabbed the package out of the saleswoman's hand. "We'll take them." She hugged the sheets as if she were drowning and the package was a life jacket.

"Are you sure? I thought I saw some blue . . ."

"No, we like the red ones." Jessica imagined her face was probably the same color as the blasted sheets. "Can we please check out?"

"Are you sure you don't want to look around some more?" Conor asked.

"I'm sure," she said between gritted teeth and led the way to the cash register, hoping Conor would follow. Thankfully, he did. She held her breath and counted to ten while he took his time giving Myrtle the exact amount of money, right down to the last penny.

"It's not funny," Jessica said as they exited the store. Her stern demeanor slipped and she couldn't stop the smile tugging at her lips.

Conor's chuckles turned into deep laughter. Jessica jerked her head toward the sound. An elderly woman walking down the sidewalk even smiled. Jessica decided she liked his laughter. A lot. And that was not a good thing.

"I think because you egged her on, you should buy supper," she said. Maybe food would make the dizzy, giddy feeling go away. Besides, the egg sandwich she'd fixed this morning and only eaten half of had long since worn off and she was starving. Her stomach was starting to rumble.

"What? You mean you're not going to buy mine?" His eyebrows drew together. "I did let you pick the sheets. The least you can do is buy *my* dinner."

"Yeah, well, after having to listen to the duel of the yelling salesclerks, you should buy mine. And breakfast tomorrow morning."

He opened the car door for her and she slid inside. After tossing the sheets into the backseat, he went to the driver's side and climbed in. But before starting the car, he turned toward her.

"How about if I bring you breakfast in bed instead?" he drawled.

It took a few moments for his words to sink in. He was doing it again—trying to make her see that this arrangement couldn't possibly work and she'd be better off crying uncle. Well, she wouldn't do it. She could be just as stubborn.

If the truth was known, she should've been angry that he was blatantly flirting again, but a vision of the kind of meal he'd serve sent treacherous little spasms of pleasure dancing up and down her spine. It was tempting to ask exactly what he had in mind.

A temptation she'd resist if it killed her. She didn't eat breakfast, anyway. Not that she didn't mind a piece of toast now and then—especially if a sexy undercover cop wearing only a smile served it to her.

She turned toward him and quirked an eyebrow. "Don't you think that might interfere with the sting operation? And I thought you were so professional."

His eyes narrowed. "Look, I'm just trying to make you see this isn't going to work out. These people are serious. They're hardened criminals, and they wouldn't think twice before killing either of us, and you're too much of a distraction."

Lord, he was even more tempting when he was irritated.

His eyes darkened to a deep, sexy green. And she loved the way some of his hair fell on his forehead. He thought *she* was a distraction? When all she could think about was kissing him? Hell, more than that. Kissing wouldn't come close to what she wanted to do to him.

She reined in her thoughts before they could get past the lip-lock stage. This was no time to think about how it would feel to have his mouth on hers. He was right about one thing: business before pleasure. And with him being a cop, she'd better forget about any fantasies involving Conor.

What a shame.

She drew in a deep breath. "Then quit flirting with me, Officer Richmond."

"Remember our deal. We'll have a fight and you run . . . run somewhere." He gripped the steering wheel.

"As soon as it won't cause our neighbors to be suspicious, that's exactly what I'll do." She was already going to hell for lying. One more wouldn't make much difference. "I don't want to be here any more than you do, but I won't put my father's job in more jeopardy than it already is."

"Okay, just so we're clear about it."

Conor started the car and pulled away from the curb. Jessica was more stubborn than he'd first thought. Cute and stubborn. The only hardship he'd have over the next day or so was the fact he'd be working. Any other time or place, it wouldn't take much stretch of his imagination to picture her naked and in his bed.

Like that would happen. Mike was right when he'd said Jessica was pure and innocent. She'd been pretty embarrassed just being in the store when they were buying sheets.

Guilt washed over him. He did feel bad she'd had to see the scantily clad mannequins—even if they were made of plastic. But then, maybe he'd have to open her eyes to a few of life's realities before she realized she was way out of her league. Damn, he really hated the thought of shattering some of her ideals, but he wouldn't have her in harm's way.

The thought of being alone again didn't sit well. She was starting to grow on him. Not only had she made him smile . . . she'd made him laugh. It had been a while since he'd done either.

"Where do you want to eat?" he asked. The least he could do was let her choose. He doubted she'd last more than one night.

"Take-out is fine. Pizza?"

He nodded.

They stopped at a grocery store and grabbed a few items before driving to the nearest pizza place. In less than an hour, they were on their way back to the house.

Jessica was silent on the ride home, and he wondered if she was thinking about the suspects. She seemed to be interested in the passing scenery, but he knew she was nervous by the way she twisted her button. He'd love to tell her everything would be all right and that he wouldn't let her come to harm while she was with him, but he didn't want her getting any ideas that she'd be staying longer than was absolutely necessary.

So he kept his thoughts to himself and made the last turn down their street and into the driveway. He cut the engine and stepped out, popping the trunk open as he walked to the back of the car.

"I'll get these," he told her when she grabbed a bag of groceries.

Jessica brushed aside his protests and grabbed a bag. Conor grinned at her independence. She was a feisty little thing. He grasped a couple of the blue plastic bags and followed behind her.

The woman was going to drive him to drink. She frustrated the hell out of him, but he couldn't stop his gaze from constantly straying in her direction. She was the most tempting woman he'd ever met.

Even when she'd looked like a street-person-turned-hooker, he'd been intrigued. A smile pulled at his lips. Then when she was dressed so casually at her father's home, with her blond waves pulled into a ponytail, she'd reminded him of a little kitten: soft and cuddly. He certainly wouldn't have minded snuggling next to her . . . both of them naked.

And now she was dressed like a lady. A very sexy lady. She wore a skirt that was fantasy short, and he was having a lot of fantasies right now.

That's why she had to leave. How the hell could he concentrate on what needed to be done with her perfume swirling around him, reminding him she was there?

He glanced toward the house next door, and this time he really did see a curtain flutter. Someone watched them. Were they judging if they really were newlyweds?

Jessica set her bag down and turned toward him. "Is your key handy? Mine's in my purse."

He didn't answer, but set his bags on the porch and gathered her in his arms. Before she could protest, he lowered his mouth to hers. Lord, this was nice. She tasted like the cinnamon toothpaste he'd seen in the bathroom cabinet when he'd put away his shaving gear.

She was like stormy weather. He could see the flash of lightning and feel the intensity as his arms wrapped around her and tugged her close.

This was work—just doing his job, he told himself, but she wasn't pulling away.

Their bodies were pressed so close you couldn't slide a hand between them. Her breasts crushed against his chest, her nipples tight little nubs that poked through her thin shirt, rubbing against his equally thin T-shirt.

He'd only wanted to make everything look real, but damn it, he liked holding her close, tasting the sweetness of her mouth, feeling her soft curves as his hands roamed over her body with a will of their own.

He wanted to do more than kiss her. He wanted to undress her, unhook her bra and touch her naked breasts, drawing her hard nipples into his mouth one at a time.

When she moaned, he returned to his senses and ended the kiss. Still, he didn't immediately pull away. Mainly because he didn't think he had the strength to move just yet.

"I don't know exactly what you think you're doing, but it won't work," she said.

He caught the tremble in her words and was gratified to know she wasn't immune to him. "Shh, someone's watching." He nuzzled her neck.

She stiffened in his arms. "Oh, I see. We're doing the put-on-a-show thingy. Make them believe we're really newlyweds."

A hard edge had entered her voice. Conor didn't think he liked the sound of it, but before he could offer more of an explanation, she grabbed his ass and squeezed.

He jumped, reaching for the wall behind her for support.

"Then by all means, let's give them a show they won't forget," she told him.

Before his shock had time to wear off, she began caressing and fondling his ass—anywhere her hands could reach. It was all he could do to keep from groaning. What she was doing sent him close to the edge, but when she began sliding one of her hands between the lower half of their bodies, he knew the show was over—or he wouldn't be able to walk for the next few days. Either that, or he'd embarrass the hell out of himself.

"I think we've convinced them by now," he managed to croak.

She stretched upward toward his ear and lightly nipped it. "Just remember, Conor. You're playing with a big girl. I don't scare easily, and I damn sure don't play fair."

She stepped from his arms, turned around, and dug her key out of her purse. He stood there watching her, too stunned to move as she opened the door and waltzed inside.

Then he frowned. Damn, they'd lied to him at the station, especially her cousin Mike. Jessica wasn't as naive as he'd been led to believe. No innocent would've grabbed his ass.

She'd have been flustered and scrambling inside to hide herself away in the bathroom or something.

This changed everything. Flirting wouldn't work. He bent and scooped up the two bags of groceries. He'd have to think of something else. Damn, how could he have been so gullible? He was a cop, for crying out loud. Just wait until he saw her cousin again.

A door slammed shut next door, drawing his attention. He watched as George retrieved the mail from the box, saluted him, and grinned.

At least he knew who'd been spying on them. He'd almost forgotten about the criminals next door.

He returned the greeting with a false smile and a wave of his own. "Just wait, Buster—you won't be grinning for long," he muttered before going inside.

Jessica was in the kitchen. She wasn't putting away the food from her bag as much as she was slamming it inside the cupboard. She didn't look happy. But she looked good. He discovered he was looking at her in a whole new light. One that could get them both in trouble.

"Showing affection is part of the package if we're to maintain some semblance of being newly married," he explained, knowing he was lying through his teeth. His job had been the last thing on his mind.

She whirled around and faced him. "I'd appreciate it if you'd warn me the next time you decide to be *affectionate*." She shoved her hair behind her ears and glared at him. "Don't think I don't know what game you're playing. If you can get rid of me, then you'll be able to control the surveillance operation. Believe me, a kiss doesn't scare me."

"Yeah, well, I figured that out."

She stopped for a minute, a puzzled frown wrinkling her brow. "Why would you even think it would?"

"Mike. He said you were . . . a virgin or at least almost one."

"Oh." A grin replaced her confusion.

He set his bags on the table and shifted from one foot to the other.

"And you believed him?"

"Well, yeah. He's your cousin. I figured he knew better than some, and you look . . ." He could feel the heat crawl up his face.

She rested her hands on her hips and cocked an eyebrow. "I look what?"

The words stuck in his throat. He couldn't very well tell her she looked virginal, because she didn't. She looked sexy . . . alluring. Why *had* he fallen for the line Mike gave him? His gaze swept over her. She looked anything but innocent. She looked hot.

She wore some kind of silky-looking blouse. A deep blue color that matched her eyes. Her white skirt was short and complemented her incredibly long legs. And heels. What was there about a woman in heels?

Virginal? He didn't think so.

"Let's just leave it at the fact I shouldn't have believed Mike. I'm new. I suppose everyone figured it would be a great joke."

"So maybe you've been wrong about more than one thing?"

He didn't think so, but how could he make her understand that she was jeopardizing the whole operation. "You're right about me wanting you to leave, and that I was a little underhanded."

"A little?"

He let her snide remark slide and countered with a question of his own. "How many undercover operations have you been on?"

She nibbled on her bottom lip as if she were trying to figure out if he'd come up with a new tactic. She finally took a deep breath that made it hard for him to stay focused when her breasts strained against the material.

"None."

He cleared his throat. "There, you've answered your own question. You don't have any experience. If you care about your father's job, then you'll let me do mine."

She leaned against the edge of the counter and crossed her arms in front of her. "The reason I'm staying is because I do care." She glanced at her hands before meeting his gaze once again. "If I think I'm causing more harm than good, I'll leave. You have my word, and the word of a Nelson shouldn't be taken lightly."

Now what should he do? He didn't want her here. Not because he was afraid she'd get hurt—he'd be able to keep her safe—but she was too much of a distraction. He needed all his attention on the case.

One look at her set features and he knew she wasn't giving him a choice. Jessica was here to stay, unless she thought she might be hindering the operation. He'd been afraid of this.

He took a deep breath before slowly exhaling. "Just stay out of my way," he warned and turned on his heel. "I'll bring in the rest of the bags."

Now what the hell was he going to do with Jessica in the house? Especially since he knew she wasn't innocent like Mike and the rest of the guys had sworn.

As he approached the front door, he stumbled. Visions of her naked and curled next to him in the heart-shaped bed upstairs danced across his mind. There was only one bed. Sweat beaded his brow as he fought the image and hurried outside.

Damn it, he was here to do a job. Not get laid.

He cast a disgruntled glance toward the house next door. They damn well better screw up and give him the evidence he'd need for a conviction, or he'd be the one committing crimes!

Chapter 8

Jessica reached across the kitchen table for another slice of pizza. "So what are we supposed to do? Just sit here?"

He turned from watching the house next door and looked at her. "No one ever said it would be exciting. Most surveillance work is actually pretty boring." He raised his can of soda and took a long drink, then set it back on the table.

"So what are we watching for?"

He hesitated.

"What's the matter? Do you think I'll blow your case if I know what to look for? I'm assuming, anything suspicious. Like if they all load up in a huge truck and take off."

She was a semipatient person and could wait him out. He caved under the onslaught of her unwavering stare. Worked every time.

"The less you're involved, the better. But yes, anything unusual . . . visitors. I doubt they'll be that obvious, but one never knows. They did rob Mrs. Huntley's house in broad daylight. But your father thinks someone else is calling the shots. That's the one he wants to catch." He nodded toward the house next door. "These lame-brains are penny-ante stuff. He wants the big fish."

She leaned back in her chair and stared at the house next door. At this rate, they would be here well into the next century. Maybe she could shake things up a bit. "Why don't I run next door and borrow a cup of sugar . . ."

"No."

She sat forward. "You haven't even heard my plan."

"No. This isn't your case. You're lucky I'm letting you stay here at all." He wiped his hands on a paper towel and tossed it back on the table before standing.

"I want to help and you know you're going to need it. You can't watch the house twenty-four hours a day."

He was really starting to piss her off, the way he treated her like she'd never patrolled the streets, and now she had to tilt her head to look up at him. She seriously doubted he would be willing to rub away the crick she was going to get in her neck . . . but thinking about him massaging her back was kind of nice. She bet he could do more than get rid of a tight muscle.

"I don't need your help," he countered.

Nothing like having a bucket of ice water thrown on her fantasy. The man was all business. Okay, she could be business-like, too. "What would it hurt if I just went next door and borrowed a cup of sugar?" She stood—besides straining her neck when she was sitting, she didn't like the way he towered over her. Was he trying to intimidate her?

It wasn't much better after she came to her feet. Thoughts of intimidation scattered as her gaze drifted over him. She liked the way he dressed. Sort of casual . . . relaxed . . . approach-able. Too bad it was all a facade. This man was the least ap-proachable person she'd ever had the misfortune to meet.

But a couple more steps and she could be in his arms. Would he kiss her the way he had earlier when they were on the front porch and he thought someone was watching them? How much of it had been an act? She wasn't a fool. She knew when a man wanted her, and Conor had been aroused.

"Stop."

Her eyebrows rose. "Stop what?"

"Looking at me like that."

"Like what?" Now she was thoroughly confused.

He waved his arms. "All soft and sexy. Like you want me to kiss you, to make love to you. You know . . . *the look*. I'm here to do a job, and I can't concentrate when you look at me like that."

"You really have an ego problem, don't you? I've never once encouraged your kisses. If I'm not mistaken, you haven't been able to keep your hands off me. As far as I can tell, I'm not the problem, you are."

She glared at him, but lost a margin of her anger when she saw the way he was looking at her—like he wanted to devour her. The way his glance skimmed over her body, she didn't think she'd mind being devoured. His gaze began its trek back to her face.

Heat flooded her body as his languid look lingered . . . touching . . . heating her body until it burned with need. She drew in a ragged breath.

"Stop," she whispered.

"What?" he asked.

"Looking at *me* like that."

His brow wrinkled. "Like I said, how can I concentrate with you in the house? If you don't want your father to lose his job, then you need to leave."

She shook her head. "You know that won't happen. It would blow your cover."

He scooped up the paper plates and empty cans, cramming them into the trash can. "Then we have a problem," he said, a gruff edge in his voice.

"I don't have the problem, you do." After closing the pizza box and sticking it in the refrigerator, she grabbed a paper towel and wet it, squeezing out the excess water before wiping the table. His frustration washed over her in waves, but she wouldn't leave. He'd just have to get used to her being around.

Of all the men she'd crossed paths with, why did she feel drawn to this one? A cop, no less. She didn't want to feel what he made her feel. Her only concern should be her father's job, not what Conor thought about her.

"Stay out of my way, then," he warned.

"Believe me, that won't be a problem." She clenched her teeth to keep from saying something she might later regret. On second thought, she didn't think she'd regret a damn thing. At this rate, she'd have to make a dental appointment. All her teeth would be ground to nubs before they caught the person masterminding the robberies. Maybe saying what was on her mind would be the best thing for her.

Conor turned on his heel and strode to the other room. She took a deep breath and inhaled, then counted to ten.

Didn't work.

She took another deep breath and forced herself to slowly exhale. "Yom-da-da-da-da."

That didn't work, either.

What she wanted to do was stomp her foot and throw something. She grabbed a dry paper towel instead, and, standing at the counter, began shredding it.

Oh, she'd like to rip his head off. She tore off the top half of the towel. And his arm, she thought, tearing off a corner. She pursed her lips. He was treating her like she was a civilian. She tore a leg, then the other leg. She ripped again and again.

She was left with one long piece of paper towel. Her eyebrows rose. There was only one part left unamputated. Her thighs quivered. Lightly, she stroked the last piece of the towel that was intact. It would be a shame to make it shorter. She cringed at the thought.

"By the way," Conor said as he charged back into the kitchen.

She whirled around, keeping her hands and the ripped pieces of paper towel hidden behind her.

"Yes," she squeaked.

He frowned, but didn't comment. "If you decide to leave the house, let me know first."

"Sure. No problem."

"You okay?"

"Never better." Her smile wobbled.

He nodded and left the room. She breathed a sigh of relief. It had been stupid to throw a silly temper tantrum. What had she been thinking?

Aunt Gloria had always told her that when she got angry, just shred a paper towel. She'd shredded many paper towels over the years.

Speaking of her aunt, though—she grabbed her phone and punched in her number.

Ripping a paper towel nearly always worked. She should just stick with chanting—no incriminating evidence to hide. Hmm, maybe she'd better stock up on a few more rolls of paper towels, though.

"Hello."

"Auntie, did you by any chance have a heart-shaped bed delivered? Along with chocolate and other items meant for newlyweds?"

"Is that what arrived in the truck?"

Laughter was evident in her aunt's voice. Her suspicion grew.

"Aunt Gloria . . ."

"Wasn't me, dear. I'd bet my next paycheck it was your father. You know how badly he wants to see you settled down with a family of your own."

She was right—it could only have been her father. Scammed again. She talked to her aunt a few more minutes, then closed the phone before scooping up the disemboweled paper towel and stuffing it down deep into the trash, just under the paper plates.

She had to admit, shredding the towel made her feel better. Conor would probably think she'd lost her mind, but as long as her frustration was gone, she didn't care.

Now all she had to do was persuade him she could be of some use. That wasn't going to be easy since he acted like she couldn't take care of herself. She was a damn good cop. She only had to convince him of that fact. But how, when he wouldn't even listen to her?

Her cell phone began playing "God Bless America." She grabbed it off the table and flipped it open.

"Hello?"

"Hey, sweetheart, so are you and Conor settled in okay?"

She flopped down into the nearest chair and crossed her legs. "Oh, yeah, we're all settled in. I noticed you were pretty scarce all week. You weren't hiding, were you?"

"Hiding? Why would I be hiding?"

He didn't fool her for a minute. "Let's see. Maybe because you're trying to sabotage your own stakeout? I mean, really, a heart-shaped bed? Godiva Chocolates? A bearskin rug? What exactly are you trying to do? I've already told you Conor has no interest in me."

"Should I fire him? Get someone in there who does?"

She opened her mouth, then snapped it closed. "Very funny."

"But you do like him, don't you?"

"He pisses me off. I think the feeling is mutual."

"Good!"

She could almost see him rubbing his hands together. "Dad, are you losing your hearing? I told you he irritates the hell out of me."

"Yeah, your mom said the same thing about me when we first met. It's called chemistry. I told you to pay attention in that class."

"Yeah, well, I'd bet my real estate license Conor doesn't want to get involved with our family. Did you know Mike and some of the others told Conor I was practically a virgin?"

"You're not?"

Heat flooded her face. Sometimes she forgot she was talking to her father and not her best friend. On more than one occasion, she'd had to extricate herself from a sticky situation. Like right now. "Could we change the subject? I know you didn't call just to talk about my love life." Then again, he probably had.

When their conversation ended, she still had no idea what he'd wanted. She had a feeling her first assumption was right. He'd wanted to find out if she and Conor had fallen in love. Her dad really had to stop obsessing about her love life. She closed the phone and set it back on the table. With a deep sigh she wondered what she was going to do about him.

"Jess is going to kill you for meddling one of these days. Either that or disown you," Gloria told her brother.

Joe Nelson didn't even try to stop his grin. Sure, he felt pretty smug. Had good reason, too. "You forget, sister, I checked Conor Richmond out before I hired him. He's a good cop. Exactly the kind of man our Jess needs in her life." He folded his hands behind his head and leaned back in his chair.

She straightened the papers on his desk, not meeting his eyes. "I thought you were trying to put the Meredith gang out of business along with their ringleader? Looks more like you're setting a trap for your daughter and the new officer."

He frowned. "That's exactly what Jess accused me of."

"Well, aren't you?"

"Yeah, but I thought I'd covered my tracks pretty good."

She stopped what she was doing and planted her hands on her hips. "How? By having a heart-shaped bed delivered? That's about as subtle as the Godiva Chocolate."

"How'd you find out about the chocolate?"

She cocked an eyebrow. "Just because I'm not a cop doesn't mean I haven't learned the art of observation. Besides, Jess told me. She even wanted to know if I'd been the one who set her up."

"You watch and see if those two don't fall in love before the surveillance is over."

"Aren't you even worried about your job?"

"It would be worth ten jobs to see my daughter happily married."

"I just don't think this is the way to go about doing it." She cleared her throat. "Speaking of jobs, the mayor called earlier. I told him you were out of the office, just like you told me."

"Good. I only want him to know what I tell him."

"You still think he might be behind the burglaries?"

"Let's just say I haven't ruled him out."

"I talked to Dad earlier," Jessica said, drawing Conor's attention away from the suspects' house.

As soon as he looked her way, he knew he was in trouble. The only light came from the full moon and a small lamp in the corner of the living room, making it easy to see her expression. Right now it was soft, with a sleepy-eyed look that made him want to carry her up to bed and do more than tuck her in.

She'd pulled her feet up under her when she'd curled herself in the wingback chair and was hugging a heart-shaped pillow. He couldn't help wishing she was curled in his lap hugging him instead.

He gripped the arms of his chair, trying to focus. It wouldn't surprise him if he totally blew this case. Damn, he'd always been able to gather enough evidence to get a conviction or, at the very least, enough proof that the suspects were innocent. He was afraid his clean record might get muddied the longer Jessica hung around.

"I spoke with your father, too," he told her.

She hugged the pillow a little tighter. "Did he mention anything about who he thought the ringleader might be?"

It wouldn't do a damn bit of good not telling her anything. Hell, he already knew her knowledge about the case was nearly as much as his.

"No, he doesn't have a suspect yet."

She was quiet a few minutes. He could feel her watching him.

"But you do." She spoke quietly.

She was good at reading people. He'd always prided himself on being unreadable. He briefly wondered if he was mistaken in other areas as much as he had been about her innocence. No, he didn't think so.

"Yeah, I have a few people on my list," he finally admitted.

"The mayor?"

"Your father doesn't seem to think so."

She rested her head against the back of the chair, and for a moment he lost his train of thought. A lock of pale blond hair fell forward. She casually brushed it behind her ear. God, she was so damned beautiful.

"My father says the mayor is a jerk. He doesn't think he's guilty. Not of the robberies, anyway. You know they went to school together, don't you? Same grade and everything. I don't think Dad wants past rivalries to cloud his judgment, but it might be working in reverse."

"You think the mayor might be involved?"

She shrugged. "I haven't ruled him out."

He crossed his legs and leaned back to a more comfortable spot. He'd never discussed an ongoing case with anyone outside law enforcement, but he reasoned that since her father trusted her with information, there'd be no harm, and she was right—technically, she was still a cop. Besides, he found himself curious to know how Jessica's mind worked.

"But what about the fact his house was robbed?" He watched her face and saw she kept her expression bland. She was pretty good at hiding what she thought, too. "It hurt his campaign," he went on.

"And a good way to throw off any suspicion. The criminals have cashed in on a lot of money since they began their crime spree. More than the mayor could make as a public servant."

Okay, so they'd wondered the same thing. That still didn't make her a *good* cop. "So, why is your father not convinced? I know the chief suspects shady dealings involving the mayor. Like contracts going to some of his friends."

"It's hard not to have dealings with people you know in a town of less than a hundred thousand. He wants more proof."

"That's why I'm here."

"But you can't stay awake all night, and all day, too. You have to go to bed sometime."

His heart pounded when he thought of the heart-shaped bed upstairs. "I'll be fine." He glanced at his watch. Nearly midnight. "Why don't you go to bed," he said as casually as his racing pulse would allow. He pictured her lying naked in the middle of the bed, pale skin against a background of red satin sheets. Not that he would do anything about it. "Go on to bed. You're about to fall out of your chair."

She straightened, eyes opening wide. "I'm fine . . . really . . ." She stifled a yawn.

God, she was like a delectable pastry. He was getting more hungry each minute he spent in her company.

"You're right," she admitted wryly. "Do you think anything will happen tonight?" She nodded toward their neighbors' house.

Absolutely not! It took him a second or two to realize she was talking about the suspects. He drew in a deep breath. "They turned off the last light an hour ago. Everything's been as lifeless as a morgue. They're probably sound asleep."

"Wake me up when you get sleepy, and I'll take over the watch. I can at least do that much. I'll call you if anything happens."

She was right. He would've taken turns with Angie if George hadn't walked in on him and Jessica kissing. "Okay. When I get tired."

" 'Night, then."

She uncurled from the chair, and like a cat, stretched as she stood. Languidly, she sauntered toward the stairs, but stopped and turned when she reached the doorway.

"You'll be up soon? I won't need more than a few hours' sleep."

His insides tightened at the thought of crawling between the red silk sheets and snuggling close to Jessica, then waking her up with a long, passion-filled kiss.

All of a sudden, burglars and law enforcement were the last things on his agenda. Instead, he wondered what she wore to bed.

He swallowed.

If anything.

"Yeah, I'll be up shortly." He was amazed there was only a slight crack in his voice. It was a miracle he could speak at all.

Darkness swallowed her, making him wonder if he'd imagined her slow, seductive walk. Inhaling, he caught a whisper of the fragrance she wore. Mysterious and sinful.

Shaking his head, he tried to concentrate on the facts. Number one, they weren't really married. Two, he had a job to do. Three, making love with Jessica should be the furthest thing from his mind.

Then why couldn't he think about anything else?

He heard the distant noise of the upstairs shower and had to adjust his pants as he pictured her standing under the spray of water, the soap sliding over her body, leaving tiny bubbles in its wake. Her skin would be slick, his hands could easily slide over the soapy surface of her body.

She turned off the water, but not his fantasies. A few minutes later a whirring noise came from upstairs. Blow dryer? A sudden vision of her getting ready for him, her hair soft and fluffy, sent a longing inside him that he found hard to control.

His hand shook as he raked it through his hair, imagining what it would be like with her pressed close. Her lips would graze his bare skin. Her tongue . . .

Get hold of yourself! It should be up to him to be the professional. Damn! He'd been the one to bring sex into the equation when he tried to run her off. Now it seemed that was all he could think about. He'd only wanted to scare her into running back home to her safe apartment. At the very least, make her see this situation was impossible and she'd better leave the first chance she got.

The tables had turned. Maybe she didn't realize what she was doing, but all the signals were there. His sixth sense told him that she craved this as much as he did.

Maybe she *was* the type for a casual affair. If he wasn't on a stakeout, the circumstances couldn't be better. Neither one expected a commitment from the other. She'd already told him she didn't want to get involved with a cop, and he certainly didn't want a long-term relationship. No one would be hurt.

He stood and went to the phone, dialing the number of the station.

"White Plains Police Department," the dispatcher said.

"Officer Richmond. I'm going to take a quick shower. Have an unmarked car cruise the area."

"Sure thing, Conor."

He shook his head. Coming from a large department to a smaller one had been a shock he wasn't sure he'd ever get used to. They certainly didn't stand on ceremony.

He glanced one more time at the house next door before making his way up the stairs. He combed his hand through his hair and straightened his shirt. Taking a deep breath, he eased the door open and stepped inside.

The bathroom door stood slightly ajar, bathing all but the shadowed corners in a soft, dim light. He ambled toward the bed, trying to appear nonchalant.

His steps faltered. If Jessica was under those covers, she'd shrunk. A soft snore drew his attention to the bedroom directly across from this one.

"What the hell?"

Surely she wasn't sleeping on the floor. He walked across the hall. The bedroom door was open. Apparently she shared his aversion to small, closed-off spaces. On closer inspection, he saw she was on a twin-size air mattress. No wonder her blasted suitcase had been so big and heavy.

Not a blow dryer, but something to put air in the mattress. What an idiot. It looked like she'd had the last word again. Disappointment filled him, but he couldn't be angry with her.

At least now he knew what she wore to bed. The room was a little warm and apparently Jessica was hot-natured. He grinned at the thought. Hadn't he already suspected that when she'd returned his kiss, then had the audacity to grab his ass?

She'd shoved the covers to the side. Her cotton pajamas even had feet in them. It must've taken her at least ten minutes to button the row of tiny buttons that stretched all the way to her neck.

She had one hand tucked under her head, the other curled beside her. Pale blond strands of hair had fallen forward to curtain her face. He stifled an urge to reach down and brush the hair aside, afraid he might waken her. And if he did, Conor didn't know if he could stop himself from carrying her to bed . . . cotton pajamas and all.

He wanted her too much. A shudder of longing swept through him. It had been a long time since he'd spent the night with a woman snuggled close to him.

Idiot! She'd already said she wouldn't get involved with a cop, and he wasn't about to change. His life was littered with impossible relationships. He didn't need another one to add to his list. No, best to get all notions of her out of his mind.

He glanced once more at Jessica. Then again, she might just be worth it. He took a deep breath before walking back across the hall, and going inside the bathroom. He shut the door behind him. Turning on the shower, he stripped and stepped under the warm spray, wishing the water would wash away his forbidden thoughts.

*   *   *

As the bathroom door creaked, Jessica dragged her eyelids open and watched through a veil of hair. She had a perfect view straight in to Conor's room and the bathroom. Was she dreaming? Had Conor emerged from the bathroom, a towel carelessly slung around his hips? She inched her hand to her arm and pinched, then grimaced. This wasn't a dream. Droplets of water clung to Conor's hair and slid down his chest.

Jessica had wondered if he was dark all over or only tanned. Tanned was nice, too. Slowly, her gaze traveled over him. Broad shoulders, washboard stomach, slim hips.

She tried to keep her breathing natural, but he made the simple act of inhaling and exhaling almost impossible. She devoured him with her eyes at the same time her body longed for what he could give her.

He ambled over to the bed. Just before he sat down, the towel dropped to the floor.

He was beautiful. No, gorgeous. She wanted him with every fiber of her being. Her thighs trembled with her need to feel him buried deep inside her.

Breathe!

In and out. In and out. That was worse! She almost groaned aloud. Slow, deep breaths. Stay calm, she told herself. He has a body, just like every other man. Her insides quivered. No, not like every man. The same parts, maybe. Conor would never be like everyone else. *Magnificent* was too tame a word to describe him.

Lord, she'd never be able to get that image out of her mind. Did she want to? At least he didn't know she'd been staring. She'd never be able to look him in the eye if he knew she'd seen him in the buff. Or worse, what she was thinking.

"Go to sleep, Jessica."

His words were so softly spoken that at first she thought she might have imagined them. When she realized she hadn't, that he knew she'd seen him, her face burned. Oh lord, she must've inadvertently made some kind of noise that clued him in.

How long had he known she was awake and keeping tabs on his every move? Was his goal in life to irritate her? Dumb question. Of course it was. He didn't want her here. She flopped to her other side and yanked the covers up to her chin, even though the pajamas she wore were stifling.

"As long as the show is over, Conor, I might as well go to sleep. And you could at least turn the bathroom light off. It shines right in my eyes."

The mattress squeaked as he got up. She glanced over her shoulder, then hurriedly ducked her head as he switched the light off.

Yeah, right. Like she'd be able to go to sleep now. Sleep was the last thing on her mind.

Fool! Why'd you look again?

She'd take a cold shower, but Conor would know exactly what she had on her mind. Like it would do any good after that show. Hell, he probably already knew she wasn't immune to his physical attributes.

And what attributes they were! Bronzed skin, a broad chest she could easily imagine resting her head against. Lean and hard. Oh yes, Officer Conor Richmond had very nice attributes.

Ones she would ignore if it killed her.

Damn, it was freakin' hot in here. Her pajamas were suffocating. She flipped to her back and began the task of unbuttoning her protective suit. She barely registered the light spilling from his room. She refused to look in his direction.

After finally getting each button undone, she wiggled and squirmed out of her bunny pj's. Much better, she sighed with relief, and tossed them into the corner before pulling the sheet under her arms.

"Too hot for you, Jessica?"

She jumped and turned to her side. Conor stood in the doorway, fully dressed.

"You know, it's only going to get worse. You want me and I want you. Eventually we'll have sex. Why not leave in the morning and save yourself some regrets?"

Damn it, he was reading her mind again. At least part of it. She did want to make love with him. She doubted she'd have any regrets, though. "Go to hell, Conor. Just wake me up in a few hours, and I'll take the next watch."

Chapter 9

When Jessica opened her eyes the next morning, the night before came rushing back. Could her life get any worse? Damn, he'd caught her staring. How embarrassing.

She'd been able to face him better when she was half asleep and he'd wakened her to take over the watch. After brewing a pot of coffee, she grabbed a book and sat in front of the kitchen window. She'd managed to stay awake until four-thirty when he slipped downstairs and made her go back to bed. She glanced at the clock. It was seven-thirty.

She pulled the covers over her head, wanting to stay in bed the rest of the day, but the darkness brought visions of a tanned, naked body sauntering around the bedroom. Just what she needed—erotic images for breakfast.

As delicious as those thoughts were, hiding because she didn't really want to face him in the light of day would be taking the coward's way out, and she wasn't, and never had been, a coward. Still, she cautiously looked across the hall before getting up. She didn't see him anywhere. The bathroom door was open, so he wasn't in there.

Good. At least she could put off facing him until she had herself under control. She scrambled off the air mattress and rushed to the bathroom.

"Eghhh!" She skidded to a stop, slapping a hand to her chest and staring at her reflection. It was obvious she hadn't gotten any beauty sleep last night. She'd tossed and turned so much, her hair stuck out worse than if she'd put her finger in a light socket.

She stripped out of the shorts and cotton top she'd put on after Conor went downstairs to take the first watch. Much cooler than the blasted bunny suit she'd bought. Besides the fact it hadn't worked to keep her thoughts pure.

After adjusting the water, she climbed in the shower. The hot water felt wonderful on her sore muscles. The air mattress wasn't even close to being as comfortable as her bed, but she had no alternative. She'd suffer it until they caught the burglars red-handed.

As much as she enjoyed the soothing spray, all things had to end. She got out, towel dried, and quickly brushed her teeth. After dressing in dark green tights, running shoes, and a loose white, sleeveless shirt over a midriff-hugging spandex top, she fastened her hair back with a gold clip and deemed herself presentable.

As she passed the mirror, she couldn't help frowning at her reflection. She didn't want to look stuffy. She unbuttoned the top button. Better. Then the next one. Much better. Kind of like saying, *yeah, I saw your ass. So what?*

Now she could face the day . . . and Conor. Well, maybe not Conor, but the longer she waited, the harder it would be. She groaned. Two words she didn't want to think about in the same sentence. *Conor*—and *hard*.

The rattling of pans and the aroma of frying bacon drew her down the stairs and toward the kitchen. Hesitantly, she entered.

"Good morning," Conor said, glancing in her direction, then turned his attention back to the skillet of sizzling bacon. "Coffee's on the counter. Cups in the cabinet to the left. Hope you like bacon and eggs."

It was amazing how at home he looked standing in front of the stove with a blue-striped dish towel tucked into the waistband of his jeans. She never would've thought he'd be the kind of man who cooked.

Some of her uneasiness at facing him evaporated. Conor acted as if nothing had happened.

"How do you like your eggs?"

She strolled to the coffeepot, sniffed, then opened the cabinet and reached for a cup.

"Unfertilized," she muttered, then louder, "I don't usually eat breakfast. Just coffee."

His hand stilled in the process of turning the bacon. "You're joking?"

Jessica shook her head. "No, that's all I eat. I like to run every morning. Jogging and a full stomach don't mix."

"You won't make an exception? I cook a mean egg."

I bet you do. In fact, she figured he did most things extremely well.

"No, nothing." She poured herself a cup of coffee. The thought of food sent an uncomfortable rumbling in her stomach. Or maybe Conor made her stomach turn inside out.

"Okay. But you haven't lived until you've eaten the famous Conor Richmond breakfast."

She had to admit the man was irresistible when he grinned. A smile tugged at her lips as she took a sip.

"Ugh. This is awful." She grimaced as the dark liquid hit her taste buds. "It's always better if you add water."

His eyebrows drew together. "Too strong?"

"That's an understatement." She poured half down the drain and added hot water to her cup. "Maybe we should invest in another pot. Then we can each make our own."

"That reminds me, we should know a little about the other's likes and dislikes. Just in case we need the information."

He made sense. Of course they should know more about each other. After all, they were supposed to be married.

"You're right. It'd be a shame to ruin your cover just because you don't know which side of the bed I prefer." She froze. As soon as the words were out of her mouth, she wanted to call them back, but it was too late. Why the hell had she brought up sleeping? He was probably remembering she'd seen him naked—at least, his backside.

She cleared her throat. "That is . . . I mean . . ."

"Absolutely. The little details can blow a cover quicker than the big stuff."

She breathed a sigh of relief that he'd let her blunder slide by without commenting and embarrassing her further. It made her reassess her opinion of him. Maybe she'd misjudged.

Taking her watered-down coffee with her, she sat at the table. Conor added the eggs to his plate and joined her, grabbing the catsup bottle as he straddled a chair, then pounded out a good portion on top of his eggs.

His breakfast looked like a bloody massacre.

Surely he didn't plan to eat that mess. It made her sick just looking at it.

"By the way, which side of the bed *do* you prefer?" he asked.

"Both." She smiled sweetly.

He cleared his throat and concentrated on stirring the conglomeration in his plate. "Yes, well, uh, if we think about it—" he met her gaze across the table "—there's already a lot we know about each other."

Was he referring to last night? She'd certainly seen more than she'd anticipated. Would he be that blunt? "What do you mean?"

He bit into a slice of bacon and chewed. "Well, like when you get nervous, you fiddle with your buttons."

"I don't . . ."

With half a slice of bacon, he pointed toward her shirt. Glancing down, she saw that she was indeed twisting the button. With a snort of disgust, she straightened the wrinkled material.

"Okay, so maybe I do have a couple of bad habits."

"I'm not faulting you for it. And by the way, you snore."

"I do not!" She sat straight up in her chair, chin jutting out.

"Don't worry. The sound didn't vibrate off the walls or anything."

Conor Richmond was definitely no gentleman. Especially after he'd dropped his towel to the floor last night with little concern that she was just across the hall and would see so much delicious, sexy, irresistible, and very naked skin.

Oh lord, was she drooling? She cleared her throat and squared her shoulders.

He placed a hand over hers, his expression turning serious. "That's what I mean, though. The little stuff is what we need to learn. I know you don't eat breakfast, but what sort of food do you enjoy?"

So, he wanted to get down to business. That was fine, but his hand on hers was a little too warm. Too pleasant. If she didn't keep her distance, she'd have to turn the thermostat down again. She pulled her hand away and stood.

Suddenly the lukewarm coffee had as much taste as a can of drain cleaner. She needed to concentrate on something besides how he made her body tingle. She went to the sink and poured her coffee out.

"Mexican and Chinese." She glanced over her shoulder.

Conor looked confused. "What?"

"You wanted to know more about me," she reminded him. "I love Mexican food and hate Chinese."

"How can anyone hate Chinese food?"

She curled her lower lip. "Ugh. No, thanks. Even as a kid, I hated it. I rate it on the same scale as liver. So what about you? Is there something I should know?"

She rinsed her cup and placed it in the drainer, then looked around for a towel to dry her hands.

"What do you like? Sports? Football? My father and brother always hogged the remote if there was a game on. I finally began to like it through osmosis." She knew her words were coming out faster than she intended, but the man made her crazy.

He grinned, and her heart did somersaults. The room got smaller and smaller as his presence filled every tiny space.

A towel. She needed something to dry her hands on. Anything to concentrate on besides Conor. She scanned the cabinet. Where were the blasted paper towels?

"I like sports," he told her. "But I like other things as well. I'd rather participate than watch it on TV. You know . . . touch football." He stood and ambled over to the sink, tossing her his towel.

While she dried her hands, he turned the water on and squirted soap on his dishes before rinsing them and placing them in the drainer alongside her cup.

"I also like picnics on a warm spring day." He tugged the towel out of her hands and began drying his. "A blanket on the ground, a beautiful woman, a bottle of wine, and some cheese. And maybe later, making love beneath the trees. You like picnics, Jessica?" His gaze held hers as he pitched the towel on the counter.

The birds outside the kitchen window grew silent. Even the everyday sounds, like the refrigerator running, all quieted to a mere murmur as his presence enveloped her in a cocoon. "I love fried chicken," she whispered.

She needed space. The man had cast a spell over her. What was he, a magician or something?

"I'm . . . um . . . I'm going out. I mean, jogging. My morning run."

"I don't want you to go."

Did he want her to stay with him? What did he have in mind? An image formed of naked limbs twined together. Sweating bodies straining. His hands caressing. Lips joining.

Maybe she could skip her run this once.

"Was there . . . something . . . uh . . . you had in mind?" She tried to make her words sound casual, but to her ears they sounded anything but normal.

"Well, I can't very well protect you if you're off somewhere else. What will you do if one of the suspects approaches you?"

Boy, had she misjudged him this time. Always the cop. That was Conor. "I know you mean well, Officer Richmond."

Her lips thinned. "But I don't need you to run my obstacle course. You were right earlier. There's a lot you don't know about me. You just assume I'm a sitting duck for every burglar, bank robber, and jaywalker because I'm not as experienced as you. In fact, I happen to know more—"

"Okay, okay." He held up his hands. "I know you've been through the academy, and even worked the streets for a while, but be careful. Run in the opposite direction from their house or something."

Jessica opened her mouth, then snapped it closed. Explaining anything to him was like talking to a brick wall. Impossible. She whirled around and stomped from the room, unbuttoning her shirt as she went through the house, then tossing it on the sofa before she went out the front door.

Once outside, she took a deep, cleansing breath to clear her head. Running would do her good. She needed to work off some energy. Anything to get her mind off Conor and how he affected her senses. He could make her angrier quicker than anyone she knew, then, in the next breath, turn around and have her wanting to have sex with him.

Good grief, she hadn't thought so much about sleeping with anyone before she'd met him. Must be all that testosterone that oozed from his pores. At least six-feet, four inches of living, breathing, raw maleness constantly invading her space.

She turned her attention to the peaceful street. It seemed quiet and lazy as she stood on the front porch and glanced up and down the sidewalk. Too quiet. One wouldn't know a gang of burglars had set up shop in the neighborhood.

Raising her hands above her head, she stretched upward as far as she could, then leaned to the left, then over to the right. A few leg stretches, and she started off down the street at a slow jog. The air on her face was invigorating. Soon she'd blocked out all thoughts of the stakeout and Conor.

She set her pace for the small park about half a mile away. As she went around the corner, she picked up speed, but it wasn't until she reached the tree-lined running trail that she lengthened her stride and a rush of adrenaline flowed through her veins.

The world ceased to exist. She could feel the beat of her heart. Trees blurred. She ran faster and faster, escaping her treacherous thoughts. But Jessica knew she couldn't run forever. Sooner or later she'd have to face Conor again, and the feelings he stirred deep inside her.

No, she didn't want to think about him. Free her mind, that's what she needed to do.

A man stepped from the trees in front of her. She skidded to a halt, bouncing on the balls of her feet so she wouldn't lose her momentum. He didn't look like someone who was out for a brisk walk in the early morning air. More like a transient. Scraggly hair, dirty, ripped clothes, and as he ambled closer, she realized she was downwind and the man had a really bad body odor. He smiled, showing yellowed teeth.

She moved to the right, so did he. This didn't bode well. Damn it, all she'd wanted was a nice run to blow off a little steam. Deep breath. She'd try one more time to reason with him.

"I happen to be running. I'd appreciate it if you would move out of my way." She'd give him the benefit of the doubt.

"No," he growled. "I know you joggers carry a little money on ya. I want it."

His gaze slid over her, making her want to run back to the house and take a bath.

"And maybe I want more from ya than your money. You're a pretty little thing." He rubbed his crotch.

Gross. "You stink, you're ugly, and I work for my money. Why in the hell would I give it to you or let you put your hands on me?"

He glowered at her. " 'Cause I'm bigger. I take what I want and no one tells me any different. They call me Mack—as in truck. Ain't nothin' can stop a big rig."

You have got to be kidding.

"Like I said. Just step aside and let me go by."

He grabbed her arm instead.

His first mistake. She was ready to kick ass and get rid of some of the tension building inside her.

She twisted around, grabbed his arm, bent over for leverage, and tossed him over her shoulder like he was nothing more than a bag of trash. He landed with a loud grunt, but for a big man, he came back up pretty fast.

And he was past the point of anger, but then so was she. *Come on you sleazeball!*

Shaking his head, he barreled toward her like an enraged bull. She bounced on the balls of her feet, sidestepped at the last second, and stuck her foot out. He hit the ground with a hard thud.

"Gawd-damned bitch. When I get through with you, you're not going to look so pretty. Right after I fuck your brains out."

He lurched to his feet, but before he could make a move toward her, she twisted her body and swung her leg up and out, connecting with his face. He staggered into the tree behind him, wiping blood from his mouth.

She was tired of giving him the chance to back off. When he lumbered toward her, she gave one swift punch to his nose, he doubled over, and she landed a perfectly executed karate chop to the back of his neck. Like felling a big oak, he crashed to the ground. She didn't think he'd be getting up any time soon.

"Wow! Too cool!" A voice spoke behind her.

She whirled around, arms up, ready to fight this new intruder.

The young man stumbled backwards. "Whoa, lady. I was hurrying over to help, but before I could, you kicked his butt." He looked at her with awe. "Good job, too."

She relaxed. "Thanks." The kid couldn't be more than sixteen. Cute, with a very disarming grin. She bet the girls drooled over this one.

"I called 9-1-1 a couple of seconds ago." He held up a cell phone. "What was that you did, anyway? Karate? What belt?"

She laughed at his exuberance. "I'm a black belt." What

he'd said flowed past the adrenaline still rushing through her. He'd called 9-1-1. The cops would be here any minute. The newspaper, radio, and TV stations would hear it over their scanners and probably show up, too. She didn't need any publicity.

"Hey, I'm in kind of a hurry, and I really don't want my picture taken. Do me a favor and tell them I took off before you got a good look at me."

His eyes widened. "You're not like superwoman or anything, are you? I mean, I've been reading a lot about people with superhuman powers and stuff." He must have realized how he sounded, because he blushed and lowered his head.

"Nope, I'm just an average woman whose father made her take self-defense classes right along with her brother."

Sirens sounded in the background.

"And one who'd better take off. Thanks for calling the cops, kid. The world could use a few more Good Samaritans."

She turned and left in the opposite direction of the sirens. Damn, she felt good . . . she felt pumped.

Okay, so maybe she did miss being a cop sometimes. But it still didn't change the fact that she desperately needed to feel like a lady, and didn't.

Drat! She wanted to feel feminine. All soft and pretty and whatever the fuck a lady was supposed to feel like. How the hell could she be feminine when bad guys were practically falling out of the trees? Especially when she had to kick their asses. Life was really complicated sometimes.

Conor paused in the bedroom when he heard the front door open and close. Jessica must be back. He smoothed the bedspread and straightened his pillow. She couldn't accuse him of not picking up after himself.

He surveyed the nice, orderly room. He'd even straightened the bathroom, hanging Jessica's damp towel over the shower rod so it could dry. Thinking about the terry cloth rubbing over her glistening skin had given him a damn hard-on. What the hell was his life coming to?

And what the hell had he been trying to do this morning? Talking about picnics and touch football and making love under the trees. He hadn't been trying to run her off. Hell, he wanted to have sex with the woman.

He planted his palms on the bathroom counter and stared at his reflection. "You're going to blow the whole operation if you don't quit thinking about having sex with Jessica."

Voices drifted up the stairs. Frowning, he went to the door and opened it a crack.

Jessica?

What the hell was she wearing? When she'd walked out of the kitchen, she'd had on a white shirt. Now she was wearing some kind of stretchy . . . thing. He frowned, forcing his gaze away from the amount of skin she was displaying, and turned his attention to the woman who'd come inside with her. He'd known Jessica would get into trouble going off by herself.

"Oh, I couldn't show you the upstairs, Trudy. I haven't cleaned it yet."

The flaxen-haired woman waved away Jessica's protests. "Oh, honey, don't worry about that. George and me are still newlyweds ourselves. Hell, we practically live in the bedroom." She slapped Jessica hard on the back, nearly sending her to the floor.

So this was the bride. Connor let his gaze roam over her. *Buxom* was a mild word. Her shirt fit like a glove, the horizontal stripes emphasizing the girth of her chest. And he'd heard of short shorts before, but never thought they could be that short without being illegal.

The woman looked about as fake as her husband's Italian accent. They were obviously made for each other. George with his gold chains and patent-leather shoes, and her with her bleached-blond bouffant hairdo and high heels. They made the perfect couple. He stifled a laugh, jerking back when George's bride glanced up the stairs.

Irritation quickly replaced his humor. How in the hell had Jessica gotten herself into this fix? He shouldn't have let her go running. Instead of the woman it could easily have been the old man or George's brother, Barry.

Jessica was a sexy, vibrant young woman. They were sleazeballs, and with their background, anything could've happened if she'd met up with one of them. How would she defend herself against someone four times her size? He'd talk to her first chance he got.

"I just love that little balcony upstairs," Trudy drawled. "And I've always wanted to see it up close."

Jessica grabbed the other woman's arm. "Let me show you the downstairs first."

Conor quietly closed the door. His gaze darted around the room as he surveyed the tidy bed—damn, the air mattress across the hall! He couldn't let her see the extra bed or she'd know something was up.

He slipped into the hall and hurried across to where Jessica had slept. He pulled the plug. Nothing. Damn, a safety valve. It would be nightfall before the mattress deflated.

Now what?

The closet.

He shoved, but it wouldn't fit. No choice. He'd hide it in his room.

After opening the door and checking to make sure the coast was clear, he scrambled across the hall to his room. He dragged the mattress inside and squished it under the bed—at least one corner. That was all that would fit.

Their voices were getting louder. He shoved again. Nothing. If George's wife saw the air mattress, she'd immediately know something was wrong. What if she told George and the rest of the clan? They'd be suspicious. Probably drop out of sight. Jessica's father would lose his job. There was only one thing to do.

He slipped his knife from his pocket.

Chapter 10

Frrrrrrrrrrrrrrrrrrttttt!
"What was that noise?" Trudy barged up the stairs.

Before she had climbed more than two steps, Jessica grabbed her arm. "Noise? What noise?" She didn't even want to imagine what Conor could possibly be doing.

"Are you going to try to tell me you didn't hear that? Sounded like a big whoopee cushion. You coming?" Her eyes narrowed. "Unless you have something to hide."

There was no way around the woman. Suspicion lurked in her eyes. Whatever Conor was doing, she hoped he'd be ready for Bulldozer Trudy.

"Why would I have anything to hide?" Nonchalantly, she pushed past her neighbor and up the stairs.

When she entered the bedroom, Conor stood in the middle of the room, spritzing the air with a bottle of her favorite perfume. He was breathing heavily, his hair rumpled. A breeze fluttered the window curtain behind him. He continued to fill the air with her expensive mist.

"We got anything for gas, honey? Must've been those beans we had for supper last night. I told you how bad they mess up my stomach."

Trudy shoved her way into the room and came to a grinding halt. Her gaze slowly roamed over Conor, strayed to his low-riding jeans, then back to his face.

"Oh . . . my," Trudy stuttered.

"Sorry, didn't know we had company." Conor set the perfume on the nightstand.

Trudy blinked several times and seemed to come out of the fog she'd momentarily slipped into. "Hell, sweetie, we all got to let loose now and again."

Jessica wanted to die! Gas? Beans? His implication brought a rush of warmth to her face. Change the subject. Do anything!

"Uh . . . this is my husband, Conor," Jessica introduced him. "Conor, this is George's wife, Trudy. You remember, the man we met the day we were looking at the house."

"Actually, his name is Georgio, but you can call him George for short." Trudy sucked in a deep breath, increasing her bust size by a good two inches. Any second now she expected Trudy's boobs to burst free.

Jessica glanced around the room. Her gaze fell on a bit of blue vinyl peeking from under the bed. *Very flat* blue vinyl. Her eyes narrowed. Whoopee cushion, her foot! Damn it! That was her bed. Why hadn't he shoved it in the bathroom behind the shower curtain or something? Did he have to pop it?

"I just knew I'd love that balcony," Trudy said, interrupting Jessica's murderous thoughts.

"The *balcony* is behind Conor," she informed Trudy through gritted teeth. The hussy wasn't even looking toward the damn door. Her gaze had been glued on Conor ever since she'd shoved her way into the room.

"Oh, yeah, I guess it is." She fluttered fake eyelashes. "I told your wife that I've been admiring the way your upstairs porch looks so cozy and romantic. I bet you can see a lot of stars at night sitting out there."

Conor smiled and eased sideways, giving her access to the door.

She slithered past, her shoulder brushing his chest. After

only a cursory glance, she turned her appraisal back to Conor. "Very nice."

"I'm glad you like it." His husky voice dripped honey.

They were flirting with each other! Right in front of her! So much for him feeling guilty about popping her bed. "Didn't you say something about being bloated?" More like his ego than his stomach. "Maybe you should look downstairs for the Tums." She smiled, forcing her lips to curve upward. "Heaven forbid you explode."

When he smiled at her, it didn't quite reach his eyes. What was his problem? In fact, he looked really pissed, though he was covering it fairly well. Hell, he should be excited that one of the suspects was in their home.

He glanced at Trudy. "I think we have some baking soda. That should work."

"Yes, why don't you do that," Jessica said. He needed to leave before he blew the case. If Trudy looked close enough at him, she would know that everything wasn't perfect in paradise. He really needed to learn how to control his emotions.

Could he be upset that Trudy was in the house? No, surely not.

After he left, Jessica turned to Trudy. "You have drool on the side of your mouth."

"Yum, yum. You hit the jackpot with that one, sweetie." She glanced at Jessica and apparently noted her less-than-happy expression. "Oh hell, you better get used to those kinds of looks from women. You just keep him happy in that big, heart-shaped love nest." She motioned toward their bed. "He won't even think about straying. Of course, if y'all are into swapping . . ."

"We're not." If it weren't for her father's career and the fact that this marriage happened to be a farce, Jessica would throw the slut out. But it wasn't real, this wasn't her home, and Conor wasn't her husband.

"That green-eyed devil sure did sink his claws in you, honey. No harm asking."

Jealous? Her, jealous? The idea was ludicrous. She hardly knew the man. Trudy was way off the mark.

Her thoughts jumbled about inside her head. Sure he had a devilishly sexy grin, and he was built . . . a deep sigh escaped . . . very nicely.

She squared her shoulders. He was still a cop, and she wasn't about to get involved with him.

"Honey?" Trudy snapped her fingers. "Where'd you go?"

Jessica pulled herself back to the present. "I'm sorry. What were you saying?"

"Just that you don't have to worry about me and your husband. George wouldn't go for swapping, anyway. Man's so damned jealous he can't see straight." She patted her platinum-blond curls. " 'Course, he knows I'd better not catch him looking at another woman, either."

"I don't think you'll have to worry about anyone stealing him." No other woman would have him.

"Thanks, honey." Trudy preened, misinterpreting the comment for a compliment. "All that Italian charm draws women like a fly to shit. They can't resist him."

A shiver of distaste swept over Jessica. She pushed back the nausea and tried to focus on the reason why she was even talking to this woman. "I hope he has the kind of job that doesn't put him in the path of many predators."

Trudy's hand flew to her chest. "Wouldn't that be scary? I'm lucky, though. He works mostly at night. They're movers. His father and half brother live with us. They're not Italian like my George. The old geezer is all American."

She strolled in front of the open closet, her fingers running over the clothes hanging inside. Scrunching her nose, she looked at Jessica. "Honey, we've got to go shopping. Put a little pizzazz in your wardrobe." She reached up and touched the large, sparkling bangles dangling from her ears.

Now might be a good time to change the subject back to

the Meredith men. She'd do a lot for her father, but dress like Trudy? She didn't think so. Besides, Trudy might be in on the burglaries. Even if she weren't, maybe she'd unknowingly let something slip.

"So, it's you, George, and your father-in-law? You also mentioned a brother?"

"Barry," she said, looking like she'd just sunk her teeth into a lemon. "George had a different mother. A hot and spicy Italiano." She cast Jessica a knowing glance. "You can tell, too. Good breeding shows."

"So I've heard." Jessica didn't care about their parentage. She wanted to know more about what they did for a living. As casually as she could, she asked her next question. "You say they work at night?"

"You seem awfully interested in what my George does." Suspicion laced her words before she turned away. Like Jell-O during an earthquake, Trudy jiggled to the mirror and adjusted her shirt, pulling down the front to better display her cleavage.

"Not really." Jessica shrugged. "Just making conversation." Did Trudy know about their illegal activities or was she afraid Jessica wanted George? Ugh! Revolting thought.

Trudy turned, her stare calculating.

"Conor's away a lot at night, too." Jessica's words stumbled out. She couldn't afford to have the other woman wondering why she was asking so many questions. "He has a pawnshop, you know, and does a lot of . . . uh . . . restocking in the evening." Jessica held her breath and prayed. Had she blown everything?

"Yeah, I guess you're right. I get a little touchy when it comes to George. He's one hell of a man."

Play the game. If she could make a friend out of Trudy, she might slip and reveal something important. Time to get inventive.

Jessica strolled to the mirror and stood by her. "Their stamina probably comes from the fact that they're used to working most of the night." Jessica reached for a tube of lipstick and slid the creamy red color over her lips. "But as long as they hand over the paycheck each week, I guess we can't complain."

Twirling around, Trudy's eyes widened. She began to laugh. "I knew we were two peas in the same bucket!" She rolled her gaze heavenward. "George does like to spend his money on me."

"Trudy!" A voice called from outside.

"Speak of the devil." She giggled, hopped over to the window, and leaned out. "I'm up here, Pooh Bear."

"That-sa the bedroom! Are you with another man? What-sa matter with you? Do you not-a remember what I told you the last time?"

"Yes, speak of the devil," Jessica murmured. She went and stood next to Trudy, wondering for a moment if she was seeing things.

No, that wasn't a frog on her lawn. George wore a lime, Italian-cut suit. She had to shield her eyes from the glare when the sun's rays bounced off the gold necklaces around his neck. As soon as he spotted her, his whole demeanor relaxed.

"Oh, I'm-a sorry. I did not-a know you were there with my little wife."

"How can you accuse me of being unfaithful, George?" she yelled down. "After the last time, I told you I'd never look at another man. You're all I need." She swiped the back of her hand under her eyes and sniffed loudly. "And now you're saying I've been unfaithful." She sniffed again—louder.

There wasn't a bit of dampness on Trudy's face that Jessica could see.

"Babycakes, I didn't mean to say . . . what I thought . . . uh . . ." His accent dropped completely as he tried to wiggle out of the mess he'd made for himself.

"I know exactly what you were thinking and none of it's good! I'm going home to Mother."

"No!" He glanced around as if an idea would drop from one of the trees. Suddenly, he snapped his fingers and looked back at the window. "But, *mio amore,* I wanted to take-a you shopping."

"Really?" Trudy sounded skeptical.

"But of course, *mio bel amore.*"

"Well, okay then. I'll be down in a few minutes, honey bunny."

George heaved a big sigh of relief. Turning, Trudy grinned and winked at Jessica. "That little performance should be good for a diamond bracelet at the very least."

"At least," she mumbled.

"Tell you what. Bring that scrumptious husband of yours over to the house Saturday night and I'll introduce you to the rest of the clan. I'll get George to grill some steaks."

"Yes, sure. That'd be great." Jessica followed her out of the room and down the stairs, not believing her luck. She'd have the chance to look around their home and might even discover the missing tape and some of the other stolen merchandise. She could be in her own bed by Sunday night.

The thought should've brought a sigh of relief, but it didn't. She had to admit, if only to herself, she rather liked playing house with Conor. She shut the door behind Trudy and leaned her forehead against it, closing her eyes.

"I warned you about going outside without my protection. Now see what you've done?"

Her eyes flew open, then narrowed as she slowly turned. "I just happened to get an invitation to their house, which is more than you've done."

"We're not here to interact with them. And even if we were, it still doesn't change the facts. What if it'd been one of the men instead of Trudy?" He glared at her, his stance rigid. "What would've happened then? From now on I don't want you leaving without me."

Anger began to burn inside her. "Is that right?"

"Yes, it is. Now if you don't mind, I'll get back to watching the suspects' house." He turned on his heel and marched into the living room.

She tried to slow her breathing, but it was impossible. Did he expect her to automatically follow his orders like some flunky? She glanced around the foyer, her gaze landing on his car keys. Scooping them up, along with her shirt, she grabbed her purse from the hall closet and eased out the front door. She needed time away from him to get her thoughts in order. If not, she'd be calling 9-1-1 to remove his lifeless body.

A half hour later she could still feel the pressure bubbling inside her. Even the quiet serenity of the park where she'd stopped did little to calm her frayed nerves.

What had she expected from Conor? A pat on the back because she had an invitation into the suspects' home? She ran her fingernail over the steering wheel. Would it have hurt him so much to say she'd done a good job?

The cell phone inside her purse rang. She smiled. Maybe he'd realized his anger had been unjustified. She reached inside her purse and retrieved the purple phone, flipping it open.

"Yes?"

"Hello, darling," came Al's voice over the phone. "Your boss said you were taking a few days off. Nothing wrong, I hope?"

Disappointment flooded her. Al. It was only Al. "No, nothing serious." Her mind searched for a plausible reason to give him. "Just a lot of little things that needed doing. Like the dent in my car." At least the last part was true.

"Then how about meeting me for coffee? I've missed you. Or I could come by your apartment."

She liked Al, but the thought of being completely alone with him didn't appeal to her. He wanted more from their relationship than she was ready to give. But he was a good friend. What harm would it do if she did have coffee? "I'm actually downtown doing a few errands, so why don't I meet you?"

Somewhere far away from the suspects so she didn't take a

chance running into Trudy twice in one day. That wouldn't be good.

They agreed on a spot, and fifteen minutes later, she entered the small café. He waved and stood when she looked his way.

"Oh . . . have you been out jogging?"

She cringed, not liking his tone. "Earlier."

"Well, never mind. This certainly isn't a five-star restaurant, and it seems like months since I've seen you." He smiled before lightly kissing her lips.

The warmth of his touch should've made her feel better. It didn't. Guilt washed over her instead. Her gaze skittered around the crowded room. The little old lady sitting in the next booth over had a knowing look on her face. Was that man leering at her?

What was wrong with her? The way she acted, anyone would think she was really married to Conor. Darn it, she wasn't carrying on an illicit affair. If she wanted to take a lover, she could. She slid into the booth, head held high. She had nothing to be ashamed of.

"Why so tense?" Al scooted into the booth across from her and took her hands in his.

She jumped. "Tense?" Her laugh sounded strangled. "Whatever gave you that idea?"

His hands were soft and warm against hers. So unlike the rough texture of the ones that had scooped her up and carried her inside the house.

"I . . . I haven't been sleeping well at night." At least that was close to the truth. She'd tossed and turned all night long, thinking about Conor's naked body . . . his arms pulling her close.

"Tell me about it."

Not likely!

She took a deep breath and tried to pull herself together. Al's eyes were full of concern. Here was a man any woman would be happy to fall in love with. Why couldn't she?

"Nothing, really." She decided telling a half truth would be better than an out-and-out lie. "My father is really stressed over the burglaries. The mayor is putting a lot of pressure on him to find the suspects."

"I still can't believe they were gutsy enough to rob his house—and in broad daylight. I bet that made the mayor feel like a jerk."

The waitress interrupted their conversation when she brought coffee over.

"I ordered for both of us," Al explained.

Always the gentleman. She moved her hands from his and brought the cup to her lips.

"I feel bad," Al continued after the waitress left.

"Why?" She took a drink and set her cup back on the saucer, looking into his worried eyes.

"Well, you showed me his home before it was officially on the market. What if I inadvertently let something slip about the mayor wanting to sell his house or about his alarm system?" He ran a hand through his well-groomed hair. "I don't know. I just feel in some way like I'm responsible for your father's added problems."

"I showed his home to a lot of prospective buyers after we listed it, and everyone knew he was speaking at the American Legion Hall that morning. You have nothing to feel guilty about. In fact, you should be commended for wanting to move to a bigger home so your mother will be more comfortable."

She'd never seen him this distraught before. He must care more than she realized. She reached across the table and squeezed his hand.

"She just hasn't been as happy living in my cramped apartment. She loves to work in a garden and that's just not possible where I live now, but since my father passed . . ." He closed his eyes for a moment, then drew in a ragged breath before continuing. "It's been almost a year, and Mother needs the stability a house would give her."

Why couldn't she love Al? He was such a good man. Maybe she could at least lessen some of his guilt. "Listen, I can't go into any details, but it may be over soon."

"What do you mean?"

"I'm sorry." She shook her head. "I can't talk about it. Just trust me."

He relaxed. "How could I not when you look at me like that?"

You're a fool, Jessica admonished herself. Here was a man who made his intentions very plain. He'd like to take their relationship to the next level, but she couldn't make a commitment. Al was exactly what she wanted in a man. Successful and happy. Sweet and attentive to her every need. He was perfect. But not for her, and she knew that now.

Later, as he walked her to the car, she realized the time away had done her good. It made her realize that living with Conor wasn't real. They just happened to be doing a job together. She had everything in the proper perspective, and she could focus on putting the criminals behind bars.

At least until Al pulled her into his arms and brought his lips down on hers. It was Conor's lips she thought about. It was his arms she wanted around her, pulling her close. Al smothered her.

"We could always go back to my place," he murmured.

"I can't. I'm not ready." Jessica knew she never would be, and as soon as the crooks were caught, she'd end the relationship.

"I understand." Al smiled, showing straight, white teeth.

Maybe that's what she found disturbing about him. He always understood. It wasn't human. Nobody could be this flawless. It was nerve-wracking.

Damn it, where was she? Conor glanced toward the house next door. Nothing stirred. He frowned. Not even a rat. A good thing, because he would find it hard to trail the criminals on foot.

He clamped his lips together. If worse came to worst, he could always alert someone to have a cruiser tail the suspects.

Why the hell had she left, anyway?

His shoulders slumped.

He already knew the answer. He'd been terrified for her safety when she'd returned home with Trudy in tow and he'd . . . well . . . lost his temper after Trudy left. The only thought going through his mind was, what if it had been Winston Meredith, the father? He'd read the report on him: brawls, drunken outrages, time in prison. The list went on and on.

So what if she had been a cop and probably knew a little self-defense? That didn't mean she could handle herself if she came up against the head of the Meredith clan. He'd tear her to pieces.

The front door opened. He flinched. It quietly shut. Her footsteps were almost silent as she walked across the floor. He didn't turn around.

"It was stupid to take the car."

"I knew you could call someone to follow them if they left."

"This is my case. I told you that we do it my way or not at all." He could feel her as she neared. He squeezed his eyes closed. The soft, sensual scent of her perfume wafted toward his nose. He inhaled, letting it wrap around him.

"It won't happen again."

"Make sure it doesn't."

Her scent drifted away. A sudden sensation of almost unbearable loss swept over him.

It wouldn't work, he tried to tell himself. Jessica didn't date cops, and even if she did, he wasn't on the market.

His cell phone rang.

"Yeah," he said, after flipping it open.

"Anything yet?" the chief asked.

Damn, did the man read minds? "We've had contact with George's wife." He took a deep breath. "She was in the house."

"First George and now Trudy. It might make it easier to ferret out some information, though. It's been too quiet. Something is bound to happen pretty soon."

"They're staying pretty close to the house. Other than George and Trudy, that is."

"No one said surveillance work was exciting." He cleared his throat. "You and Jess getting along okay?"

He cocked an eyebrow. "You have a very stubborn daughter, sir."

He chuckled. "Yes, I know. She takes after me. Doesn't like taking no for an answer."

They talked for a few more minutes before hanging up. Conor shook his head as he closed his phone. The chief seemed more concerned about his daughter's love life than the stakeout.

He smiled. He bet the chief was a great dad. He'd only met Gabe briefly, but he was very likable. Hell, the whole Nelson clan seemed to be a lot of fun.

Including Jessica.

He sat in the chair and crossed his ankles. There was a lot about Jessica he was starting to like. She was a damn good kisser. He wondered what else she did well.

Not that he would attempt to find out. He uncrossed his ankles and leaned forward. He wouldn't let anything interfere with the stakeout. His job was his top priority and would remain so.

Chapter 11

Lunch was eaten in silence. Conor normally liked the quiet, preferring his own company most of the time. Today was different. He couldn't explain it, even to himself, but after only a couple of days around Jessica, hearing her laughter, listening to the softness of her voice, watching the way she moved from room to room . . . he was addicted to her.

Like any addiction, he needed more. More information, for starters. What made her tick? Why had she wanted to become a cop? Why did she then quit and go into real estate?

He had the perfect opportunity to discover more when she took the chair next to his in the living room, but where did he start? She still wasn't talking to him, since her escapade with Trudy. He'd pissed her off. No doubt about that. Why else would she have taken off in his car? That had been a stupid stunt.

Okay, she'd apologized, and he didn't think it would happen again. What was done was done. It was time to end the stalemate. Her silence was driving him nuts. When she did talk, it was with a minimal number of words.

Hell, after his anger evaporated and he took a little time to think about it, he realized Jessica was pretty damned slick in getting an invitation to the suspects' home. He hadn't planned on actual contact, but hey, maybe that was the way to obtain more information, and as long as she was with him, he'd keep her safe. In fact, if Jessica were his partner, he'd say she was doing an impressive job.

He almost grinned, but at the last moment stopped the upward curve of his mouth. He didn't want her getting any ideas. If he weren't careful, she'd be trying to run the sting operation.

When she crossed her legs, his gaze traveled downward. She'd changed from her running clothes to a sundress splattered with fat strawberries. She wore sassy little sandals and her toenails were painted a bright strawberry red. She had really sexy legs. He found it took quite an effort to pull his gaze away.

Damn it, she was doing it to him again, and without really trying. He cleared his throat and looked out the window. "You don't have to sit with me."

"I know. I thought you might want to take a nap or something. I can watch the house." She paused. "I promise I won't leave without telling you."

At least she'd said more than two words. He nodded. "In a bit." He should be exhausted. What little sleep he'd had last night hadn't been restful. The smart thing would be to go up and lie down, but he couldn't summon the energy to stand and walk away from Jessica.

It wasn't like something major was happening right now. The house next door was quiet. He'd seen Barry go out back, smoke a cigarette, then go inside once again. Nothing out of the ordinary.

So maybe now was a good time to ask questions and learn more about her. The information might prove useful if anything were to happen. Besides, it would get his mind off wanting to tug her into his lap and kiss her until she was panting and begging for more.

He drew in a deep breath. "Why did Mike tell me you were practically destined for sainthood?"

She looked at him and grinned. His hands grew moist. He casually folded them and tried to concentrate on her words rather than carrying her to bed.

"Because I Saran-wrapped the toilet seats. It took him longer to get even than I thought it would." She looked thoughtful for a moment. "He probably had help. I have to admit, this was a good one."

Jessica smiled in a way that made his gut clench. From saint to sexpot. Odd how he could view someone through different eyes when he stopped listening to what other people said and saw the truth.

A mischievous twinkle entered her eyes. "I still can't believe you fell for his stories."

Heat crawled up his face. Conor quickly looked out the window. "Mike had help. I might not have believed him if a couple of the others hadn't added their two cents. Hell, by the time they finished feeding me their bull, you practically had a halo around your head. What else was I to think?"

"Oh, but I do have a halo. I'm a perfect angel." She smiled innocently, raising her hands and making a circle above her head.

"I just bet you are," he mumbled.

It wasn't her hands that captured his attention, though. Her chest thrust forward, expanding by a couple of inches. The thin white material of her dress stretched taut, outlining her nipples.

More than that, she had that look on her face again, the wanton one. The one that said she wanted to have sex. He had a feeling her thoughts were anything but angelic as the conversation took on a subtle, sexual tone.

Back off, Conor.

He cleared his throat. "Do innocent bystanders usually get caught in the crossfire of your family's pranks?" At least this was a safe enough topic. Maybe.

Her expression turned solemn. "A casualty of war."

The corners of his mouth tugged upward and this time he didn't even try to stop his smile from forming. She returned his smile. Her whole face lit up. An odd warmth filled him from the inside out.

"So, do you have a big family?" she asked. "I mean aunts

and uncles? You said you have a sister, but she lives in New Jersey. What about cousins?"

He shook his head, unable to draw his gaze away from her. "A couple of distant cousins. Like I said before, my sister moves around a lot. I might see them once or twice a year. Since my parents moved to Florida, I see them about as often." He felt strangely detached.

"It must get awfully lonely. Is that why you moved to a small town?"

She was damned astute. Hell, he'd never really thought about why he'd wanted to move. Telling himself he was tired of the city, the fast pace, but Jessica was right. He was lonely. He could've moved to Florida, but his parents always seemed to be lost in a world of their own, and without meaning to, they excluded him.

That was a part of himself he really didn't want to delve into right at this moment, so he switched topics. "Why does everyone call you Jess rather than Jessica?"

She curled her feet beneath her. He really liked looking at her legs. Imagining how they would feel wrapped around his waist, pulling him deeper and deeper inside her hot body. A shudder swept over him. Now they were hidden beneath the full skirt of her dress and maybe that was for the best. He returned his attention upward when she began speaking.

"There are more men in the family than women. I guess I became one of the guys. They tagged me with Jess, and it sort of stuck."

His gaze slowly traveled over her. "You certainly don't look like one of the guys."

She even blushed prettily. He could only stare as she turned her face away and looked out the window.

Suddenly, she jerked straight up in her chair. "Visitor."

He quickly looked out the window. Damn, he had to remember he was on duty and not on a date. Jessica had a way of making him forget a lot of things. His gaze fixed on the house next door and the woman approaching it.

She was skinny, almost to the point of anorexia. Dressed as a UPS employee and clutching a package, she walked to the front door. Looking first to the right, then the left before pushing thick, horn-rimmed glasses higher on her nose, she then rang the doorbell.

"What do you think?" Jessica whispered, as if the woman might hear her. "She looks sneaky."

He'd thought the same thing, but didn't voice his opinion as the door opened. The UPS worker handed the package to whoever opened the door. He grabbed the camera and snapped off several pictures before picking up his cell phone and punching in the speed-dial number that would take him directly to the chief's cell phone.

"Yeah," the chief answered.

"We have a suspicious UPS person. About five-three, dark hair, in uniform. Let's get a tail on her. See if she's actually delivering packages."

"I'll have an unmarked in the vicinity in less than five."

"Wouldn't the radio have been faster?" Jessica asked after he folded the phone.

He shook his head. "Every scanner in the city would've picked up our conversation."

"A different channel?"

"Even some of the so-called safe frequencies aren't clear."

He moved to the front door, opening it just a crack. "She's in a UPS van. Everything looks legit." So what had she been delivering?

She climbed back in the van, again looking around as if to see if she was being watched.

Something was definitely suspicious.

"Did you notice the size of the package?" Jessica asked as she came and leaned around him.

She filled his senses as she tried for a better view through the crack in the open door. He certainly knew the size of *his* package was rapidly growing larger as the softness of her body pressed against him. He swallowed past the lump in his throat, then blinked several times while trying desperately not to turn and pull her into his arms.

"So did you notice the size of it?" she repeated.

Lord, had she brushed against him? He had a major hard-on.

"The size of the package?" she clarified. She turned and looked at him. "You okay?"

She had noticed. No, that wasn't the package she meant. She referred to the UPS person. He breathed a sigh of relief. *Think with your head,* Conor!

"A large package," he said.

She let out an exasperated sigh.

He shrugged.

"Okay, medium-size."

His glance swept over her. *You're on duty,* he told himself. Think *suspect.* Burglars.

What had she seen that he hadn't?

"The exact-size box a video would fit inside," she elaborated.

She was right. The mayor had a video stolen. Could the delivery woman have something to do with the robberies? But why would she have the video? On the other hand, who would know better than a delivery person when someone wasn't at home?

His cell phone rang.

"Yeah?"

"We have someone following her, but so far it looks like she's just delivering packages. Everything appears to be on the up and up. We're doing a background check just in case."

Something was up . . . besides him, he thought with more than a little sarcasm. He'd stake his career on it. The woman had looked too damn suspicious.

He spoke with the chief for a few minutes, then flipped his cell closed before turning back to Jessica. The phone conversation with Jessica's father had effectively drained his desire. Funny how talking to a woman's father could do that to a person.

"Right now everything appears legit. We'll know more

after they run a history on her, but if she does work for UPS, it's doubtful they'll find anything. Since no one has stolen a UPS truck recently, she's more than likely employed by the company. Maybe she's decided she wants a little extra cash."

She nodded. "Okay, so what do we do now?" She began to pace the small entryway.

He smiled inwardly, thinking of a lot of things they could do. Like having hot, sweaty sex on a heart-shaped bed. He was quickly coming to the conclusion that being a cop could be damned difficult at times.

"We go back to the window and watch."

"Oh." Her face fell.

Damn, she was cute. And sexy. And definitely a temptation.

Night had fallen hours ago. Jessica had gone upstairs and Conor was taking first watch, but the house next door wasn't on his mind as much as Jessica was right now.

He rearranged himself in the wingback chair, adjusted the pillow beneath his head, fixed the blanket in his lap, checked to make sure his cell and the camera were on the table, and tried to concentrate on his job.

Not an easy task. The movement upstairs was drawing all his attention. Everyday sounds to most married couples, but he wasn't married . . . Jessica wasn't his wife.

If he were married to her, he'd be upstairs right now rather than sitting in one of the hardest chairs known to man. He closed his eyes for a moment and could see himself sitting on the bed, waiting for her to emerge from the bathroom.

He swallowed past the lump in his throat. She'd step from the bathroom completely naked. Her skin would glisten with the oil she'd applied. Her breasts would be full, her nipples tight little nubs begging for his mouth to cover them.

The thatch of dark hair between her legs would cover her sex, tempting him to look closer, to see what secrets lay behind the curls.

Son of a bitch! She was doing it to him again. He shifted in his chair, tugging at the front of his jeans to make more room for what was becoming a constant ache, a constant hard-on. When the surveillance was over he wasn't going to miss Jessica and the torture she was putting him through one little bit. He would be glad to see an end to all this.

Yeah, right.

He ran a hand through his hair. How the hell had he let her get under his skin so quickly? All this would eventually end. A relationship wouldn't work between them. She'd told him that she didn't want to get involved with a cop.

Damned if he didn't want to convince her otherwise.

He had the time. It didn't look like the case was going to be solved any time soon. The chief had called him with the UPS worker's background and she'd checked out. No criminal history of any kind.

Still, he'd swear it wasn't a routine delivery. She'd had all the signs of being nervous: looking around furtively, hugging the package close to her body, short, quick steps. No, there was more going on. At least they had her picture on file now.

So far, the UPS worker was their only real lead. Not that he'd crossed the mayor off his list. He'd gone to a political rally once and heard him talk. The man had charm. Hell, he'd even kissed a couple of babies.

The guy gave him the creeps. But like the chief said, other than a few suspect contracts, the mayor was clean. Conor knew the chief hadn't ruled out the mayor, though.

There was also the possibility the person calling the shots was someone not on their list. But how were they getting their information? There were a couple of times when the burglars had come close to being caught, but the culprits were warned . . . or just got lucky.

Ring. Knock. Knock. Knock.

"Jessica, open up. Jessica are you awake?" Trudy cried.

"Son of a bitch." Conor jumped to his feet, grabbing the

falling blanket and scooping up his pillow. He hurried to the hall closet.

"What's Trudy doing here?" Jessica whispered frantically as she flew down the stairs.

Conor shoved the pillow and blanket inside the closet, slammed the door, and wheeled around. His breath caught in his throat when he took a good look at Jessica as she skidded to a stop beside him.

Forget trying to talk. Hell, he could barely breathe. The flimsy blue gown was a far cry from that damned bunny suit. Wispy satin outlined every curve and hollow. The lace-trimmed neckline dipped low, accentuating full breasts. He could only stare at the vision clinging to his arm.

"Conor, didn't you hear me?"

Mentally shaking himself, he tried to keep his mind on what was happening around him and not what stood so temptingly beside him. He tried to tell himself he was on the job, but the mental warning didn't quite reach his brain. Right at this moment, his thoughts weren't focused on putting criminals behind bars.

She frowned. "Quit staring. Surely you've seen a woman in her nightgown before."

"A few," he admitted. "I like what you have on now a lot better than that other thing you wore."

"I . . . uh . . ." She tugged at the material.

He enjoyed seeing her flustered. Made him wonder if she was immune to him after all. He'd begun to think he'd imagined the signals she sent out. Even if Jessica didn't realize it, she wasn't unaffected by his presence.

He liked that thought. He probably shouldn't. She was an obstinate, opinionated female, and she didn't want to get involved with a cop, and he wouldn't give up law enforcement—an impossible relationship.

Another explosion of noise erupted. *Ring. Ring. Knock! Knock!*

"Are you awake in there?"

Jessica turned the lock and opened the door a crack. "Trudy, is everything okay?"

Conor hoped Trudy talked a long time. Jessica was using the door to shield her body from any curious neighbors. The way she'd angled herself, her short gown rode up in the back. A lot. The sweet cheeks of her ass were rather delectable. Leaning against the doorjamb, he admired the view, which got better and better.

Trudy slammed her way inside.

Jessica hopped to the left.

Conor caught the door before it banged him in the face.

"Oh, Jessica," Trudy blubbered into a tissue, stopping just short of bumping into the banister. "George doesn't love me anymore."

Jessica turned pleading eyes toward him.

He shrugged. What was *he* supposed to do? Shoot George? He'd like to catch him with the stolen goods before he resorted to violence.

After sending him a men-are-good-for-nothing look, Jessica put her arm around Trudy's shoulders and guided her into the living room. "Now, now, I'm sure you can both work out any misunderstanding you've had."

"No! It's over. He accused me of flirting with the salesman at the jewelry store. It was only a little harmless teasing, but George blew up. And he refused to buy me the bracelet," she finished on a loud wail.

Conor wondered what she was more upset over, the loss of George, or the bracelet?

"Please, can I stay? Just for tonight? I'll sleep on the couch. And I promise I won't be a bit of trouble. You won't even know I'm here."

Stay here? Downstairs? The couch? His hormones raged, causing his brain to malfunction. This was going to be his lucky night! He wanted to kiss Trudy . . . on second thought, he didn't think he would go that far.

Damn, what was he thinking?

He reined in all the testosterone flowing through him before he went berserk. He was on duty.

But Trudy couldn't know that. What would any normal husband do for a neighbor's wife who had nowhere to go?

"Of course you can stay," Conor told her. He hurried to Trudy's side and patted her on the back. "We can't have you sleeping on the sidewalk, now can we?" He glanced up and met Jessica's glare. His eyebrows rose. "Can we, dear?"

Play the game, Jessica. One wrong move and Trudy would suspect something wasn't quite right between him and Jessica.

"Of course not," she responded between gritted teeth.

Okay, that was better than nothing. A sudden, malicious gleam entered Jessica's eyes. He backed up a step. What was she plotting?

"But I'm sure Conor won't mind sleeping on the sofa. You can sleep in our bed with me." She smiled triumphantly.

"Oh no, I wouldn't hear of any such thing. I'll be fine on the couch."

Conor breathed a sigh of relief. The sofa was at least a foot shorter than his frame.

And there was only one bed upstairs. His mouth went dry as once again erotic thoughts swept him away—right into a fantasy of Jessica's hot little body pressed tightly against his.

On duty! On duty! On duty!

"But . . ." Jessica began.

Trudy shook her head. "It wouldn't be right. You two go back to bed, and I'll be fine. And come first light, I'm going home to Momma." She sniffed loudly.

Jessica looked ready to blow their cover. He couldn't let that happen. "Don't we keep an extra pillow and blanket in the closet, sweet pea?" He rushed over and pulled them out. "Here they are."

His smile faded when he turned around. Jessica's eyes had narrowed to mere slits. Was it his fault Trudy had decided to come over, dragging her problems with her?

"Now go on, you two," Trudy said, taking the blanket and pillow. "Just pretend I'm not even here."

Bringing the tissue to her nose, she blew loud enough so the windows rattled. Okay, Conor conceded, the wind might have picked up just a little at the precise moment she snorted into the Kleenex.

"Maybe I should stay here with you." Jessica took a step toward Trudy.

Conor grabbed Jessica's hand. He didn't want any unnecessary interaction between Trudy and Jessica. She just wasn't experienced enough. "I think she wants to be alone."

"You don't know that." She squeezed his hand.

The woman had a grip! His little finger was slowly being crushed. He yanked. Jessica stumbled into his arms.

"See, dear?" He smiled down into Jessica's furious eyes. "You're so tired you can't even stand. I'm sure Trudy understands."

"He's right. Y'all don't pay me no mind. I'll be okay." She tossed the pillow and blanket on the sofa.

"Let's go to bed, hon."

Conor slid his arm around Jessica in what he was sure would be construed as a husbandly gesture. Her shoulders stiffened. No, *stiff* was a mild word. Her shoulders felt as tight as a rusty gun barrel. Maybe insisting Trudy stay hadn't been a good idea, after all. Then again, the alternative would've been to kick her out.

Jessica jerked away and stomped up the stairs.

He followed. Even in anger, Jessica's hips moved seductively, the blue satin brushing across the back of her upper legs. He tugged at his jeans. Her shoulders weren't the only thing stiff.

At the door of the bedroom, Jessica spun around. He stopped right before he plowed into her. She glared at him. With that look, she should've stayed a cop. Freeze criminals right in their tracks. Sure did a lot to ease the ache in his lower regions.

She stepped across the threshold without another glance in

his direction. Hesitantly, he slipped in behind her. As soon as the door closed, he realized his phone was downstairs. He had no connection with the chief. He strode to the window. Damn it, he couldn't see the suspects' house from this angle.

He ran a hand through his hair. What were the odds that anything would happen with Trudy in the house? What choice did he have? The idea of going downstairs to retrieve his phone didn't appeal to him. The way Trudy looked at him made him more than a little nervous.

One look at Jessica's expression and he was tempted to go back downstairs and insist Trudy sleep in here and he'd take the sofa. Jessica didn't look at all pleased with the turn of events.

But then, he knew the signals were there. She wanted him. Was that what worried her about them staying in the same room? Was she afraid something would happen? He'd give anything to know exactly what she was thinking.

Anger slowly coursed through Jessica. She wanted to kill him. A hundred different ways came to mind.

Conor had manipulated the situation, and she didn't like being coerced into doing anything. How could she have been such a fool? And to think she'd been harboring romantic thoughts about the man.

Oh, he'd pulled out all the stops tonight. Maneuvered his way upstairs and into her bed. Okay, technically it was his bed, but he'd destroyed her air mattress! And it damn well wasn't fair.

Going to the closet, she reached up and yanked down extra pillows, flinging one at him. He caught it in one smooth motion like there hadn't been a bit of force behind her throw. That irritated her even more. The least he could've done was stumble backward a step. Instead, he frowned at her like she was the one in the wrong.

"What'd you want me to do? Throw her out the front door? That would've looked real good. Don't forget the reason we're here, Jessica."

That didn't make the situation any less difficult. Or her any less angry. She didn't want him in her bed. She wanted him on the sofa. Where it would be safe.

Safe for whom?

The thought scurried through her mind. She could easily get used to him snuggled in bed next to her. The full length of her body pressed against his. Her hands exploring his chest, his back, his . . . she swallowed. A flash of heat stole over her. And him a cop. Someone she'd sworn to keep at arm's length. Someone she *would* keep at arm's length.

She jutted her chin and met his gaze. "No, I didn't want you to throw Trudy out. And yes, I know why I'm here. But that doesn't mean I have to like the circumstances I now find myself in."

"I'll sleep on the floor."

"Damn right you will!"

He reached for the blanket she still held, and flinched. For a brief second his face screwed up in pain.

A little niggle of fear swept over her. Conor always seemed so strong, but there was definitely something wrong. "What's the matter?" She put her hand out to steady him.

"Nothing." He grimaced and shook his head, pulling away from her.

"No, you're hurt." It had been a fleeting look of discomfort but it was there long enough for her to notice. When he'd stepped away, he favored his right leg.

"It's not a big deal. I injured my back a few years ago when I was taking down a perp and every once in a while it acts up. Must be the change in beds. Mine is a little softer at home. Don't worry about it, though. I've slept in worse places than the floor."

Guilt felled her quicker than an axe to a tree. She nibbled her bottom lip before finally coming to a decision, but she couldn't look him in the face when she told him what she was thinking. She certainly didn't want him to read more into the situation.

"Well, you won't be sleeping there tonight. We're adults."
She pulled the covers back and bent over to arrange her pillow. "I'm sure we can act in a mature fashion."

When she straightened and turned, Jessica caught the expression of longing on Conor's face. His gaze had fastened on
the lower half of her body. As soon as Conor realized he'd
been caught staring, he cleared his throat.

"Yes, I'm sure for one night we can manage to sleep in the
same bed."

Cops were supposed to be people you could trust. They
were good at instilling that feeling. Trained, in fact. She
should know. But in this case, Jessica didn't trust Conor any
more than she would trust George inside a bank with the
vault door open and everyone gone to lunch.

Going back to the closet, she grabbed three more pillows
and lined them end-to-end down the middle of the bed.

"What are those for?"

"A reminder."

"Don't you trust me?"

She didn't give him a second look as she crawled beneath
the covers and pulled them to her chin. "Not as far as I can
throw you, Officer Richmond."

Was that a chuckle? Was he laughing at her? Well, as long
as he stayed on his side of the bed, she didn't really care.

Dresser drawers opened before Conor went into the bathroom.

When she was starting to get comfortable, the mattress
shifted and Conor crawled under the covers.

"Go to sleep, Jessica."

Sleep? That was the last thing on her mind. She probably
wouldn't sleep a wink. No, what she would be doing is thinking about the man on the other side of the bed. That was another thing. How could the mattress have shrunk? She could
almost feel each breath he took. In and out, in and out.

Oh, this was going to be a really long night.

Chapter 12

Heat swirled around Jessica. Nice, snuggly warmth, pulling her closer. She rubbed her face against her pillow and vaguely wondered how it could've grown hair.

And it thumped.

A steady thump, thump rhythm.

What did she care? She was having the most erotic dream. In her dream someone was stroking her breast. Gently massaging, scraping his finger back and forth across her nipple. She strained closer to her fantasy lover's hand as the itch for just a little more grew inside her.

But damn it, voices kept trying to intrude upon her delicious fantasy. Very annoying voices. Well, she wasn't into a threesome or group orgies. No more than two people were allowed in this dream, so they'd better go away.

They didn't. She yawned, struggling past the last vestiges of sleep.

"Trudy! Trudy, my leetle buttercup! Pleeze forgive-a me!" George yelled.

"Go away, George. Tomorrow I'm going home to Mother! I should've listened to her and never married you." A loud wail followed.

Ee-yuck! How did George and Trudy get in her dream?

She dragged her eyes open, then blinked rapidly. Where was she? It was clear to her that she wasn't on her air mattress. If she were, it had grown a wide chest and a very large, warm hand that cupped one of her breasts. Apparently, her gown had ridden up after she went to sleep and someone had placed a nice heating pad on one cheek of her ass, too. Had she walked through a looking glass?

She really wasn't at her best when awakened in the middle of the night. Damn it, and she'd been having a really good dream.

Last night's events came creeping past her muddled, sleep-induced fog.

Or was it a dream?

Realization slowly dawned. Her fantasy lover wasn't a fantasy, after all. She should move away. She really should. It was obviously Conor who caressed her breast. She really should—*God, that felt good*—move away. She gasped as his hand again brushed across her nipple, this time bringing it to perky life. She inched closer, biting her bottom lip.

"Pleeze, my leetle love muffin, you are-a breaking my heart. Pleeze, come home."

Conor's hand suddenly stilled, as if he, too, realized something wasn't quite right in his dream world.

Damn George and Trudy. Her body ached with unfulfilled need, but apparently George and Trudy yelling at each other had awakened Conor, too, because the mattress shifted slightly and his hand disappeared. She bit back a groan of disappointment. The worst thing about the situation was that she cared more about Conor moving his hand than the fact it was there in the first place.

"What's going on?" she finally managed to ask, but wished they could go back to cuddling . . . and stuff.

"I believe George is on our lawn, and he's come to collect his bride," Conor explained in a voice still heavy with the last dregs of sleep. "If he can talk Trudy into opening the front door."

She rubbed the sleep from her eyes and focused on Conor's face. Plenty of moonlight streamed in through the window, so she could clearly make out his features. It was kind of hard not to. Their noses were almost touching.

And their lower limbs intertwined.

He'd changed into pajamas before climbing into bed. Very thin pajamas. So thin she could feel the heat radiating from his body. Or maybe that was her heat, because she was definitely feeling warm. Okay, more like hot, as in heat wave, as in an inferno, as in she really wanted to get laid.

Deep breath, she told herself. She wasn't *involved* with the man lying next to her. She was only sleeping with him. Not exactly *with* him, more like *next to him.* Crap, she couldn't even make sense to herself. She drew in a calming breath.

She was only here to help her father out of a sticky situation. Speaking of which . . . she was in one right now. At least, she might have been if George hadn't interrupted.

Deep breaths! Lord, he would think she was panting for him. Brain to respiratory system: stop deep breaths.

Meditation. That's what she needed. Think of the spiritualist's soothing voice. She closed her eyes.

Yom-da-da-da-da, she silently chanted, letting her body become one with the universe.

"Are you going back to sleep?" Conor whispered.

The spell was broken. Not that the short meditation had helped. No wonder the stupid CD was in the bargain bin.

"No," she murmured, at the same time slowly extracting her leg from between his.

They would just forget that any of this ever happened. Of course she'd gotten a little horny when Conor caressed her boob. It could happen to anyone. Now that she was wide awake, she wasn't even thinking about having sex . . . well, maybe she was still visualizing it just a smidgeon, but that didn't mean she'd act out her fantasy.

When she brought her leg upward, her knee brushed against something hard and unyielding.

Conor grunted.

She hoped her face wasn't glowing bright red. Jeez! She

hadn't just . . . She had. Without a doubt, she knew exactly what her knee had bumped. "Sorry," she murmured and scooted a safer distance away.

Lot of good the pillows were. She'd practically thrown her body over them. Well, it wasn't her fault. She'd forgotten her stuffed huggy bear. The barrier between them made a good substitute. The living, breathing man on the other side had been even better.

"I will-a buy you the bracelet tomorrow. I promise."

"You accused me of flirting, George."

"I'm a red-blooded Italiano. You are a hot-a woman. You make-a me crazy with the lust-a! Can you blame me that I am so jealous, *bel amore*?"

"The lust-a?" Conor asked.

"Shhh. I want to hear what they're saying."

"He promised her the bracelet. Ten dollars says she'll take him back."

"You're on." She'd already pegged Trudy. "I say she'll hold out for the necklace."

"How can you be jealous when I told you I'd never look at another man?" Trudy wailed.

"And what about our-a wedding night?"

"Trudy was unfaithful on their wedding night?" Jessica whispered.

"Do you blame her?"

Conor had a point.

"I told you that was a mistake, but you can't seem to forgive me. Mother was right. I should've married an American."

"Pleeze, my love. *Mio amore*. I will-a buy you the earrings you wanted so much-a, too. The bracelet and-a the earrings. Both of them-a. Just pleeze come home to-a me."

"The big diamond earrings?"

"Ha!" Jessica exclaimed. "You owe me ten dollars."

"Diamond earrings are not the same as a necklace."

"Are, too!"

The front door opened and closed. Apparently, Trudy had decided she'd stay with George and was going back home.

"Trudy, *mia cara*. I will-a never, never hurt-a you again."

Their voices drifted away from the house.

"She's gone." That had to be the dumbest observation she'd ever made. Of course Trudy had left.

Conor raised on one elbow. "I guess I can go back downstairs and watch the house next door."

"You could."

Clear your mind, she told herself. Yom-da-da-da-da. *You do not want to have sex. You are not horny.* Yom-da-da-da-da.

Her breasts ached for his touch . . . for his lips. She wanted him to taste her, to fill her body. She wrapped her arms around her pillow and pulled it close. It came in a poor second. But the fact remained: he was still a cop.

The mattress shifted as he started to get up.

He was also a hot man, damn it! She didn't want another night dreaming about having sex with him. Tonight she wanted the reality and screw the fantasy! Or better yet, screw her. "Or you could stay," she blurted before she could change her mind.

The rational part of her brain warned her to bite her tongue and not say another word. She sighed. When had she ever been rational?

Moonlight cast a dim illumination of its own in the room. He had his back to her as he sat on the side of the bed, so she couldn't read his expression.

"What do you mean?" he quietly asked, breaking past the sudden silence of the room.

"Nothing. Forget it. I'll see you in the morning."

But how could she forget when she knew he needed her— when they needed each other? There'd been a connection from the start, but she'd been denying it . . . denying herself.

Without considering why she was doing it, Jessica reached

across the darkness and touched Conor's shoulder. She felt the shudder that swept through him. He turned his head, taking her hand in his and pressed his lips into her palm. Warm tingles skittered up her arm. This was right. She didn't want to think about what tomorrow would bring. She didn't really care.

"Stay," she whispered.

"I should go downstairs. Watch the house."

"They won't do anything tonight."

He hesitated and she knew he was torn between duty and her. Guilt whipped through her, but she couldn't stop what was going to happen any more than he could.

She sighed with relief when he crawled back in bed, pulling her close, until her body was pressed intimately against his. One night, she thought to herself. They could share a night together. It didn't have to be anything permanent. It would mean nothing to either of them in the morning. Except maybe a great sexual experience. That's all, nothing more.

He slipped his hand beneath her gown and cupped her breast. All thoughts of what tomorrow would bring scattered as naughty sensations erupted inside her. The kind that made her feel wanton and unmindful of what she did or was about to do. Her focus was on getting and giving as much pleasure as she could.

She bit her bottom lip when his thumb lightly brushed across her tender nipple. Her breasts swelled, pushing toward him. Yes, that was it. This is what she'd dreamed about almost every night since Conor had arrested her. She just hadn't wanted to admit he'd affected her that much.

"God, I think I've wanted to do this from the moment I saw you standing on that street corner," he said as if reading her thoughts. He nuzzled her neck, then gently tugged at her earlobe with his teeth.

"When my skirt was torn, hose shredded, a button missing from my blouse, and looking like a hooker. Gee, thanks." She sucked in a deep breath, pressing her hips closer to him.

His breath tickled her neck when he chuckled.

"You looked damned sexy to me. I had a hard time remembering I was a cop."

She snaked her hand between them and stroked. "It doesn't feel like you're doing a very good job of it now, either."

He groaned. "Can you blame me? You've been teasing me for way too long."

"Me? I've been teasing you?" Right now, teasing was out of the question! She wanted the real thing.

"Yes, every time you walk into the room. It's time for a little payback."

He made it sound like she would enjoy every second of his revenge.

He gently pushed her onto her back, tugging her flimsy little nightgown over her head and pushing the covers to the foot of the bed. She lay exposed to his view, and she imagined he was getting an eyeful with the moonlight streaming into the room, making it almost seem like early morning rather than the middle of the night. The only thing she still wore was the thong, a tiny triangle of silky white material.

He ran his hand from her neck, between her breasts and across her abdomen. She arched toward him, wanting him to continue in the direction he'd started, but his hand veered to her hip and down her thigh and stayed there to lightly stroke. If she were a cat, she'd have purred.

"How did you tease me?" he asked. "When you look at me, your eyes tell me you want to have sex. Every movement of your body is an invitation to touch...to caress...to taste."

"I...I..." She closed her eyes. She had done exactly that, but it wasn't all her fault, and it hadn't been intentional.

At least, she didn't think so.

"And you haven't been sending out signals? What about scooping me up and carrying me inside the house that first day? You weren't in any hurry to put me down, either. And what about when you licked the chocolate off my finger?"

For a moment she forgot what she'd been reminding him of as she remembered how he'd licked every bit of the chocolate and raspberry from her fingers. The way his mouth had sucked at her tender flesh. She bit her bottom lip. Just thinking about it made her damp. She mentally shook away the image . . . for the moment, and frowned at him. She wasn't the only one doing the arousing. "You can't tell me all that had to do with trying to run me off."

"You're right. I enjoyed it as much as you did."

She opened her mouth, then snapped it closed. He didn't have to agree with her that quickly.

"One night," he said. "One night together, and then I'll be able to concentrate on my job." He slowly drew his hand back up and cupped her breast, tugging on the tight nipple before moving to the other one and giving it equal attention. "Shall we let bygones be bygones?"

"Oh . . . yes, uh-huh, sure." Her bygones were already out the window as her eyes drifted closed and she lost herself in what he was doing to her nipples and the erotic sensations washing over her, wave after delicious wave. She didn't want to think, she only wanted to feel what his hands were doing, the pleasure his touch gave her. Had she ever been this turned on? She didn't think so.

He lowered his head and sucked on the tender nub, drawing it into his mouth. She pulled his head closer, wanting him to take more into his mouth, but he pulled back instead. A frustrated moan escaped between her lips. Not fair. Not fair at all.

"You've told me you wanted nothing to do with a cop, but your body tells a different story with each touch of my hand. I think you're a liar, Jessica Nelson."

Enough—his teasing had to stop. She rose to her knees and pushed him onto his back, taking him off guard, then straddled him.

"What do you want to hear me say? I was wrong?" She rubbed her crotch against his hard, hot length.

He arched, grabbing her thighs for a tighter fit against him. "I don't think I care what you admit, as long as you don't stop what you're doing."

A smile lifted the corners of her mouth. Conor needed to learn that she fought dirty. Not that she wasn't getting just as much enjoyment. The friction their clothes created was nice, but being completely naked would be even better. She wanted to see his body as much as he'd wanted to see hers. The pajamas he'd slipped on before coming to bed were more than a hindrance. They were in her damn way! She wanted to feel naked skin . . . his. She quickly unbuttoned the top, pushing open the sides, her hands running across the hairs on his chest.

Oh, God, yes. This was exactly what she wanted. She loved touching him. She'd dreamed of this . . . feeling his muscles tighten and relax beneath her hands, but when she moved to pull his bottoms off, he stopped her.

"It won't work between us," he warned. "You don't want to get involved with a cop and I don't want a long-term relationship. I just want to make sure we're on the same page here. Nothing beyond tonight . . . right?"

She stared at him. Nothing beyond tonight? She knew he waited for an answer and would go no further until he had one.

Chapter 13

"Hell, I don't want to marry you. I only want to have sex with you," Jessica told him in a voice throaty with passion. "I need an orgasm really bad."

His laughter filled the room. She was so glad he'd found his sense of humor. She certainly didn't want to have sex with a stodgy, never-laugh-at-anything man. Two people joining together should be exactly that—having fun. Giving as well as receiving. Just living in the moment.

And she planned to do a lot of giving.

"Sometimes I don't know what to do with you."

Had there been just a hint of wistfulness in his voice? Yeah, right. Her sexual deprivation was making her hear things that weren't there. This was sex between two consenting adults . . . nothing more. Lots and lots of sex, if she had anything to say about it.

She slipped out of bed and very slowly tugged her thong over her hips, stretching the elastic out at the sides. He groaned. She rolled her hips to the right, then left, savoring the exquisite torture she put them both through. Finally, she bent at the waist and tugged the thong all the way down.

A stripper couldn't have done a better job. When she straightened, she faced him without shame or embarrassment. Why should she? Not when this felt so damn right.

Closing her eyes, she ran her hands up her thighs, over her

abdomen and cupped her breasts before sliding her hands back to her waist. Her skin was hot and so ready for a different set of hands to caress her.

She opened her eyes and ran her tongue over her lips. "Honey, if you don't know what to do with me, then you're in a lot of trouble. I guess I could show you, though. You just *might* be worth the effort."

For a second she wondered if he had heard her. Then his eyes narrowed. She knew a second too late he was going for revenge.

She bit back her scream when he barreled off the bed and came at her. She twirled and ran to the other side, but he apparently anticipated what she was going to do and lunged across, grabbing her by the waist and hauling her back onto the bed. Laughter erupted from her.

"You tell me if I know what I'm doing." He jerked his top off and tossed it to the floor.

She expected him to pounce, but he didn't. It threw her completely off guard, heightening the thrill when he slowed his actions and lightly stroked his fingers between her legs. God, that was wonderful. She arched toward his hand, but he didn't increase the pressure.

"You feel like every wet dream I've ever had. All soft and silky . . . hot and ready for me to slip inside you," he breathed close to her ear.

She drew in a deep breath, not wanting him to stop. Needing more. Wanting to give as much pleasure as she was getting. Before she could touch him, he stayed her hand.

"Not yet," he whispered. "I want to taste you . . . every last inch."

Yes! She wanted just that.

He moved off the bed.

Not fair! He was going to torture her. He kept his gaze on her face as he took his own sweet time and shoved his pajama bottoms over his hips. Her mouth was so dry she couldn't swallow as her gaze drank in the sight of his perfect and very male body. From his tanned, broad shoulders to an amazing washboard stomach. The ache inside her grew stronger. And the best was yet to come.

He stood still so she could get her fill looking at him. Not that she would ever, ever get tired of staring at his magnificent form. Every muscle was honed to perfection, and she did mean every muscle. He was big and hard and she wanted him more than she'd wanted any man in her entire life.

Her gaze stalked him as he moved to the foot of the bed. Her heart skipped several beats. His hands circled her ankles and began spreading her legs apart, seeing everything she had to offer, and then some.

Tremors swept up and down her body as his hands inched their way up her calves, over her knees. Closer . . . closer . . .

She bit her bottom lip, waiting for the first touch of his tongue . . . his mouth, but all she felt was his warm breath blowing across her mound. Her hands knotted in the sheet. An aching need built inside her. She spread her legs even more for him. She was beyond thinking. She knew only that she wanted everything he had to give.

His weight shifted as he changed positions. "Ahh, sweet," he whispered.

When he touched her, moving back the folds to reveal her sex, she whimpered. He soothed her with a gentle murmur. Then his mouth closed over her and he kissed her.

Fire rushed through her veins as spasm after spasm of pleasure washed over her. He sucked, pulling the nub of skin into his mouth at the same time his hands massaged the inside of her thighs. He took her to the very edge. She reached, strained to fall over, but he pulled her back. Oh, God, her body trembled from head to toe. There wasn't an inch of her that didn't scream for more.

When he slid up next to her, she moaned, unable to contain her disappointment. Before she could do much more than that, he began stroking her again.

Her breathing slowed. Hell, she hadn't even realized she

was panting. Conor brought her away from the edge. Sexual hunger enveloped her. She'd never felt like this—so out of control. Almost in a frenzy to explore Conor's body as a sweeping need to touch him, to taste every inch, plunged her into what felt like a scorching furnace.

"Shhh, just take a deep breath," he said, guessing her thoughts and the turmoil he'd caused. "It's going to be a long night. We have plenty of time."

She scooted to her knees. "Sorry, babe, but it's been too damn long since I've had the big O. We'll go slow next time." Once more she pushed against his shoulders. "And you can wipe that self-satisfied smirk off your face."

"You enjoyed what I did."

She cocked an eyebrow, straddled him, but then scooted down his thighs before he could stop her. With one long stroke of her tongue she licked down his hard length, then back up before taking him into her mouth. She sucked, liking the way he tasted . . . the way he felt inside her mouth . . . and maybe the sense of power that swept through her, knowing she was giving him as much enjoyment as he'd given her.

He groaned at the same time he grabbed her head. "Ah, damn. That feels . . . oh, jeez. Maybe . . . damn . . . you'd better stop, though."

Grinning, she raised her head. "Did you like it?" she asked innocently.

Something between a growl and a groan came from deep in his throat. He scooped under her arms and pulled her toward him until their faces were only inches apart; then, in one swift movement, he flipped her on her back.

"Yeah, too damn much. I'm about to explode." He reached over to the nightstand and scrambled around until he found his wallet and jerked out a foil packet. It only took him a couple of seconds to slip on a condom.

When he entered her, the heavens opened up and stars exploded all around her. She arched her back, her legs wrapping around his waist so she could take all he had to give.

"Damn, you feel good. Tight and hot," he told her.

She moaned as she met him thrust for thrust. Talking stopped and they lost themselves in the moment. The only thing heard in the room was their labored breathing as they strained toward completion.

He slid deep inside her, heat spiraling downward, engulfing her in the flames. It had never been like this. Not this all-consuming need to reach for more. To hang on a little longer, knowing it would be worth the effort. To give a little more. She clenched her inner muscles, sucking him further inside her body . . . again . . . and again. Raising her hips upward, clenching her muscles, sliding back down. Heat built inside, the flames licking, teasing.

He moaned and plunged deeper.

Coherent thought fled. Her body tightened as she climaxed. Seconds later, he stiffened as a low growl came from deep in his throat. She squeezed herself around him, holding him tight as sweet release washed over her in waves. Her body trembled and shook.

Never . . . never like this. Never in her life. God, what had happened?

She breathed in deep gulps of air as the world came back into focus. She'd never seen stars like the ones he'd just shown her. Hell, he'd taken her into another galaxy. She rather liked flying in outer space.

When he rolled to his side, the connection was broken, but he quickly pulled her close to him, cradling her next to his body. Somehow she knew it would take more than separating their bodies to break their connection.

Fuck, that wasn't supposed to happen. This wasn't fucking supposed to happen. She'd only wanted an orgasm. One tiny, little climax. Was that asking too damn much? No. But what she got was earth-shattering. She'd not only gotten the big O, she'd gotten the *big ohhhhhhh!*

Absently, he caressed her shoulder, slipping lower to lightly massage her back, her hip. There were no words be-

tween them. Thank goodness. What the hell was she supposed to say? Or him? Gee, thanks for the orgasm. That felt
great? I think I'll catch a quick nap now.

Yeah, right.

A few minutes later, he kissed the top of her head and
eased from the bed. She couldn't help herself—she rolled to
her stomach and watched as he walked to the bathroom and
shut the door. God, he was magnificent. Tanned skin and
hard, sinewy muscles, all wrapped up in a nice, tight package. Until she'd pulled the string and unwrapped him.

She smiled and rolled to her back. She felt like a cat that'd
just licked the last drop of cream from the bowl. She tugged
the covers closer to her body and realized the saleslady was
right—the satiny sheets felt wonderfully wicked against her
naked skin. Almost as wicked as Conor's naked skin had felt
against her.

The bathroom door opened. Disappointment filled her.
Conor was once again dressed in his jeans, although he'd left
his shirt unbuttoned and he wasn't wearing shoes.

"I thought I'd run downstairs and just make sure all was
still quiet next door. You want anything?"

She lazily let her gaze sweep over him. "Only you."

He grinned. "I think I can oblige. I'll be back before you
know it."

She snuggled her pillow close to her body and smiled as he
left the room. While he was gone, she made a quick trip to
the bathroom, then scurried back to bed. She stifled a yawn
and pulled the covers up to her neck.

In a few minutes Conor would return and she had a feeling
he could take away her sudden chill. He could do a lot of
things to get her toasty hot. She burrowed deeper. The heart-
shaped bed was much nicer than her air mattress. Even better
when she was curled next to Conor.

She yawned, her eyes drifting closed. She'd just rest a
minute. Catch a couple of winks until he joined her. She

grinned. Literally joined her. She sighed deeply. Her breathing slowed.

Conor had to bite the inside of his cheeks to keep from whistling as he hurried downstairs. He felt as if a weight had been lifted from his shoulders. One night, that was all he'd needed. Now he could get back to doing his job without the stress of wanting to bury himself inside Jessica. The mystery was gone.

Wasn't it?

He took a deep breath as he reached the last step. Her light scent seemed to linger in the air. He paused, closing his eyes. Damn, she'd been worth every minute he'd spent away from watching the house next door. His hand massaged the banister, his thumb lightly tracing the rounded top. He could almost feel her breast, the way the nipple had peaked when he barely flicked his finger across it.

He swallowed past the lump forming in his throat.

And the way she'd tasted. The essence that was woman . . . that was all Jessica. Fire and heat. Sweet and sultry. A temptress, to say the least.

When he realized where his thoughts were taking him, and the fact he was fondling the banister, he frowned. Damn it, he was hard as a rock. Having sex with Jessica had taken away the mystery, but it created a new set of problems. He knew exactly what having sex with her was like, and he wanted more. Son of a bitch. If he weren't careful, he'd blow the surveillance. And cause himself a hell of a lot more prob lems.

Bright lights suddenly illuminated part of the living room. It took a few seconds to switch his brain from thinking about Jessica to what he was supposed to be doing. Conor rushed to the window as a black car pulled to the curb next door and a man climbed out, his hat pulled low on his forehead. The stranger looked both ways and hurried up the sidewalk.

Conor strained to see, but there were too many shadows and not enough light from the street lamp. Something was going down, though.

The mystery man approached the Merediths' door, glanced around furtively, keeping his head low, then rapped twice on the frame.

The hair on the back of Conor's neck twitched. The man was too cautious, and for it to be late at night, the door opened awfully fast, to Conor's way of thinking.

Barefoot, he made his way through the house and slipped out the back door. He crept across the lawn, wishing he had his shoes on, and peered through one of the windows. Not even a sliver of light escaped past the partially closed curtain.

Staying next to the side of the house, Conor eased down to the next window. He gritted his teeth when a thorn stabbed his foot. Balancing on one leg, he pulled it out, sucking in his breath. He should've put on shoes, but they were upstairs. Stupid—there was no other explanation for his actions tonight. Any of them.

He eased down to the next window. The blind was up about an inch and he could see into the foyer. The stranger had his back to Conor.

"Damn," Conor muttered under his breath. "Come on, turn around. Let me see your face."

There were three people in the room. He recognized George's brother, Barry, and their father, Winston. Then there was the stranger. He didn't see George or his wife.

His gaze returned to the unidentified man. Something about the way he stood, the way he moved his hands, nagged at him. Could it be the mayor? He was the right height, but the long black coat and the hat pulled low obscured his features. Hell, he even wore black leather gloves.

Conor reached for his phone, then remembered it was still downstairs next to the chair. This was what he got for thinking with his dick rather than his brain. No time to go back and get the phone now. He didn't want to take a chance he'd miss seeing who was behind the disguise.

Suddenly, Winston laughed and slapped the mystery man on the back. If Conor hadn't been watching so closely, he might not have seen the stranger flinch and take a half step away from the older man.

He didn't like them, Conor mused. He might be using them to do his dirty work, but he couldn't stomach their company. They started for the front door. Conor eased to the corner of the house. Maybe he'd get lucky and catch a glimpse of the man as he left. That was the only hope he had. The way things stood, he didn't have any reason or evidence to question the stranger. Not unless he wanted to blow his cover.

The door opened and light spilled out.

"Then it's set. Don't screw this one up."

"Yes, Mr.—"

"No names, you fool. How many times do I have to tell you not to use my name?"

"But . . ."

"No, you listen and listen good. There won't be any more jobs after this one. Don't take stupid chances. I'm not giving you a warning—that's a threat." Spinning on his heel, he strode briskly back to his car.

Conor still couldn't see the man's face, and the car windows were tinted. As the black sedan pulled away from the curb, Conor squinted his eyes to catch the license number. The plate was dirty. Done on purpose? Probably.

The stranger was the ringleader. No doubt about it. At least, they hadn't sounded like they were planning anything legit. He'd bet his last dollar this was the gang pulling all the robberies.

But apparently not for much longer, if he'd understood right. They'd be making their move pretty soon, and if Conor didn't catch them in the act, he might never be given another opportunity.

Maybe the Merediths would give him some more information. He went back to the window. Barry and his father had
left the foyer. He slipped down to one of the other windows
and looked inside. Inky blackness filled the room.

He started to turn away when a door opened, emitting a
beam of light. George came strolling out of the bathroom in
a pair of pajama bottoms with big red lips splattered all over
them. He sported two gold chains around his neck. They
only emphasized his scrawny frame.

Conor's eyes widened when Trudy sat up in bed. She was
actually wearing . . . leather? "Come here, my hot little Italiano.
I know exactly where you can put your spicy sausage."

His stomach churned. He'd seen more than he cared to see
in this lifetime or the next.

"I will show you just-a how much I care for you, my leetle
cuddle bear."

Conor shook his head. It didn't look like they'd be going
anywhere tonight. He had a gut feeling the other two wouldn't
be causing any more mischief, either. Crouching low, he made
his way across the lawn and back inside the house.

As he entered the living room, Jessica was coming down
the stairs, rubbing the sleep from her eyes.

"I thought you were coming back to bed."

Even knowing he'd screwed up tonight, all he could think
about was tangling his hand in her hair and pulling her close
to him. He wanted to tug her gown off, cup her breasts in his
hands and suck on her tight little nipples.

Fuck, what the hell was she doing to his head? It was always the job before anything else. If he didn't stop what they
were doing right now, he might as well call the chief and tell
him that they could both start looking for new jobs.

"The Merediths had a visitor tonight."

Her face paled. She jerked her head toward the window
and hurried the rest of the way down the stairs.

He stopped her before she even got close to the window.
"He's gone."

"Did you call my father?"

"Too late. My phone was next to the chair, my shoes upstairs. By the time I got to the phone the car was long gone. All I had was a color and a dirty license plate. That could be just about all the cars in the state." He turned away from her before she could see his anger.

It wasn't Jessica who infuriated him, but himself. He should've kept his wits about him. He planted his fists on his hips, his body tense as he tried to bring his emotions under control. He'd screwed up, and that didn't happen to him. Not when he was on a case.

He jerked when her hand lightly stroked his arm.

"We made a mistake. We're human. We'll get him next time."

"Then we'd better do it fast. I heard enough to know they're only pulling one more job. The next one will be their last." He sucked in a deep breath. "We should've had them tonight. A car could've tailed him. I fucked up."

She dropped her hand from his arm. "You mean I did, don't you?"

He stopped himself just short of turning around, of telling her it had been as much his fault, but maybe this was the only way to end what had started between them. He clamped his lips together. Even though he told himself it was for the best, a sick feeling churned inside his stomach.

He sensed more than heard her leave the room. She left a feeling of emptiness in her wake. He sank into a nearby chair and rubbed a hand across weary eyes.

This didn't feel like the best possible solution. It felt like hell.

No, hell would be a lot easier to bear than what he felt right now.

Chapter 14

The next morning, Conor slipped out of the house, his thoughts on Jessica as he retrieved the paper. Just like any normal married man—except he wasn't married to the woman upstairs.

He'd sat in the chair the rest of the night, staring out the window, but not really seeing the house next door. His mind had been focused on something else. Namely, the way it had felt to finally hold Jessica in his arms, to kiss her, to know she wanted him as much as he wanted her.

She'd invaded his territory.

No, that wasn't exactly right. He'd known what would happen when he crawled into bed with her last night. Back injury? Yeah, right. He'd lied, then tried to convince himself sleeping with her wouldn't hurt a thing. That he'd just wanted to feel her body close to his. He'd excused his reasoning by telling himself the floor was too hard to sleep on.

They shouldn't have had sex.

Sex? No, it was more than sex. He didn't know what the hell it was, but it was more than sex, and he should feel ashamed. After all, he was the senior officer.

Then why didn't he feel any remorse?

The answer was easy. For the first time in his life, he felt whole. As if he was a part of someone's life.

His parents had each other. Hell, even his sister was besotted with her husband. Growing up, he'd never been what he'd call close with his family. Jessica was giving him something he never really knew he'd missed.

Now he had to end what he'd just found. Either that, or take a chance of blowing this case. His job had to come first. The badge represented everything he stood for, everything he was, and it had for a long time. He couldn't betray it. Hell, he already had.

"Pssst, Conor."

He turned. George. Just fucking great.

George glanced over his shoulder before traipsing across the lawn toward him.

This was all he needed—more contact with a suspect. "Hello, George."

"*Ciao*. I wanted to thank you for-a last night. If-a not for you, my Trudy, she would-a went home to her mama. You are a very good friend." He lowered his head. "I . . . I've never-a had a friend. I owe you for last-a night. It is something that will-a not ever be forgotten. Her mother would-a not have been so easy to deal-a with." He shook his head. "She is a real-a bitch, as you would-a say here in America."

When George raised his head, Conor saw the sincerity clearly mirrored in the smaller man's eyes. What had been in George's file? Something about his mother dumping him on his father's doorstep and taking off to parts unknown. It couldn't have been easy having a father like Winston and a brother like Barry.

Damn, he almost felt sorry for him. Why the hell did he have to be one of the bad guys?

Hell, George was starting to grow on him. First Jessica, and now George. This wasn't good.

He was on duty, George was a suspect, and he still had a job to do. Conor wouldn't take any more chances screwing up this surveillance.

"Tell you what," he cast a sideways look at George, "If you run across any deals on merchandise that someone might want to unload in a hurry, I wouldn't be adverse to taking it off their hands. It would be easy to get rid of pretty fast at my pawnshop. No one would be the wiser."

George glanced behind him as if he expected his father or brother to come storming outside any second and drag him inside the house. Hell, the little guy's shoulders even shook and his hands trembled.

"That would be—" He coughed. "That would-a be illegal."

Conor reminded himself that he had a job to do, then continued. "But you know how expensive these women are." He let his shoulders sag. "Even owning my own business and with the money I bring in, Jessica keeps wanting more. If you could help me out, buddy, I'd really appreciate it."

"I will-a see what I can do." George stood taller. "*Amici* have to-a stick together."

His neighbors were suspects—and the reason the chief's job was on the line. So why the hell did he feel guilty for lying?

George's front door opened and an older, unshaven, barrel-chested man stepped out, his faded green T-shirt stretched taut across his wide girth. He glared in their direction and then spat off the side of the porch.

Winston Meredith in the flesh, and he had more than an ample supply.

"I have to go," George muttered and scurried away.

The old man growled something as George bounded up the steps, but Conor couldn't make out his words. The wiry young man glanced back once, his expression frightened, then hurried inside.

Before Winston turned, he cast a warning glance in Conor's direction. Conor squared his shoulders and met his glare head-on. Winston might frighten George, but his intimidating tactics didn't touch Conor.

As soon as the door shut behind them, Conor knew there was one thing that did intimidate him. He had to call the chief. He had to tell the chief that he'd missed a chance to discover the identity of the ringleader, and he had to do it in a way that didn't incriminate Jessica.

Conor was standing too close to her. Okay, he was actually a few feet away, but that was still too damn close. Especially when all she could think about was the way he'd held her in his arms last night. Or the fire he'd started inside her when he'd touched her . . . when his hands . . . she swallowed hard . . . and mouth had made her body come to life.

She drew in a shaky breath.

"Quit twisting your button," he told her.

Jessica glanced down. "I can't help it."

She should've worn a shirt without buttons, but she liked her red top. It was long, loose, and very comfortable. Besides, she was quickly running out of clothes, and the house didn't have a washer and dryer.

Her father hadn't provided one. He probably thought if they ran around naked, she would have a better chance of snagging Conor for a husband. She was going to have a long talk with him when all this was over. A really long talk.

Conor slid the bowl of potato salad across the kitchen counter toward her. She yanked the plastic wrap from the box and ripped it across the row of metal teeth. She didn't like the way his gaze lingered on her. Well, maybe she did.

After last night, who could blame him? She'd certainly been wrong about one thing. Conor wasn't even close to being out of her system. The memory was too vivid.

And she wanted him again. She wanted the thrill, the excitement. Once was supposed to be enough. That wasn't the case. Hell, she wanted him more than ever. He was like a bag of chips—she couldn't eat just one.

"Damn it!" she muttered. Both ends of the plastic wrap were firmly stuck to each other.

"You don't have to be nervous about the cookout tonight. I won't let anything happen. In fact, I can tell Trudy you have a headache if you'd rather stay here. That might be the wisest move, anyway." He took the plastic wrap from her and quickly covered the food they were taking, flattening the edges with the palm of his hand.

Surprised, she met his gaze. Nervous? About tonight? Jessica almost laughed at the thought. Maybe she'd been a little on edge when she'd first arrived to show the house, but after seeing George, the thought of being scared of him was ludicrous. She could take him any day. And Trudy? Piece of cake.

Didn't Conor realize he was the one making her so jittery? Even though he hadn't mentioned the fact they'd made love, she'd been unable to think of anything else. But if he believed the cookout was the cause of her skittish behavior, that was fine with her. A lot better than telling him the real reason. Especially after the fiasco they'd made of their one night together. Who would've thought someone would actually show up at the Merediths after the ruckus Trudy and George had caused earlier in the evening?

Guilt filled her. It had been as much her fault as his. The scales might even tip a little more in her direction. And here she was supposed to be helping her father. Yeah, right into an early retirement.

Stop beating yourself up.

It wouldn't happen again, and that was the main thing. They were both professionals.

She drew in a deep breath. "No, I'll go. We might discover something in their house that will give us a clue about the identity of the leader."

"Not *we*, Jessica. *Me*. Understand?"

He was right . . . again. She was only there to make an appearance. His case, not hers.

"Okay, I'll play the role of the quiet, unassuming wife."

She'd acted in a couple of school plays. Not the lead or anything, but she could pull this off. The thought of being a doormat didn't appeal to her, though. Her acting abilities didn't stretch that far. Maybe she could find a happy middle ground.

Conor frowned as if he'd suddenly thought of something. "If burglars make you nervous, why did you want to be a cop?"

Nervous? She choked back her laugh. Okay, he'd asked a reasonable question, except she didn't want to admit the burglars didn't bother her as much as he did. She thought about it for a moment. Why had she wanted to be a cop? Her father had almost started crowing when she'd told him her decision to go through the academy.

"Hero worship," she admitted. "I doted on my father. I don't remember much about my mother. She died when I was four." Jessica had a vague image of soft blond hair and a warm smile. She remembered the questions she'd asked when her mother didn't come back from the hospital. Her father's tears had mingled with theirs when he told her and Gabe a story of how God needed a very special angel in heaven.

"Not having a mother must've been rough."

She pulled her thoughts back to the present. "Time healed the wound and we were able to enjoy the memories she left behind. Dad became the center of my world. I knew he wanted me and Gabe to follow in his footsteps, and I guess at the time, I thought it was what I wanted." She leaned against the counter.

Being a cop wasn't the life she wanted, though. She needed more than pagers constantly going off, phones ringing, sirens blasting through the stillness of the night. Not to mention that wearing a gun and cop uniform hadn't helped her social life. What did she say to men who filtered through her life?

I'd love to go out with you Saturday night. Oh, and by the way, I'm going to give you a ticket for speeding. Pick me up at seven?

Oh, yeah, her love life had been great. No wonder her father had resorted to finding her a husband.

"Speaking of your father . . ." He cleared his throat. "I called him about last night."

She could feel the color drain from her face. "You did what?" she croaked.

He straightened. "I didn't mention what happened between us," he quickly interjected. "I told him Trudy came over, forcing me to stay upstairs while she was here."

After this week she'd have to make an appointment with her hairdresser to get rid of all the gray hair Conor was giving her.

"And?"

"I said I fell asleep, Trudy left, and when I did go back downstairs, the Merediths had a visitor."

Her glance moved over him. He'd taken all the blame. "It was as much my fault as yours."

"It doesn't matter now."

It did to her.

He looked away. End of discussion. He was playing the hero. Lord save her from another one. She came from a family of heroes, and they had the medals and decorations to back up their deeds.

Except her.

"What changed your mind?" he asked, drawing her attention once more. "About being a cop, I mean."

Along with taking the blame, he'd also effectively dismissed their night together. Maybe it was for the best, but did it have to bother her so much? She thought it had been more than a casual one-night stand. Apparently, she'd been wrong.

She shrugged. "Does it matter?"

"I think it does to you. Maybe more than you want to admit."

Psychology course? She didn't need analyzing and she didn't like the turn in their conversation. She opened her mouth to tell him to mind his own business, but the words wouldn't come. Her eyes met his and she found she couldn't look away.

It wasn't like it was that big of a deal, and she didn't want to make more out of the situation than was there. "I was tired of wearing a uniform. Somewhere along the way I lost my identity. I wanted to know what it was like to be feminine." God, she hadn't just told him her deep, dark secrets. It sounded so lame when she said the words out loud. She bit her bottom lip.

He didn't look convinced that was her only reason.

"I don't think that's all of it. Maybe partly, but you left something out."

At least she knew why he was a detective. Either that or he could read minds, but if that was the case, she'd already have been in really big trouble because she certainly hadn't forgotten their night of hot sex.

Wicked visions suddenly invaded her mind. Her body tingled, starting at her lips where he'd kissed her, his mouth hot and sensual. Moving to her breasts where he'd teased sensitive nipples and down to the juncture between her legs where he'd caressed and stroked until she'd cried out that she needed more. The ache was tangible . . . so damn real it was all she could do to keep from throwing herself at him.

Don't even go there! No, he couldn't read minds—he was just good at reading people. Conor didn't have any special powers.

"If you don't want to talk about it, that's fine with me," he said. "It's not really any of my business why you wanted to quit."

Now he was making a big deal out of an insignificant matter. At least, it wasn't that important to her anymore. Time had helped ease the traumatic experience. Now she just thought of it as the catalyst that helped her move forward.

She shrugged mentally. What the hell. He'd find out sooner or later. She was surprised no one had told him, but then, her family was loyal. They wouldn't have spilled the beans.

"I let an arsonist get away." She watched his expression closely, waiting for condemnation. Not that she really cared what he thought.

Liar.

"Is that all? No one can catch the bad guy every time."

Jessica wished that was the end of the story. It had happened over a year ago, but it might as well have been yesterday. She'd let her family think it hadn't affected her, but it had. A lot.

"I rescued a goat." She cringed. Okay, so it bothered her a little more than she liked to admit—even to herself.

Conor crossed his arms in front of him and leaned his hip against the counter. "A goat."

She nodded, took a deep breath, and continued. "The dispatcher came over my portable radio with a call—a suspicious-looking character lurking around a house. About the same time, I heard a child's cry for help."

The wail *had* sounded human, damn it.

"The wind was blowing, children were just starting their summer break—it was early afternoon. I was afraid a kid had gotten a little too rambunctious and might have injured himself. I told the dispatcher to send the next closest officer to the suspicious-person call while I investigated the cry for help." She hesitated.

"Go on."

His expression revealed none of his inner thoughts. He had to think she was a fool. No, that would probably come later.

"The two local television stations were apparently listening to their scanners that day. I guess they figured it might make a good human-interest story. They showed up just about the time I began trying to free the goat from the barbed wire fence he'd gotten himself tangled in. They were able to get most of the rescue-of-the-century on film."

Jessica glanced out the window. She'd never been so embarrassed and humiliated in all her life.

"Is that all?"

"No." She sighed. "After I freed him, the wind tore my cap off. The ungrateful beast butted me when I bent to grab it. They got that on tape, too."

Silence filled the room. She still couldn't look at him.

"They dubbed me 'The New Kid on the Block.' "

"After the goat, or the musical group?"

"Go ahead and laugh. Everyone else has." She might as well spill the whole story. "The arsonist got away, but not before he'd torched the vacant house."

"Anyone hurt?"

"No, thank goodness, but what if someone had been living there?"

"What if it had been a child instead of a goat? What if a child's life had been in danger? What if the arsonist hadn't been an arsonist, but instead, looking at the house because he was interested in buying it?"

"But it didn't happen that way." Why couldn't he see? She'd screwed up.

"It didn't happen your way, either."

Now he was talking foolishly. She'd seen her picture flashed across the television screen. She'd heard the snickers.

"Was anyone hurt?" he asked again.

She opened her mouth, but no words came out.

"You've condemned yourself more than anyone, Jessica. Do you think all cops are perfect? Everyone has made mistakes."

"But I'm a Nelson. The chief's daughter. Nelsons are heroes, not duds."

"Does that mean you're not allowed to goof up?"

"Did you ever goof up?"

"Lots of times."

She angled her head so she could look up at him. "As bad as I did?"

"Yeah, last night."

Pain ripped through her.

"Don't look at me like that." He stepped closer, raising her chin until she had to look him in the eye. "I don't regret what we did. I regret the timing wasn't right."

He stared into her eyes for a few seconds, but then something changed. There was a subtle difference in the way he was looking at her. She didn't even attempt to stop him when he lowered his mouth to hers. The warmth of his lips felt so right against hers. She leaned closer, letting him invade her senses, letting the moment wrap around her. When he pulled away, she was left wanting more.

He looked a little dazed himself when he stepped back. For a moment they could only stare at each other. Then he shook his head and strode to one of the cabinets, opening the door. Conor replaced the plastic wrap before he turned toward her again.

"Apparently, I can't even kiss you without wanting to carry you to bed. I apologize. It won't happen again while I'm on duty."

Disappointment stabbed at her. Before she could tell him that was fine with her, he began to speak.

"But it *will* happen again. You're the most ravishing woman I've ever met. I don't plan on our relationship ending this soon."

She drew in a ragged breath as images of them lying naked in bed swirled around inside her head. She could almost feel his hands gliding over her body, his mouth covering first one breast, then the other.

He's a cop! She had to end it now before either one of them got hurt.

"This isn't real," she began slowly. "I'm here to keep my father from losing a job he loves. You're here to catch criminals. I really like you. Probably too much. And you're right, what we did last night was wrong. But when this is over we'll go back to the way things were. It won't happen again. Remember, you're the one who warned you didn't play for keeps."

He hesitated, as if weighing his words. "There's something between us. You know it as well as I do."

No, there couldn't be. She wouldn't allow it. Once they were no longer pretending to be married, they wouldn't see each other again.

"When this is over, I'll walk away without ever looking

back." She didn't need another hero in her life, and reliving the goat incident made her realize that what was starting up between her and Conor had to stop.

At least, that's what her brain told her. Her heart was another matter entirely.

He stepped in front of her, searching her face. When he lightly caressed her arm, she couldn't stop herself from leaning toward him.

"I think you're a liar, Jessica Nelson," he murmured.

He was right, but she detected a hint of uncertainty reflected in his eyes. He wasn't as sure about her as he'd like to be. Maybe that was a good thing. A relationship with Conor would be doomed from the start. He was married to the badge, and she would be no man's mistress.

Chapter 15

Jessica supposed Conor's idea that she carry the potato salad wasn't bad. At least she couldn't twist her button loose. He looked way too tempting and his aftershave had her leaning closer, inhaling the tantalizing scent. Damn, didn't he realize how hard it was, trying to concentrate on what she was supposed to be doing and not what she wanted to do when he looked and smelled so delicious?

Probably not. Except for the kiss earlier, he'd kept his distance. The rest of her day had been spent mentally chanting. It mellowed her. Enough so that she was transported to a place of peace, an island far away where ocean breezes caressed her naked skin as she lay on a sandy beach. A place where tropical birds serenaded her from high above in palm trees or whatever the fuck kind of trees tropical birds hung out in.

It hadn't mattered, because Conor had shown up, shattering everything as he paraded across the sand bare-assed naked, bronzed even darker by a sun that never burned.

The caress of the ocean breeze was replaced by Conor's skillful hands as they massaged lotion on her back, over her hips, between her legs. Just when his mouth was about to replace his hands, he'd asked if she was ready to leave for the Merediths.'

The damn ache between her legs still hadn't stopped throbbing.

She covertly glanced in his direction. How could he look so cool and calm and so . . . so . . . unhorny? He'd turned her whole world upside down. Having sex again with him was all she could think about. And this from the woman who said she wouldn't be having a relationship with him after her father's job was secure? Like that wouldn't happen. She squared her shoulders. No, she could and would be strong.

He suddenly looked in her direction and smiled. She jerked her gaze away. Not when he looked at her like that. Damn, he had a sexy smile. Hell, he looked pretty sexy all over.

They stopped in front of their neighbors' door and Conor pushed the bell.

From lowered lashes, Jessica cast a sideways glance in his direction. He'd swapped his usual jeans for beige slacks and a short-sleeved, white shirt. He looked good enough to nibble on.

Her skin grew warm. She faced the door, wishing her heart didn't flutter quite so much every time she looked at him. They'd better hurry and get enough evidence, or she was going to be in big trouble.

Heavy, lumbering footsteps approached and the door was jerked open.

"Yeah?" the man growled.

The arm at her back kept Jessica from stumbling off the small porch. This wasn't a man. A big, burly, ugly, smelly bear had opened the door. He was unshaven and wearing a grungy black T-shirt with words that had long ago faded.

This had to be the father, the so-called head of the Meredith gang. He was an ugly bastard. The kind of ugly nightmares were made of.

Conor squeezed her arm. Probably to reassure her she wasn't alone. She wanted to tell him that she'd been surprised at first, but she was okay now. The bigger they were, the harder they fell. Size didn't mean a lot to her.

Well . . . except in some cases, and in Conor's case he didn't have to worry about that department.

Pay attention, she warned herself.

"Conor! Jessica!" Trudy's voice came from behind her father-in-law. She squeezed past the mongrel.

And she'd thought they might've overdressed. If anything, compared to their hostess, they were very understated. Trudy wore a leopard-print blouse that clung to her generous curves and a tight, black leather miniskirt. Silver earrings dangled to her shoulders. Black hose and spike heels completed her outlandish ensemble.

"Now you didn't have to bring food." She took the bowl from Jessica's hands and looked at the dish. "But I'm glad you did. I can't cook for beans." She stopped and laughed. "Beans. Huh! That was funny."

Conor hugged Jessica close. Did he think she'd run back to the house and hide under the bed? She sighed. The Merediths didn't scare her.

"Move out of the way, Pop. I invited Conor and Jessica over." Trudy eyed the older man with a look of distaste. "And go change your shirt. You look worse than a busted sewer pipe and you don't smell much better. Either shower or sit downwind from us."

"You know how I feel about company." He reached up and scratched the stubble of whiskers on his face. His eyes narrowed on the unwelcome visitors.

"Oh pooh, you don't like anyone. Then go back to watching your TV. I'll have George take your steak off the grill since you don't want to be sociable."

"Didn't say I wouldn't join the party. I just want to finish watching my show. I'll be out later."

Trudy rolled her eyes after he left. "That was Winston, leader of the Meredith clan." She winked. "Or so he thinks." Jessica narrowed her eyes on Trudy. Interesting the way she'd phrased that statement.

"Are you sure this is a good time?" Conor stepped into the house.

Trudy laughed. "If I waited for the right time to invite

someone over, I'd never have any friends." She motioned them to follow her.

They entered a foyer. An elaborate Chinese carpet covered the hardwood floor. An abstract painting hung on one wall and on another a field of pastel flowers. There was a clutter of knickknacks scattered on a shelf, and a set of deer antlers mounted on the wall held several baseball caps. *Amazing.* She tried not to stare as they followed their host down a narrow hallway.

"I keep telling them we need to socialize more, but even George acts funny about it. You'd think it was a sin for me to have anyone over." At the end of the hall, she bumped her hip against a door. As it swung open, she proudly exclaimed, "And this is my kitchen."

It took a minute for Jessica's eyes to adjust.

"Astonishing," she mumbled, trying to grasp the color scheme.

Black-and-white-checked floor, fluorescent orange cabinets, a center island that had been painted red, white, and blue, and Jessica wasn't sure, but it looked like the refrigerator leaned to the left. Optical illusion? She'd gone to an amusement park one summer. A man had placed a ball on a table and it rolled uphill. Trudy's kitchen had the same effect. It was rather unnerving.

"I designed it myself. My taste runs electric."

"Very . . . unusual." Conor appeared thoughtful.

"I tried for a modern decor, but I added my own imagination. George says I should've been an interior designer."

"I could tell from the start, George has a good eye for style," Conor told her.

Thankfully, Trudy didn't catch the sarcasm in Conor's observation. Jessica wanted to poke him in the ribs, but George chose that moment to open the back door. With him came the tantalizing aroma of grilled meat. How could she think about food? She pushed thoughts of her empty stomach to the far recesses of her mind and focused on George.

This might be a good opportunity to question him. "It must have cost a fortune to remodel. Maybe Conor will let me spend a little money on our place." She cast a glance in his direction.

"Now, honey, you know we have to keep track of every penny if we're going to do more than rent." He nodded toward George as he picked up the cue. "Maybe you can give me some business tips that will help us financially. Looks like you're doing pretty good for yourself."

A rooster couldn't have puffed out his chest more than George. And in less than a minute, he began to crow.

"I do not like-a to brag, but *si*, I am considered very good when it-a comes to matters in our family business." He smoothed his fingers across his eyebrows.

"What exactly is your business? I don't think I've heard anyone really say." Conor smiled innocently.

Jessica held her breath, waiting to see how George would answer. She knew he wouldn't come out and say they were burglars, but he might accidentally let something slip.

"Business?" his voice squeaked. He cleared his throat and straightened his spine. "We are-a movers."

"Movers. That's interesting." Conor tapped his fingers on the Formica counter. "What exactly do you move?"

"Uh . . . my steaks! I have-a to check on the meat. Excus-a me, pleeze. I would-a really love to continue this wonderful-a talk, but we wouldn't want-a to burn our supper." He hurried out the door.

"Don't you just love that sexy accent?" Trudy beamed as she took a pan off the stove. "Macaroni and cheese," she said as she dumped the contents into a bowl. "I think I was born to marry an Italian. I just love pasta." She winked. "And I have a bottle of Boone's to go with it. Y'all like strawberry- or peach-flavored wine?"

They didn't get a chance to ask anything else. Trudy kept everyone busy carrying food and drinks to the picnic table in the backyard. Then it was time to eat, and George's father wasn't exactly opening any conversations about what they did for a living.

Barry didn't seem very impressed with them, either. Although he resembled George more than his father, she could see their personalities were miles apart. Barry had a cold, calculating gleam in his eyes. And the way he watched her every move made Jessica squirm in her seat. The farther she stayed away from him, the better.

"So, how long have you lived here?" She shifted her position on the bench when Winston turned his attention from his steak to her. As he glared at her, he stabbed a piece of steak and stuffed it into his mouth, chewing with his mouth open.

The small bite she'd put in her mouth suddenly turned rancid. It was all she could do to swallow it down with some of the carbonated peach wine.

"Not long," Trudy finally answered. "Only 'bout three months. Barry found the work and—"

"Shut up, Trudy." Barry might have meant his words for his sister-in-law, but his gaze was glued on Jessica.

"Don't be so damn rude, Barry!" Trudy tossed her green linen napkin on the redwood picnic table. "I was only makin' small talk. You should learn how to do it sometime."

Trudy glanced across the table, and for a brief moment Jessica felt a little sorry for her. George's bride actually looked embarrassed by her in-laws' behavior. Who could blame her?

An uncomfortable silence filled the air. Trudy looked close to tears because her dinner party wasn't turning out the way she'd planned. George kept looking from his father to his brother, who in turn had narrowed their eyes on the two guests. Jessica was starting to feel decidedly uncomfortable.

"So what do you think about football season? We going to have a chance this year?" Conor casually asked as he cut his steak.

"*Si!*" George grabbed at the change in conversation and smiled from ear to ear. "I cannot-a wait for the first-a game. I always watch the Dallas Cowboys."

Conor had effectively calmed the sudden turmoil that had erupted, but Jessica was frustrated that she hadn't found out anything. What was worse, the men seemed to gather in their own group as the talk about football intensified. Jessica was left discussing fashion with Trudy. Her sympathy quickly drained away, leaving a bad case of boredom in its wake. And it didn't get any better as time passed.

Then it was too late to discover anything. The evening was obviously drawing to a close. Her shoulders slumped. She could see the surveillance stretching into weeks.

But then, what had she expected? They would confess? Her father's job would be saved? She wouldn't be drooling over Conor all the time?

Well, maybe there was something more she could do. Abruptly, she stood. Conor looked surprised by her sudden movement.

"Trudy, do you mind if I use your bathroom?"

"Sure, I'll show you the way."

"Oh no, don't trouble yourself. I'm sure I can find it. Just point me in the right direction." She hoped her smile was warm and friendly.

Once inside the house, Jessica hurried down the hall and made a quick detour from the way Trudy had told her to go. She opened the first door she came to.

A linen closet. Sliding her hands underneath towels and sheets, she searched for anything that felt out of place. Nothing.

Closing the door, she hurried to the next room. As soon as she slipped inside, she knew this had to be George and Trudy's bedroom. It looked as if a huge cauldron of Pepto had boiled over, coating everything pink, from the walls to the shag carpet. Sickening. She blinked several times to get her equilibrium back in kilter.

The pink bed, walls, and floor were bad enough, but pink lace ruffles and feathers adorned everything from the canopy to the curtains to the frilly chair that had been placed against one wall. Trudy had created the first Pepto infinity bedroom. It was enough to make the most stalwart stomach queasy.

She went straight for the closet and opened the door. A walk-in. Nice, except it overflowed with Trudy's unfashionable wardrobe and George's rainbow of suits. It was still better than looking at all the vomit-pink color.

Shaking her head, she stretched her arms upward, her nimble fingers darting around and under boxes on the top shelf. Nothing.

She knelt on the floor, careful not to disturb the shoes neatly lined against the back wall. There had to be at least fifty pairs. But something was shoved in the far corner that didn't look like it belonged.

Her pulse quickened. Was it going to be this easy? Just half an inch more and she'd be able to reach . . . there, she had it. Exultation filled her. The tape! Why else would they have hidden it? Her father's job would be saved. This was plenty of evidence to put the burglars away. Her dad would be able to get a confession and make them name the ringleader.

"Is there something you were lookin' for?" Barry's voice came from behind her.

Her heart plummeted. Damn it! She should've been listening for someone to enter the room. Slowly, she came to her feet and turned around to face him, keeping her arms and the tape behind her. She had to think—and fast!

Barry's eyes narrowed to mere slits. Cripes! He would have to be the one to catch her prowling around. She could've handled George. But Barry? She wasn't so sure about him.

Batting her lashes, she smiled coquettishly. "Oops, caught red-handed."

What to do? She couldn't drop the tape and let it clunk to the floor. There was only one solution that she could see. Carefully, she inched up the back of her shirt.

Oh lord, she was stealing evidence. This wasn't good. Conor would strangle her. She took a deep breath. She'd get the tape back somehow. Besides, she had to make sure this was the right tape, anyway.

If she didn't screw everything up.

She had to convince Barry she was doing no more than snooping. Okay, here goes nothing.

"I got lost looking for the bathroom. When I stumbled into this room I just knew it had to be Trudy's. The best way to find out about another woman is to look in her closet." She sucked her stomach in, keeping her smile in place, and slipped the tape inside the elastic waistband at the back of her slacks.

Her smile faltered. The weight caused the tape to slide downward to the seat of her pants. *This must be what hemorrhoids feel like.* She was never so glad she'd worn a long shirttail as she was today. It would easily hide the evidence. If she didn't move too suddenly.

Praying her tactics didn't get her into more trouble, she sauntered forward. "I just wanted to see what kind of person Trudy is. You're not going to tell, are you?" She pouted.

When he hesitated, she reached out and trailed a fingernail down the front of his shirt. "I promise I won't ever go where I don't belong again."

Stay calm, she told herself. Remember what you've been taught. But she couldn't use any of her self-defense training. As sure as she did, their cover would be blown. Then she'd have to explain everything to Conor. He'd kill her, and her father would lose his job.

"I been watchin' you all evening." His nostrils flared like overinflated balloons. "I saw the way you was lookin' at me. I knowed you wanted me. I got this really bad itch for you, baby."

Maybe he just had fleas.

Instead of offering to buy him a flea collar, she smiled prettily. "I wondered if you had noticed." Now she was going to be sick.

"There's a soft place we can do a little scratchin'." He motioned toward George and Trudy's four-poster bed.

Her eyes widened. She briefly wondered if George and Trudy would think anything about a dead body in their room. She could paint Barry pink. Maybe they would just think he was a rasp-*Barry*?

He took a step toward her. "Why rile Conor when we don't have to, sweetie?" Her words spilled out as she tried to think of something that would waylay his advances. "We can meet somewhere and he wouldn't have to be the wiser. Just you and me."

She almost gagged. Not only on her lies, but the sour smell of his breath. Was the man afraid of vampires or what? He smelled like rotten garlic.

His chuckle echoed through the room. He'd bought her act. *Don't relax yet*, she told herself. She had to stay on top of the game.

"I thought you was newlyweds?"

She shrugged. "He's boring in bed. I need a real man." Her voice was husky and reminded her of an old B-movie starlet. She wondered if she should bat her eyes again for more effect. No, she didn't want to push her luck.

"Well, you found a real man here." He latched on to her hand.

Ugh! Slimed. She'd picked up a frog once that was less clammy.

"Jessica! Where'd you go?" Conor called.

"Oh, no. He can't catch me here with you." She almost did panic when Barry didn't loosen his hold.

"Where we gonna meet?"

"I'll call you, sugar." That seemed to appease him, and he let her go. Without a backward glance, she hurried from the room, scrubbing her hand on the hem of her shirt. When she reached the hall, Trudy and Conor were just coming from the kitchen. She screeched to a halt and tried to slow the erratic beat of her heart.

"There you are, hon—I was starting to worry."

Jessica met Conor's gaze and saw more than worry mirrored in his eyes. She had a feeling she'd catch hell as soon as they got home.

"Uh . . ." She frantically sought a plausible explanation for her long absence. "It must have been the beans. I'm a little queasy." That excuse had worked for him, why not her? At least she hadn't popped his bed and used most of his aftershave!

"Y'all sure you're from Texas? I haven't ever seen two people with as sensitive stomachs as the both of you." Trudy shook her head in amazement.

"It was a lovely supper, Trudy," Conor politely stated.

His jaw twitched. Definitely irritated. Conor wasn't as calm as he appeared. Trouble brewed, and she didn't have an escape route. She squared her shoulders. Nothing to do except face the storm head-on.

"Yes, lovely," she quickly chimed in.

She could probably think of some reason to stay a little longer, but that would only delay the inevitable. Besides, the tape was uncomfortable in the seat of her pants.

Going off to investigate had been crazy. It wasn't as if she'd had any real surveillance training. And she'd very nearly blown their cover—again. But she had to admit the intrigue was exciting. Maybe she'd given up on being a cop a little too soon.

And then, maybe not. Now she had another problem to contend with—Barry, and the tape she had to return. This was the one, though. She could feel it all the way down to her bones. Her father wouldn't lose his job.

Excitement bubbled inside her. She'd done it. Barry didn't matter in the least.

How could Conor berate her when she'd found some of the evidence? A little longer, and she probably could've found the jewels that were on the list of stolen goods.

"Conor, I . . ." she began as he hurried her across the lawn like a disobedient child. Jeez! The tape was bouncing around in her pants worse than a pickup on a country road.

"Save it until we get inside." His words were short and clipped.

Conor's hand tightened on her arm. She didn't think he realized how hard he squeezed.

"Could you at least loosen your grip?"

Without even an apology, he eased his hold, but didn't release her until they reached the house, and then only long enough to jerk the door open. As soon as she was free, Jessica slid around him and inside to the living room. He slammed the door and followed.

"What the hell did you think you were doing back there?" He didn't make any attempt to hide his anger.

"Well, *you* didn't seem to be getting anywhere. I just thought I'd investigate a little on my own."

Conor couldn't believe it. Of all the stupid, female stunts! He raked a hand through his hair. "Not getting anywhere? What the hell did you think I was doing, Jessica? Maybe you should've stayed on the streets long enough to know we don't play games when we're on a stakeout."

Why didn't she look apologetic? His eyes narrowed. He'd been around her long enough to know she was up to something. Hell, she looked as smug as a cat that'd just caught a fat mouse.

"At least I came up with something concrete," she stated with a self-satisfied smirk.

"What?" he asked cautiously.

Reaching behind her, Jessica began to squirm. Finally, she pulled a tape from the back of her slacks. "I have the mayor's tape! This should get my father off the hook—at least until we can find more proof they're behind the burglaries." She was almost jumping with excitement.

"You stole evidence?" Didn't she realize she could never get a conviction that way?

"I didn't actually steal it." She didn't meet his eyes. "More like *borrowed it*. I'll get it back."

He closed his eyes and counted to ten. "Are you sure it's even the right tape?"

She tugged on the hem of her shirt. "Well . . . no. Not positively, but it was the only tape 1 saw in the whole house. It has to be the right one. Why else would it be hidden?"

A flicker of doubt crossed her face.

"No better time than now to find out." Taking the tape, he strolled across the room to the VCR and popped it in. He turned the television on and pushed a button.

When he started to step back he almost stumbled over Jessica, who'd sat on the floor right in front of the TV. She scooted over. He continued to stand.

The screen went from black to the interior of a bedroom. A man suddenly jumped into the camera's eye, arms flung outward, wearing what looked like a caveman's costume.

"I am-a Tarzan, King of the Jungle! Where-a is my little slave-a girl?"

Okay, he'd been wrong. It hadn't been a caveman's suit, after all. He should've guessed from the leopard print. The costume looked two sizes too big, but it still wasn't long enough to hide George's knobby knees or his bony arms.

George brought his fists to his hairless chest and did a fair imitation of a jungle man, even if it sounded a little on the soprano side.

Conor glanced down at Jessica and felt a moment of pity. Her mouth had dropped open. Apparently sensing he watched her, she glanced up, confusion written across her features. She turned back to the TV screen.

"Here I am, my big strong he-man," Trudy said, out of the camera's view.

"Okay, Trudy. Now we need you to come in right after you say your line. Let me adjust this just a little."

Conor took a step back as a face zoomed in and filled the entire screen. Kind of scary-looking. Kind of familiar, too. His eyes narrowed. "Isn't that the—"

"—UPS worker. Looks like her."

At least now they knew why she was hugging the box that was about the size of a VCR tape. They were making porn movies. His attention returned to the screen as Trudy bounced into view, wearing a tiny G-string and barely hiding her ample breasts behind her hands.

"Turn it off. Turn it off!" Jessica shrieked.

Conor pushed the Stop button and the screen went black again. Jessica covered her face with her hands, her shoulders shaking.

He should let her know how furious he was that she'd taken such a stupid chance, but how could he when she was obviously so upset? At least this had been a good lesson for her to learn. She probably wouldn't take matters in her own hands again.

Had that been a laugh? "Jessica?"

She moved her hands away. Tears streamed down her cheeks, but her shoulders shook with unmistakable mirth.

He frowned. "You think almost blowing our cover is funny? And all because George and Trudy make porn movies?"

"No," she squeaked, then began to laugh in earnest, not even trying to cover the fact she thought the situation humorous. She fell over sideways on the carpet, holding her stomach. "Oh, my belly hurts." Her gaze fastened on his. "And it's not from beans!" She went into another fit of giggles.

Conor didn't even crack a smile, although it wasn't easy as he watched her merriment. That only seemed to make her laugh harder.

"George, George . . . George of the jungle," she sang off-key, and then took off with more gales of laughter. "He could be the next Italian Stallion. Or more like the Italian Shetland."

"There's nothing funny about this."

He really tried to keep a straight face, but the more he thought about it, the more a picture of skinny George swinging on a vine through a jungle came to mind. Trudy's arms wrapped around his middle. Her bouffant hairdo catching on every tree limb they swung past.

There hadn't been any real harm done. Maybe he needed

to lighten up a little. He'd talk seriously to Jessica later. Right now she looked so damn cute, he couldn't be angry with her.

He was still smiling when he went to answer the ringing phone on the hall table.

"I want to speak with Jessica," a gruff voice said.

"Just a minute and I'll get her." He set the phone on the table.

Even though he'd tried to disguise his voice, Conor knew exactly who was on the other end. He opened and closed his fists and took a deep breath.

Maybe he'd have that talk with Jessica a little sooner than he'd planned. He wanted an explanation and he wanted it damn fast. He strode into the other room.

"Barry's on the phone. He wants to speak with you."

Chapter 16

Damn! She'd hoped to tell Conor in her own way and time about Barry. Now she'd have some explaining to do. She didn't think he'd be happy, either.

Stall.

"Barry's on the phone?" she asked with feigned surprise.

"Isn't that what I just said?" He glared at her.

"Gee, I wonder why he'd be calling me."

"Yes, I wondered the same thing. Especially since he went inside the house not long after you. Is there something you'd like to share?"

Not if she could get out of it.

"I'd better see what he wants." She rose from the carpet and dusted the seat of her pants, even though the rug was clean. It bought her a few extra seconds, though. To do what, she had no earthly idea.

Her feet dragged as she walked across the room. Conor went with her, picking up the phone and handing it to her. She had a feeling the smile on her face was a little sickly, but her hesitation was barely noticeable as she took the phone from his outstretched hand and put it to her ear.

"Yes?"

"When can I see you?"

Great! This was all she needed right now. Getting the wrong tape wasn't bad enough. Now she had to deal with

Barry. How in the world was she going to get out of this mess?

"This isn't a good time," she frantically whispered into the mouthpiece. She turned on her heel to make sure Conor had given her some privacy and rammed her elbow into his stomach. He grunted and stepped back. Startled, she almost dropped the phone. Jeez! He didn't have to stand so close. She could handle—okay, maybe she couldn't handle everything, but she'd think of something to wiggle out of meeting Barry alone. Just the thought made her nauseous.

"I want to see you."

After casting Conor a dirty look, she focused her attention on the problem at hand.

"This isn't a good time," she repeated between clamped teeth.

"Is he there?"

What a moron. "Yes."

"Meet me tonight."

"That's not possible." Stall. She had to put him off. "Day after tomorrow." Surely she'd be able to think of something by then.

He hesitated. "Monday? Can't. What about Tuesday?"

"I'm not sure." She didn't dare look in Conor's direction to see what he thought of the conversation.

"Tuesday!" His tone left no room for argument. "Meet me behind the house by the picnic table. No one will be there after it gets dark." He paused. "I'll make you feel real good," he added in a husky voice.

Gag!

Barry didn't wait for her to agree. An unmistakable click ended the conversation. He was about as romantic as a bouquet of wilted flowers. Barry would make some woman a lousy husband. A shiver of revulsion ran down her spine.

Under any other circumstances, she wouldn't dream of meeting him anywhere, but she felt sure she could extract some information.

She had three days to figure out exactly how she would be able to do that. Surely Barry would let something slip. If she obtained any information whatsoever, it might even make up for the fact she'd messed up when she and Conor had sex.

Well, not the sex part, only that it interfered with the investigation. And she'd goofed again when she sort of stole the tape.

It wasn't all her fault, though. Her father should have to take some of the blame for having a heart-shaped bed delivered to the house. She rolled her eyes and replaced the phone.

"Now, would you like to tell me exactly what happened after you went inside?"

Darn, she'd forgotten for a moment that Conor was standing beside her. From the look on his face, she didn't think she had a choice except to tell him exactly what happened. Taking a deep breath, she began. "Barry caught me rummaging through Trudy's closet."

He stalked back into the living room without saying a word, stopping at the window. Jessica hurried after him, not liking the way he kept his back turned or the way his hands clenched into fists. This didn't bode well. Damn, if she could take back what she'd done, she would, but that wasn't possible.

"Did he touch you?"

Surprise flittered through her. He seemed more concerned that she might have been violated in some way than the fact she could've bungled the whole operation.

A gentle tenderness filled her. She hadn't expected him to think of her first. An urge to wrap her arms around him and hug him tight washed over her, but she forced herself to stay right where she was. "No, he didn't touch me," she told him softly, her heart swelling inside her.

"Pack your suitcase. I want you out of the house. I won't have you put in harm's way again. Anything might have happened."

Stunned, she could only stare at his back. The tender feeling of only a moment ago quickly melted into a puddle of pissed-off. Conor had wanted her out of the house since she'd arrived. Now he was using this as an excuse to get rid of her. It didn't seem to matter that nothing had happened. Boy, he must really hate it that he'd screwed up and had sex with her.

She dug her heels in. "No."

Even when he spun around, his expression fierce, she stood her ground.

"I'm not leaving until the real tape is found and the criminals are behind bars. Especially when we're this close." She'd make Barry slip up if she had to use every feminine wile in the book. Ugh, disgusting thought.

His eyes narrowed. "What do you mean?"

"Barry wants me to meet him Tuesday night."

"You're not meeting anyone anywhere. Especially a sleazeball like Barry," he growled. "I won't let you risk your life or anything else over this case."

"But I think I can find out what we need to know. Like maybe when they're planning to rob another house." She paced the floor. How could she make him listen to reason? This could be their only chance to get the information.

"They're pulling another job on Monday," he told her.

Her head jerked up. "How do you know?"

"While you and Trudy were discussing clothes, we were talking about other things."

"Football! I heard. How could you have switched from sports to knowing when they're pulling a heist?"

"We didn't talk about football the whole time. I asked them about moving some stuff for me Monday night, but it seems they have other plans."

She snapped her fingers. "That's why Barry told me to meet him Tuesday. I should've known something was up. Conor, you're a genius."

He planted his fists on his hips. "Now that we have that settled, you can pack your things. I'll tell Trudy and George we had a fight and you went running home. That shouldn't be hard for either of them to digest since it seems all *they* do is fight."

"If I leave now they might get suspicious." She had to make him understand. "I have to stay."

A long silence filled the room. Jessica waited for his answer.

Myriad emotions warred on his face. He looked out the window, his gaze narrowed on the suspects' house. For a second or two she wasn't sure if she'd convinced him it was better that she stay.

She knew the second he capitulated.

"Okay, for the time being you can remain here," he finally said, his words clipped.

She let out a sigh of relief.

"But if you don't stay out of the way, I'll have you packed and on the way back to your apartment before you can blink an eye."

"Anything you say. You won't even know I'm here." This had worked out perfectly. Not that she intended to stay out of the way. She hadn't really lied. As long as nothing important occurred, she would. And if something did break, she'd be more careful and make damn sure she didn't get caught.

Besides, this was getting interesting. The adrenaline rush was almost as good as when she ran. She might've made a pretty good cop after all.

She froze.

Heaven forbid she'd have second thoughts. Or tangle herself up with a cop. Cops didn't have lives. She still clearly remembered how many times her father had to rush out of the house when new evidence would break open a current case.

Damn it, she wanted more out of life. She wanted her husband to leave work at five and concentrate on her, not his job. She wanted . . .

That was it. Why hadn't she seen it before now? She wanted stability. That's why she'd dated nice, dependable Al. She wanted the white house and the picket fence and the two children when she married. She wanted a husband who came home at night.

A cop's life was exciting, she wouldn't deny it, and for just a little while she did have a twinge of regret, but now that she knew what her problem was, she could move forward.

Monday night should bring an end to the surveillance, and then her life would return to the normal routine she'd managed to carve for herself as a real estate agent. Great—she felt better now that she had everything worked out in her mind.

She looked at Conor. "So, what do we do until Monday night?" she asked.

When he opened his mouth, she knew exactly what he was going to say and raised her hand. "I know. Sit and watch the house next door."

The harsh planes of his face relaxed as a slow grin spread across it. It made her wonder if he'd been thinking about the house next door or the two of them in bed together having hot, sweaty sex.

Delicious warmth flooded her body as sensuous images filled her mind. His hands gliding over her naked body . . . parting her legs and stroking. She drew in a ragged breath. Jessica had a feeling Officer Conor Richmond wasn't quite as serious as she'd first thought. But no matter where his mind had just wandered, he was still first and foremost a cop.

Instead of voicing whatever he'd been thinking, he only said, "I'll take first watch."

She nodded. "I'll straighten up the kitchen." It was a couple of seconds before she turned to leave—even then, she had to force her feet to move. She grabbed her cell phone off the end table as she left.

When she thought about it, the best possible solution would be to put some space between them. She'd screwed up royally by taking the tape and putting the stakeout in jeopardy. She doubted he would let things go as far as they did the night of Trudy and George's fight. He'd slipped up. She had a feeling that had never happened to him. Lord, she felt like Delilah to his Samson.

Where was this attraction to each other coming from? Surely there had to be some explanation.

Maybe they were starting to like each other because of the enforced proximity? She couldn't seem to get enough of Conor. Why? Raging hormones or something. Would she feel the same way if it were Al? Her stomach churned. She didn't think so.

There was an awful lot to like about Conor. Just thinking about him made her skin tingle almost as if he were caressing her. But it was more than just sexual awareness. She liked the way he smiled, and the way his eyes sparkled when he did, as if his humor came from the inside first and worked its way to the outside.

He was still too immersed in his work, but he was beginning to lighten up some. Hell, he even had a pretty good sense of humor—at times.

She went to the sink and washed up what few dishes there were before sitting at the table, still lost in her Conor fantasy. She wanted to talk to someone, but she wasn't quite sure who. Her father would think it was terrific she was starting to like Conor. Hell, why wouldn't he, when he'd plotted for them to be together in the first place.

Dad probably wouldn't be happy she'd messed up when she'd had the brilliant idea of taking the tape, and she certainly wouldn't mention the sex part.

Maybe she should call Aunt Gloria? Or maybe Gabe? She picked up her cell phone and turned it over and over in her hand. It wasn't Gabe or Aunt Gloria that she wanted to talk to, though. She chewed on her bottom lip; then, before she could change her mind, she called her father.

"Hi, sweetheart—I'd recognize your ring anywhere."

She smiled. "That, and the fact you have Caller ID."

"Nope, your ring has a subtle difference. Much sweeter than Gabe's and a lot softer than your Aunt Gloria's."

Her dad was like chicken soup on a cold winter day. Just the sound of his voice was like a warm hug. She leaned against the back of her chair and propped her feet on the other one. "I love you, Dad."

"You're okay, aren't you? I mean, it's not that bad returning to law enforcement, is it?"

Her smile flipped, becoming a frown. "I'm not back on the force, Dad. I've already told you that I'm only here to help out. When the bad guys are behind bars, I'll go back to being a real estate agent." Odd but she didn't sound quite as convincing.

"So what's on your mind?"

She was thoughtful for a moment. "I sort of screwed up."

"Sort of?"

"Yeah, I stole a tape from the suspects' house, but it wasn't the one taken when the mayor's home was burglarized." She drew in a deep breath. "I think I might be messing up the case for Conor."

"Nonsense—things can go wrong on any investigation. This is nothing like the billy goat escapade."

She cringed. Before she could comment, he hurried on, his voice softening.

"Listen, baby girl, I know that bothered you a lot and you never really got over feeling bad, but you can't dwell on what's in the past. You're not perfect and no one expects you to be. None of us are, and none of us ever will be. You can only do your best. No one can ask for more than that. You were a damn good cop."

"Have I mentioned just how much I love you?"

"A time or two." He chuckled. "So, do you like the fella or not?"

She mentally shook her head. "Yeah, he's starting to grow on me." She could almost see her father beaming on the other end.

When this case was over, she was going to explain the facts of life to her dad. She did not need a man in her life to make her happy. She could take care of herself. If and when she decided to get married, it would be her choice.

Did every daughter have to go through this?

Chapter 17

Conor leaned back in the chair. Jessica was champing at the bit, and had been all morning and into the afternoon. Hell, she'd been pacing the living room floor for the last twenty minutes. Maybe he should've let her go for her run. He just couldn't take a chance Barry might see her leave and decide to make his move a little early.

The thought of Barry even going near Jessica made his blood boil. If he laid one hand on her, he'd smash his face in.

Damn it, he had to relax. Think about something else, or he might storm next door and cram Barry's sleazy smile down his throat. That wouldn't do this stakeout a whole hell of a lot of good.

Relax? He wasn't used to relaxing on the job, but then, he'd never had a partner quite like Jessica.

His gaze was drawn to the bearskin rug. Sex would relax the both of them. He closed his eyes for just a moment as he savored the fantasy image of her lying naked on the white rug . . . legs spreading . . . inviting him to join her on the plush fur. Begging him to kiss her, to knead her breasts, to draw the tender nubs into his mouth.

A shudder swept over him. God, she was killing him. Slowly torturing him until he couldn't think straight.

He shifted in the chair, but his ache wasn't relieved. It was an image he'd had much too often. Every time it was his turn to watch the house next door, in fact.

One night with her had not been enough to get her out of his system. He wasn't sure a dozen nights would be enough.

"How can you just sit there? Aren't you bored out of your skull?"

Thinking about her lying naked on the white rug? Not in the least. Watching the house next door? "Yes, I'm bored." Maybe if there was a little action, he wouldn't be thinking about having sex with Jessica every time he turned around.

She opened her mouth, then snapped it closed. "Well, you could've fooled me. You look pretty damned relaxed."

She sighed, plopping down in the chair next to his. Her perfume wafted to his nostrils. He inhaled, liking the way her fragrance enveloped him in a light, flowery scent. She wore shorts today. Was she getting tired of playing dress-up?

When she'd slipped up and said she left the force because she wanted to be a lady, that she wanted to find herself, he could've told her that changing what she wore would only make her different on the outside. If she was meant to be a cop, that was what she would come back to.

Not that he thought she was meant to be a cop. Jessica was like a delicate flower opening her petals to the sun. Someday she would find her place in life.

He didn't really mind that she had put away the dresses and heels today, though. Shorts were nice, too. His gaze roamed over her long legs. Yeah, shorts were real nice.

He liked the white T-shirt even better. That and her bra were just thin enough so he could make out her nipples. He was tempted to turn the thermostat down a few degrees, but figured that bordered on some kind of perversion.

"At least talk to me or I'll go crazy. Tell me something profound about undercover work."

He grinned. Damn, she was cute. "What do you want to know?"

"Are all stakeouts this boring?"

He chuckled. "I tried to warn you. And no, most surveillance work isn't this slow. Usually, there's a lot more activity. If it wasn't for their visitor the other night, I'd begin to wonder if the Merediths were the right suspects."

"Have you been on many stakeouts?"

"I've done my share."

She curled her feet under her and said, "Tell me about some of them."

He folded his arms in front of him. At least it would pass the time. "Once I was on a stakeout that involved drug trafficking. I was on that one for a month before we had any activity. Talk about mind-numbing. My partner sleepwalked, too. I ended up handcuffing him to the bed so he wouldn't wander off while I watched the house across the street."

"I guess you haven't had much luck with partners."

"Well, you're a lot cuter."

She blushed, turning her gaze away from him, then frowned. "Isn't that the mayor?"

He was going to have to stay focused. He looked out the window. Sure enough, the mayor was walking up to the Merediths' door . . . in broad daylight. He reached for the camera, but Jessica was already snapping off pictures.

"I'm going to slip next door and see if I can hear anything." He cast a warning look in her direction. "Stay put."

She didn't say anything.

"You may need to call for backup if I run into any trouble."

"Okay, I'll stay." He could be really anal at times.

She watched him leave the room, then turned back to the window. Her eyes narrowed on the house next door. She'd known the mayor had something to do with the robberies. He had weasel eyes . . . and he was shifty.

The mayor rang the doorbell, but this time Trudy stepped onto the landing. She glanced over her shoulder, then placed a hand on the mayor's arm. He didn't seem to mind, either. In fact, he acted pretty friendly. As if he knew her.

Jessica took some more pictures. They might need them for evidence.

Her attention was drawn to the side of the house as Conor crept along the hedges, keeping low. Just before he got to the front door, Trudy and the mayor went inside.

Conor spied through one of the windows. She held her breath and silently prayed he wouldn't get caught.

Her gaze moved to the back of the Meredith home when Barry stepped into the backyard and lit a cigarette. She looked at Conor. Only a few feet separated the two men. Her pulse sped up. If Barry walked around the side of the house, he'd see Conor.

She stepped from behind the curtain and waved her hands at the same time Barry looked up. Oh no, she'd gotten the wrong man's attention. What the hell was she supposed to do now?

Barry waved back at her, then blew her a kiss right before he rubbed his crotch.

Vomit! Puke! Eeeyuck! Barry was so gross.

"Not in this lifetime, imbecile."

She brought her hands up, indicating he shouldn't come over. Then she swallowed past the lump in her throat and blew him a kiss. He nodded that he understood while she wiped her hand down the side of her shorts. It felt as if he'd actually touched her. A shiver of revulsion washed over her.

She didn't breathe easier until he flicked his cigarette away and strode back inside. Her attention turned back to Conor. She frowned. Where had he gone?

"Now you know why I didn't want you to go running. The last thing you need is to bump into Barry."

She jumped, whirled around, arm raised to defend herself. He easily caught her wrist in his hand. When it sank into her brain that it was only Conor, she relaxed.

But he didn't let go.

Trembles started where his hand grasped her arm and fluttered down to her stomach . . . before moving lower.

"The mayor?" she said in a voice laced with need.

"He left. He gave Trudy some brochures. I think he was campaigning. Or he might have been passing on information about the next heist and using the election as his cover. Trudy might be the one running the show, for all I know."

Whether consciously or unconsciously, he stroked her wrist, running his thumb lightly back and forth.

The sharp peal of the doorbell echoed through the house.

"That would be the mayor," he said as his eyes darkened and he pulled her close. "Even if he is the one calling the shots, he'd want to make it look like he was out trying to round up votes."

"Shouldn't we answer the door?"

He shook his head. "He'd recognize you for sure, maybe me. We can't take the chance."

The doorbell rang again as Conor's mouth lowered to hers. She melted against him, a deep longing to have more than just a kiss filled her. His mouth was hot against hers. He pulled her closer, as if he couldn't get enough, but then, neither could she. Both strained toward the other. Wanting the connection to be complete.

He cupped her breast, his thumb tracing the outline of her nipple. When he did scrape across the tender nub, she arched toward him.

"I want you. Damn it, I know it's wrong, but I want you," he growled from low in his throat and pulled her T-shirt over her head.

None of the reasons why they shouldn't have sex came to mind. The only thing she knew was that she wanted Conor as much as he wanted her. Later. There would be time later for self-recriminations. Right now she wanted to feel his hands on her naked skin.

"We'll listen," she panted. "If we hear anything, we can stop . . . uh . . . whatever we're doing." Please, God, don't let anything happen. Her body felt as if it were on fire. She unhooked her bra and tossed it to the floor.

He cupped her breasts.

She moaned. "God, that feels good."

"And this?" he asked, brushing the pad of his thumb across her tight nipple.

Pleasure shot downward, spiraling to the vortex of her being. He wedged one of his legs between hers and nudged against her at the same time he lowered his head and drew her nipple into his mouth. Instinctively, she rubbed against his leg, grasping his shoulders so she wouldn't fall. The throbbing inside her grew, but before her satisfaction was complete, he pulled away.

"Ahhh, Conor." She sighed with regret and pent-up desire. "Don't stop right now. I was almost . . . almost . . ." But she couldn't voice her thoughts aloud. She'd been so close to an orgasm and he'd pulled back. Not fair at all. Now she was frustrated and wanting more.

"Shhh," he whispered against her ear, the warmth of his breath tickling. "I'm not stopping. Only taking a short break."

"No breaks. This isn't a union."

"Not yet, anyway."

The smile was evident in his voice. He had really bad timing when it came to discovering his sense of humor. All her frustration died when his teeth latched on to her earlobe. He gently tugged before letting go and swirling his tongue inside.

She leaned her head to the side, giving him easier access. If this was some kind of torture, she wouldn't complain. Not one little bit.

With a will of their own, her hands began lightly trailing up and down his back. It wasn't enough. She pulled his shirt away from his waistband, sighing when her hands encountered the smooth surface of his back.

His sinewy muscles felt rugged beneath her hands. Firm muscle and tough skin. She kneaded his back, memorizing the texture. When she was lying in her lonely bed, after the stakeout was over, she wanted to remember how it felt to touch him, to breathe in the musky scent of his skin, to hear the steady beat of his heart. She wanted to remember it all.

He raised his head.

"Coast still clear?" she asked, her voice shaking.

He inched the two of them toward the window so he could peek around the curtains. "Clear," he croaked.

"Good." She unhooked his belt and slid it out of the loops, dropping it to the floor. "Then let's get naked."

His smile was slow and sexy and oh-so-lethal.

"I like the way you think."

He grasped the waistband of her shorts and tugged her closer, slipping the top button through the hole before sliding the zipper down. He pushed the shorts over her hips as she unsnapped his pants, then unzipped them. His arms tangled with hers.

She laughed, realizing having sex with Conor was fun. She enjoyed seeing him naked, exploring his body, his exploration of hers. And she wanted to see all of him. She shoved his pants downward.

In one easy motion, he turned her around.

The way she was angled, she could see the house next door, but they couldn't see her. There was no movement whatsoever.

"All clear," she moaned as his hands cupped her breasts and squeezed.

"I'm glad. I'd hate to stop."

"You and me both," she said as his hands roamed over the front of her body. He tweaked her nipples, then cupped both breasts and massaged. She leaned against him, his hardness nudged against her backside.

His hands were everywhere at once. Gliding over her stomach, slipping inside her panties. She bit her bottom lip, but he didn't come near her secret spot. The spot that itched like crazy and wanted his touch so badly she almost cried.

"Touch me," she begged, the sweet ache building inside her to the point she didn't think she could bear another minute of the exquisite torture he inflicted.

"Where?" he breathed close to her ear. "Here?" He trailed his fingers over her thighs. Bringing them close to the spot, but not quite touching her.

She shook her head and clasped his legs.

"No?" he asked. "What about here?" He lightly ran his fingers just above her mound . . . back and forth.

The silky material of her panties made his touch more sensuous . . . more erotic. She whimpered, unable to do more.

"Or maybe you want this." He moved his fingers over her sex.

She gasped, arching forward. "Yes, that's the spot."

"I rather thought it would be."

"Ass. What goes around comes around."

"I can't wait."

"Ummm . . ."

He massaged her sex. Instinctively, she rubbed her backside against him in the same motion. Her ragged breathing filled the room. She tightly clasped his thighs, wanting him to take her all the way, but his motions began to ease. She grabbed his hands, but his greater strength wouldn't let her increase the pressure.

"Slow, now."

She shook her head. "No, I need you to touch me. Please, Conor. I can't stand any more." She forced her brain to focus on the house just across the way. "See? Nothing going on. We don't have to stop."

In one motion, he laid her on the bearskin rug. Still standing above her, he said, "I'm not stopping, baby. Hell, I'm just getting started." He stepped the rest of the way out of his briefs and pants, kicking them aside.

Not stopping was a good thing. She wouldn't have to be committed to a state institution for sexually starved women after all.

Her gaze moved over his body. She was staring and she didn't care. Good lord, he was magnificent in all his naked glory. "I want to taste every inch of you."

His pupils dilated and there was a slight tremble in his hands as he knelt beside her. Had she really said the words out loud? It didn't matter. Sex wasn't just about her enjoyment, but his as well. Okay, so maybe the idea of tasting him caused a ripple of pleasure to chase down her spine.

"You're beautiful," he said, drawing her attention away from his tanned torso and back to his face.

"I run." Now that was a really brilliant thing to say.

"I know."

"You are, too. Beautiful, I mean." He was on his side, facing her, and she couldn't resist circling her finger around his areole before tasting the nipple. She turned on her side and leaned forward, taking him into her mouth. His nipple tightened in response and she heard him draw in a sharp breath. She sucked, laving her tongue across the hard nub. He hugged her tight, moaning.

A feeling of power swept over her. Conor had been in control of the whole operation, at least as much as she'd let him, but now she felt as if she was the one in charge.

"Do you know how many times I've envisioned you lying on this rug, just as you are, completely naked?"

"No more than I have you." He gasped when she moved her hand downward and stroked her fingers over his hard length.

Before she could revel too much in her power, he reciprocated and began caressing her between her legs. Because he'd taken her so close to the edge, her body betrayed her by immediately responding. Not that she really cared. She closed her eyes, continuing her assault on his body as well.

"I don't think I can hold off any longer," he whispered and grabbed a condom from his pocket.

She smiled when he fumbled with the foil packet. She loved knowing that he'd been taken to the edge as well. He rolled the condom on before moving between her legs, easing into her.

"God, you're wet and so damned tight," he said.

He slid deeper. She wrapped her legs around his waist and clenched her inner muscles around his heat. He began to move slowly. She arched toward him, savoring the fullness of him inside her.

His movements increased. She closed her eyes and threw her head back. He thrust in deep and slid almost all the way out. Then again and again. Fire burned inside her and coursed over her, washing her in a hazy, erotic dream world, except she wasn't asleep and Conor was moving faster and faster.

When she thought she could stand no more, lights exploded around her. She cried out, her body tightening as the orgasm gripped her. She only vaguely heard Conor's cry as he arched toward her. He slumped forward, then apparently realized he was still on top of her and rolled to his side.

The simple act of drawing in enough air so she didn't suffocate was almost too much trouble. If she died now, she knew it wouldn't get better than this. She closed her eyes and let her body settle back to earth, and as it did, realization sank in.

"You still alive?" she finally managed to ask.

"I think so."

"Have you ever had sex like this before?"

"Never."

"Me, either." She hesitated. "I don't want to get involved with a cop. I told you that from the very beginning."

"I think I mentioned I wasn't into long-term relationships."

"This is going to get complicated."

"I think it already has."

How could she have been so stupid? A relationship wouldn't work between them. It just couldn't. He was a cop. When this was over he would go back to the streets or another undercover operation. She would merrily sell real estate. They'd probably never cross paths again.

She raised her chin and turned her head toward him. "This can't happen again." When she turned on her side to make sure he understood exactly what she meant, her breasts brushed across the hairs on his chest. Instantly her nipples sprang to life.

He glanced down. "Never is an awfully long time," he told her.

"Nevertheless, you do know why we've got to end whatever is happening here and now."

He ran a hand over her shoulder and she cursed the tingles that followed in the wake of his touch.

"I know what we should do. I know it as well as I know my name." His gaze roamed over her body. "But it's going to be damned hard to tell my brain one thing when my body wants to do the exact opposite."

She understood the feeling. "It doesn't matter. We have to be strong." With what little strength she had left to muster, Jessica stood and walked away. Only she knew how much of an effort it took or how damned bad her legs trembled from the effort.

She went up the stairs and down the hall to the shower, but the cool spray couldn't wash away his touch or the lingering smell of his skin.

It couldn't wash away what she was feeling, either. Damn, this wasn't supposed to happen. She shouldn't feel this horrible sense of loss or that she was totally screwing up her life.

She wasn't meant to be a cop, any more than she was meant to have a relationship with one.

Chapter 18

"I don't like leaving you here alone," Conor said. "Your father said there were some new developments and he wanted me down at the station."

Jessica knew he thought she'd get into some kind of jam. And why wouldn't he think she was incompetent? Especially since she'd told him how she'd let an arsonist get away so she could free a goat.

Then set about seducing Conor.

He'd made the first move the second time, though. Like that exonerated her. She was making excuses. She didn't like that in other people and she damn well didn't like it in herself. She'd been making mistakes ... period.

Who could forget the infamous tape she'd stolen? Or Barry nearly catching her red-handed?

Well, she wouldn't screw up again, even if it killed her. "I'll be all right," she assured him. He still didn't look convinced.

"It's different now. We've made contact." He began pacing, then stopped and looked at her, a worried frown wrinkling his brow. "What if Barry comes over?"

"I won't answer the door. Even if the house catches on fire, I won't step one foot out the door. I'll stay close to the window and keep watch. I'll even call you if they leave. I know what to do. I can take care of myself."

How many times did she have to try to explain she really could take care of herself if push came to shove?

"Promise you won't do anything," he pleaded, finally relenting.

"Scout's honor."

He looked dubious. "You were a Girl Scout?"

"Why do you think I went into real estate? I'll have you know I sold more cookies than anyone in my troop." Of course, she also had more relatives than anyone in her troop, too. And what neighbor would say no to a cute kid selling cookies, especially when her father and at least half her other relatives were cops, paramedics, or in the fire department. Nope, they weren't about to take any chances upsetting *her* relatives.

"Well, this isn't the Girl Scouts. Don't open the door—for anyone."

"I'll be okay. Go."

She walked with him to the door and shut it behind him, reaching toward the lock.

"Don't forget to lock it," he said from the other side.

"Give me a chance and I will," she mumbled, shaking her head. She turned the lock. It clicked loud enough for him to hear.

When she heard footsteps walking away, she sighed with relief. All of two seconds passed before she gave in to temptation and pulled back the curtain and watched him climb into his car. Damn it, he wasn't out of sight and she already missed him. She didn't move from her spot for a good three minutes, then sighed deeply when she turned away.

The coast was clear. Time to get busy. Lord, she was going to hell for lying.

She hurried to the phone. If the suspects did make their move tonight, as Conor believed, Jessica had a feeling he wouldn't let her go with him. She picked up the phone in the hall and quickly punched in some numbers. It rang twice before it was answered.

"Hello?"

"Mike, this is Jessica. I need you to bring me a few things."

"This is my day off," he whined.

"Please . . ."

"Jessica . . ."

"Pretty please?"

Her cousin groaned. "Okay, okay. What do you want? And it better be legal this time."

She quickly gave him a list of what she'd need, but before she hung up, she asked him one more favor. "You still have your motorcycle, don't you?"

Silence.

"Mike?"

"No, not my motorcycle."

She frowned. "What's the matter? Don't you trust me with your toy?"

"It's not a toy!"

Oops. She'd forgotten how much the shiny red bike meant to him, but it wasn't like it was a monster Harley or anything. It was a Honda 233cc Rebel. Apparently marriage hadn't mellowed him when it came to his bike. But she did want to borrow it, so she'd be nice.

"I know it's not a plaything. I promise to be very careful, but I do need it. Besides, you taught me to ride it. The least you can do is loan it to me."

Silence.

"This isn't some scheme to get even, is it? I was only getting you back for the Saran wrap on the toilet seats. That was really low, even for you."

"Yeah, I know." She grinned. "That was a good one, but no, I'm not trying to get even. I'll take really good care of your bi . . . motorcycle. I won't put a dent or scratch on it. Swear, but right now I really need to use your bike. Please, cuz."

"That's not fair, Jessica. You're using that same tone of voice that always got me into trouble when we were growing up."

"Then you'll let me borrow it?"

There was a few seconds of silence before he spoke. "If you put one teeny-tiny dent on it, I'll hang your hide on the side of a building."

"Thanks, cuz."

"By the way, how's the stakeout going?"

"Great . . . well, at least not bad . . . except for a couple of minor incidents." She cringed. Mentioning her screw-ups would serve no purpose—so she didn't.

They talked for a few more minutes before hanging up. She sauntered into the living room and glanced toward the suspects' house. At least she'd be prepared if Conor turned stubborn, and what he didn't know wouldn't hurt him. She might not even need the bike.

Barry walked out the front door. She held her breath, but he only lit a cigarette and stood on the front porch to smoke it. He glanced once toward their house, but she kept herself hidden behind the curtain and silently prayed he wouldn't decide to drop by for a visit.

When he finished his smoke and thumped it in the grass, then went inside, she thought she'd at least feel relieved. She frowned. It had been more like disappointment. She hadn't realized just how ready she was for a little action.

"Yom-da-da-da-da," she chanted under her breath. Peace and inner tranquility were what she was striving for. Not guns and action. She wanted to be a lady and sell real estate. She didn't want to be a cop. Stability would make her happy. At least, she thought that was what she wanted. She wasn't quite as positive as she once was.

Conor walked into the police station with purposeful strides and went straight to the chief's office. Gloria glanced up as he entered.

"Joe's been expecting you."

"I left as soon as he called."

A mischievous gleam sparkled in her eyes. "You and Jess getting along?"

Heat crawled up his face. "She can be stubborn at times." He certainly wasn't going to tell her exactly how well they were getting along.

"But she's cute and funny, too," Gloria said, pushing for more.

This wasn't the time or place to start a conversation about his relationship with Jessica. He wasn't sure there ever would be a time or a place.

For reasons he wasn't quite sure about, he didn't want to talk about what was going on between them. If there even *was* anything substantial. And if there was . . . well, it could be worse. At least he hadn't noticed her stealing anything the one time they went shopping.

When he didn't answer, Gloria's smile widened. "I guess Joe was right, for once," she murmured. "Go on in." She motioned for him to enter and went back to her paperwork.

It wouldn't do any good trying to convince any of the Nelsons there was nothing serious between him and Jessica. He'd already figured out they were a stubborn bunch. It was better to just let the matter drop.

Conor rapped his knuckles on the door before he went inside.

"Record time," the chief said as he looked up from the papers littering his desk.

"You sounded like whatever you were going to say was important."

The chief motioned for him to take a seat. He cautiously sat in the chair across from the chief's desk.

Had the chief found out about him and Jessica getting intimate? No, he didn't think that was something Jessica would discuss with her father. Or any other family member, for that matter.

"The case is closed." The chief shut a file he'd been looking at and smiled.

"Excuse me?" What was he talking about? The case wasn't closed. How could it be?

"You heard right. We caught the burglars an hour ago. They robbed a house on Barnett Circle. The homeowners were away at the time, but they'd installed a brand-new alarm system. When it detected an intruder, the company called us. Caught them red-handed—two men. They'd even left a stuffed raccoon sitting on the sofa."

"They confessed to the other burglaries?" He was stunned. This was the last news he'd expected to hear.

The chief's chair creaked when he leaned back. "They're denying everything. Hell, one of the guys said they'd been out drinking and had a little too much, ending up in his *girlfriend's* home. They didn't know about the new alarm system. Said the raccoon was for her. Too coincidental, if you ask me. We haven't been able to contact the homeowners to confirm their story, but I'm not buying it."

"Do you have the mayor's tape?"

"No, but they'll talk. Their kind always does. They're still claiming the girlfriend is real."

"That's . . ." He shook his head. "That's great." Then why didn't he feel relieved? Something bothered him. Then he remembered. "What about the conversation? The one I overheard. They were planning another job."

The chief shrugged. "It was probably just that. A job. Not a burglary. There are movers who work at night so they won't interfere with the office personnel jobs."

"I'd have sworn that wasn't what they were talking about."

"We all make mistakes. I guess you and Jess can pack it up. You're probably both ready to get back to your own places."

Conor's gut clenched. Was this why he was so stunned? Had he already guessed the surveillance was over before the chief spoke the words? How did he really feel about possibly never seeing Jessica again? Just the thought left a sour taste in his mouth.

The chief picked up the globe on his desk and turned it over. Snow began to drift toward the base.

"I don't suppose you and Jessica will be seeing each other again. She'll probably hook up with Al."

"Yeah, probably." The thought of Al kissing Jessica didn't sit well with him. In fact, he'd like to punch the guy out.

Jessica didn't belong to him, though. He had no rights just because they'd had sex.

"A shame," the chief said. "I kind of thought y'all would get along."

"She doesn't date cops." Lame. Before he dug himself in a hole he couldn't climb out of, he stood. "I guess I'll go back and tell Jessica she can head home."

Conor left the chief's office, mumbled a good-bye to Gloria, and hurried out. If she said anything, it didn't sink into his brain. His thoughts were on Jessica. Damn it, he didn't want her to walk out of his life. Whatever was between them wasn't over yet. He didn't like leaving loose ends.

Jessica knew something was up the minute Conor walked back into the house. She hadn't seen him look this serious since the day he'd mistakenly arrested her for solicitation. She had a feeling she wouldn't like whatever he was about to tell her this time, either.

He went into the kitchen without saying a word and pulled a soda from the fridge.

"What?" she finally got up the nerve to ask. "You look like you wish that were a beer rather than a soda. Or maybe a stiff shot of whiskey."

He took a long drink, then went to the table and pulled out a chair.

"Actually, it's good news."

She raised an eyebrow as she sat in the chair across from him. "Yeah, you look like you're jumping for joy."

"They caught the burglars." He ran a thumb over the condensation on the outside of the canned drink. "We can go home."

Her gaze flew to the window. Had she fucked up and missed a takedown? No, that hadn't happened. No way. Nothing looked any different than it had a moment ago. She hadn't seen the Merediths leave. Or cops barreling up to the door. It was still just as quiet as it had been all day.

She turned her gaze back to Conor. "I don't understand. What did my dad tell you?"

"That it wasn't the Merediths pulling the burglaries. They're innocent. At least of these jobs."

"But . . ."

"It's over." He glanced out the window.

"What about the mayor?"

"Apparently, he was just campaigning." He shrugged. "Wrong place, wrong time."

The breath left her body. At least, that's what it felt like. Her brain stopped functioning. She couldn't think.

What did all this mean? That they could pack up and leave? She looked at Conor, wanting . . . hell, she didn't know what she wanted. That he wouldn't leave? She turned her gaze back to the window. He'd told her he didn't want a long-term relationship.

Pain ripped through her. Maybe if she groveled? No, she wouldn't stoop that low—at least, she didn't think she would.

"Jessica?"

She laughed, but it came out sounding more like a death rattle. "I guess you'd started to grow on me. Isn't that funny?" She stood, wanting to get this over with as painlessly and as soon as possible. "It'll be great getting home and back to selling real estate. It's been fun, though, and different . . . interesting . . ." *Shut up!* she told herself. She was babbling like some kind of moron.

"Jessica, it doesn't have to end here." He stood.

No, don't listen to him. "Haven't we already complicated each other's lives more than we ever intended? I still don't want to be involved with a cop and you don't really want a long-term relationship, remember? We don't have to make this more difficult than it is." She twined her fingers in front of her.

He stood and walked around the table, untangling her fingers. "Maybe I'm not so sure about long-term relationships. I was, but then you came into my life. I kind of like having you near."

She was afraid this was going to happen. Neither one wanted to walk away from the other. "Maybe we can sort of see each other occasionally."

Did he have to stand so close? Once again, he was invading her space. She took a deep breath and his musky scent wafted to her nostrils. Damn, she loved the way he smelled.

In fact, there were a lot of things she liked about him. Wouldn't her dad have a field day if he found out she was falling for . . . Oh lord, not that. She didn't want to fall in love with Conor. Not a cop.

"Maybe it would be better to end it now. Before we get in over our heads."

"I think it's too late. We at least need to explore what's going on between us." He raised her chin and lowered his mouth.

Her body morphed into a quivering mass of Jell-O. *I don't want this,* she told herself as her body screamed for more. I don't like that he takes his job so seriously, I don't like that he occasionally can make a joke, I don't like the way he smiles, the way he laughs . . . the way he makes love . . .

I do like it, I do, I do . . .

She twined her arms around his neck, and with a sigh of surrender, pulled him closer, tasting all he had to offer. He was heat and he was fire. He stole her breath away, but that was okay because he gave her back so much in return.

He picked her up, her arms tightening around his neck.

"I won't drop you," he said, setting her on the kitchen counter.

"Good. I'd hate to have to make a trip to the hospital. I

can think of a lot more things I'd rather be doing than sitting in the waiting room."

To hell with it. She didn't want to deny herself. Tomorrow would be soon enough to regret her actions. But right now, she didn't want to stop kissing him, but when he pulled away she wondered if maybe he was having second thoughts.

She leaned back, in what she figured was a blatant invitation, but her hand missed the counter and landed in the sink. She fought to get her balance and grabbed the faucet handle. When she pushed herself up, she accidentally turned the water on.

How sexy was this? she thought with derision.

"Here, let me help." Conor reached for her at the same time she moved. He missed, his hand landing on the hose attached to the sink; a shower of water squirted out, hitting him in the face.

She laughed as she pushed herself upright. What else could she do? He had water dripping down his face. He was all wet.

"You think that's funny?" He pulled the length of hose out and aimed the nozzle at her.

"It was a nervous laugh," she said with as straight a face as she could muster under the circumstances. Not an easy task. She didn't think he bought it, either.

He didn't.

Instead of hitting her in the face, the water landed on her light blue T-shirt. She sucked in a deep breath. "That's cold."

He grinned. "I can see that."

She glanced down. Her nipples poked against the material of her shirt. The water had made the cotton material transparent as it molded to her equally thin bra.

"Wet T-shirt contest?" she wryly asked.

"You'd win." His gaze slowly moved over her.

Somehow having her clothes plastered to her body made her feel sexy. Naked . . . but not.

He slipped his hand beneath her shirt, pulling her bra straps down her arms before he leaned toward her. He wasted no time pushing it down around her waist and drawing her nipple into his mouth, sucking greedily. She arched toward him, not caring that her bra was around her waist like a wet belt.

The material of her shirt rubbed against her naked skin, sending tremors over her body. When he moved, she groaned, but before she could raise much of a protest, he took her other nipple in his mouth and gave it his undivided attention.

The setting sun created an eerie glow about the room, casting the last of its warmth over them, but it wouldn't have mattered if it were the dead of winter. Conor created his own kind of heat, and she was getting damn hot.

Her body ached, and her hands itched to feel his naked skin. She reached over his back and tugged his knit shirt out of his pants before dragging it toward his head. Before she could go very far, he took a step back.

"Are you hinting that you want me to take my clothes off?" he asked.

She tossed her hair over her shoulder and tilted her chin. He was getting a little cocky. Her gaze moved downward. Make that a whole lot cocky. Her gaze roamed back to his face. "Oh yeah, a striptease would be . . . interesting, to say the least." Her body tingled just thinking about it.

He raised an eyebrow. "Striptease? As in dance?"

"Why not? Women do it for men all the time. Turnabout is fair play."

He grinned. Lord, she loved his lopsided smile. It made her thighs quiver and her belly tighten. Very slowly, he pulled his shirt over his head. Her mouth went dry. When he reached for the hose again, she thought maybe he wanted to cool her off, but rather than squirting her, he put the nozzle against his chest and pushed the lever so that water ran over him.

He closed his eyes, his body swaying to the music in his head. She bit her bottom lip, liking this side of Conor.

His skin shone as if it had been oiled. Her gaze followed his hands as they slid over his skin. His movements were hypnotic. He might as well have been swinging a watch on a chain in front of her eyes.

"More," she croaked, her gaze straying lower.

"What do you want? Tell me and I'll do it."

"Take off your pants."

He moved to his belt, taking his time as he slipped it from the notch and pulled it through the loops. Before he dropped it to the floor, he ran it across her thighs. Just a light movement. For one incredible second she had an urge to ask him to spank her. To feel the pain with the pleasure.

"Not this time," he said, reading her thoughts. "But one day I'll fulfill your every fantasy. That's what sex is all about . . . bringing the fantasies to life. Having fun."

"I like having fun." Had she just said that? He probably thought the doctor dropped her on her head when she was born. He was being imaginative, while she felt like a lump of coal.

A few seconds later, she couldn't recall what she'd said. Conor undid the top button on his pants and slowly slid the zipper down before pushing his pants over his hips. A lump of coal was okay. As long as all she had to do right at this moment was watch him slowly peel out of his clothes. Lord, she was getting hornier by the minute.

"What do you want?" he whispered, standing before her in his white briefs.

"Me . . . I mean, I want to . . ." Her face would glow in the dark if it were dark, but it wasn't, not yet. She didn't care that he saw what kind of effect he was having on her. He'd said *anything,* so she would take him to mean *anything.*

She slid off the edge of the cabinet, her feet lightly hitting the floor. The water was warm—she'd checked before taking the nozzle in her hand. She damn sure didn't want anything to shrivel at this stage of the game. She sprayed the front of his briefs, his very thin, white briefs. He might as well have been naked . . . but he wasn't. His hard length was outlined to perfection.

She dropped the nozzle and moved to her knees in front of him. "You have the sexiest legs I've ever seen on a man." She trailed her nails lightly over his thighs. His legs quivered. When she put her mouth against the cotton fabric, he groaned and grabbed the cabinet.

"This is very sexy. Tasting you through the material." She closed her eyes, scraping her teeth back and forth.

"You don't have to convince me. Ahhh, that feels good. Maybe a little more to the left. No, my left."

She'd known that. A smile tugged at her lips. "You mean, right here," she asked innocently, then ran her tongue down his length.

He caressed her head as she worked her mouth over him; at the same time, she hooked her fingers into the waistband and inched his briefs downward. Rather than touching his bare skin, her mouth trailed along with the material. She heard him suck in an anticipatory breath. She wasn't about to give in to his needs . . . at least, not yet.

"What do you want?" she murmured. "Just tell me, and I'll fulfill your every fantasy," she said, turning his words back on him. She could play on his imagination as well as he'd played on hers. His was probably running just as rampant.

Something close to a gurgle came from him.

"Having problems thinking of something? Maybe I can help." She tugged his briefs to his knees, cupping his butt, and began to massage his firm cheeks; then, with one languid stroke, she ran her tongue up his penis, flicking across the tip. He curled his fingers in her hair and arched forward. "Did that help you think of anything?"

"I think you enjoy teasing me."

She shook her head and looked up into his glazed eyes. "Oh, no, just name your pleasure and I'll do my best to fulfill it. I'd never *tease* you."

He returned her stare. "Then take me. I want to feel your tongue licking and your mouth sucking."

"I thought you'd never ask." And she was happy to oblige. Like candy that had been denied far too long, she drew him into her mouth and began to suck.

He was smooth against her tongue . . . smooth and a little salty. She swirled around the tip, French-kissing him before taking all of him again. He rocked against her, but gentle enough that he didn't hurt, letting her set the pace.

"Enough," he groaned, pulling her to her feet, kicking the rest of the way out of his briefs.

Before she could protest, he began kissing her lips, slipping her wet T-shirt over her head. He buried his face in her cleavage, kissing and licking as his fingers busily worked the clasp at her waist.

"Damn it, do you know how difficult it is to undo a wet bra?"

The situation might have been funny if she wasn't just as anxious to feel his hands . . . his mouth . . . on her naked skin. "There are other ways." In one smooth motion, she slid the bra around so she could see what she was doing. He was right. "The damn thing is wet and hard . . ." she grit her teeth.

"You're telling me?"

She stopped struggling, looked up, then laughed. He did have a wonderful sense of humor. Just not at the most appropriate times.

Before she could protest, he grabbed a knife out of the drawer and cut through the material.

Her mouth dropped open. "That was one of my new bras." She'd paid a ridiculous amount of money for it.

"I'll buy you another one." He tossed the knife into the sink and cupped her breasts. "Damn, I love touching you."

She grabbed the counter to steady herself. He leaned toward her, his mouth covering one breast while his hands worked her shorts over her hips and down her legs. Without missing a beat, he moved to the other breast while his fingers began a campaign all their own, stroking between her legs, tangling in her curls, scraping across the fleshy skin. He slipped a finger inside her; she rubbed against him, moving her body up and down.

"Oh, God, now," she cried.

He scrambled for a condom and quickly skimmed it on his rock-hard penis before he lifted her. She wrapped her arms around his neck, her legs around his middle, as he sank inside her. Her breasts were crushed against his chest as she moved to his rhythm.

As he filled her, she clenched her inner muscles around him, sucking him in further. He moved faster, going in deeper until the gates opened and the room exploded around her. She vaguely heard his cry. All she could do was wrap her hands tighter and hang on as her body trembled with pleasure she could never have imagined.

"Sweet Jesus, what have you done to me?" he whispered close to her ear.

She couldn't speak. All she could do was hold him close and wonder the same thing.

Chapter 19

"We can't stay here forever," Jessica told Conor as they lay on the heart-shaped bed.

Conor brushed a strand of hair from her eyes. The only light in the room came from the bathroom. She looked sexy as hell with the shadows playing around her.

After their kitchen adventure, they'd made their way upstairs to find dry clothes, but had only gotten as far as the bed. God, she'd been hot and more than ready for him again. He'd been happy to oblige.

Then they'd showered and fallen asleep, wrapped in each other's arms. He wasn't sure what time it was or how long they'd slept, and right now, he didn't really care. Deep down he knew he was trying to spend as much time with her as he could—before they went their separate ways.

"Why can't we stay just like this?" He turned on his side, facing her, and cupped her breast, tweaking the nipple. It sprang to life. "We're not on duty anymore, remember?"

Would he ever get his fill of her? It didn't seem that he would. They'd had the most incredible sex he'd ever experienced, and still he wanted more.

"Why can't we, Jessica?" he asked, burying his head in her hair and inhaling the peach shampoo she'd used.

She grinned. "For one thing, we'd starve."

As if to reinforce her words, his stomach growled. She grinned.

"Betrayed by my gut." He fell back against the pillow before the temptation of her breast overcame him. She was right—he was hungry.

"Okay, you win." He rolled over and sat up on the side of the bed. The illuminated dials read eleven o'clock. He hadn't realized it was that late. No wonder his stomach had growled.

He glanced over his shoulder, and his stomach did more than growl. Her hair was tousled and she had a very satisfied expression on her face as she hugged the pillow. Like a woman who'd been sexually satisfied. Her charms were hidden behind the large white pillow, but her legs, one hip, and a shoulder were tantalizingly displayed.

"Food sounds nice," she purred, squishing the pillow. She glanced toward the clock. "You know, it's too late to pack and load the car tonight, so we might as well stay until morning."

She was right about it being late, but he had a feeling she wasn't thinking about disturbing the neighbors. Her expression might be innocent, but there was a wealth of meaning in her words. He rather liked the idea of her naked body curled against his.

"You think we should eat just so we can keep up our strength?"

"Umm, that might not be a bad idea."

He stood, pulling out fresh clothes from the dresser, and was putting them on when he realized his was the only movement in the room.

He glanced toward Jessica. She was still in the same position as when he'd gotten up. "Is something wrong?"

She shook her head. "I'm staring, aren't I? Sorry. I just can't seem to get my fill of watching you." She moved languidly from the bed.

His mouth went dry. In the shadows of the room, she looked like some kind of goddess rising from her throne. A very naked goddess. His gaze roamed over her full breasts,

slim hips, and stopped on the thatch of dark hair. She sauntered past him, quite unconcerned that she was completely
naked and had just given him a world-class boner.

"Let's eat fast," she murmured as she went to what used to
be her room. He leaned around the corner and watched her
pull on a nightshirt that fell to the tops of her thighs. "I'll
meet you in the kitchen."

Now, how was he supposed to eat when he knew she was
naked underneath the nightshirt? But then again, maybe he'd
have her for dessert.

"I'm right behind you," he called out, catching up with her
at the bottom of the stairs and scooping her in his arms. His
chest muffled her scream. She weighed hardly anything at all.
The thought of her fighting crime and taking down bad guys
sent a shudder of fear down his spine.

She wrapped her arms around his neck and snuggled close,
wiggling her bottom and making it nearly impossible to think
about food. He carried her to the fridge and set her on her feet.

"What looks good?" she asked, after opening the door.

He circled his hands about her waist and pulled her
against him. She felt soft and curvy and very hot next to his
body. "*You* look good." He nibbled her neck.

She chuckled. "But I won't put meat on your bones."

"I don't know—so far you've made one bone thicker." He
nuzzled the side of her neck.

"You must be hungry. That was really bad."

"Bad to the bone?"

She grabbed the pizza box. "Quick, eat before you short-
circuit my joke receptors."

"Hey, I'm kind of a novice at this. Give me a break." He
plopped the pizza on the table while she grabbed a couple of
sodas and turned on the light over the sink. It wasn't as
bright and glaring as the overhead, but would give them
enough light to eat by.

"Cold pizza and soda. My favorite meal. Gabe and I used to
stay up late sometimes, and this was our main late-night snack."

"You're close to your brother?"

She opened the box and tore off a slice. "Yeah, we're pretty close. Like most brothers, he could be a real pain at times. But he's family and that's a bond that always keeps people together." She bit into her slice and chewed. "Unless, of course, you're in a dysfunctional family. I bet the Merediths have some great family reunions."

He leaned back in his chair, food momentarily forgotten as he watched her. He wasn't even listening to what she said. The way she moved, the way she gestured with her pizza, the way she pulled her nightshirt down so when she sat in the chair her bottom wouldn't freeze. That's what captured and held his attention.

She must have noticed he was staring, because she blushed and looked away. They'd had the most incredible sex with wild abandonment on both their parts. They'd explored each other's bodies until he knew hers almost as well as he did his own. And now she blushed when he stared at her. Amazing, contradictory woman.

"Our neighbors are up." She pointed out the window with her slice of pizza.

A light shone from one of the windows in the house next door. He casually glanced out the window. She was right. There hadn't been a light on a minute ago. For just a second, his gut clenched, then relaxed. He wasn't on duty. The chief had given him the next couple of days off. He didn't have to think about the strange behavior of the family next door. He'd much rather concentrate on Jessica. Besides, they were probably going to work.

He caught Jessica's arm and tugged her onto his lap. "Apparently, they are," he said, then took a bite from her pizza and chewed. He was so lost in her smoky blue eyes he couldn't even say what kind of pizza he was eating.

"Do you always steal other people's food?" She frowned at him. "First my Godiva candy, and now my pizza."

"Sorry." He swallowed and leaned in for another bite, but

she moved it out of his reach so he was forced to get his own slice. He was grinning when he reached inside the box. His grin slipped when he saw Barry leave the house, looking left, then right, as he stepped off the porch and slinked toward the garage.

"Strange behavior," Jessica said as she stood.

"Too damn strange."

Barry raised the garage door as Conor came to his feet.

Jessica glanced over her shoulder. "Are you sure my dad got the right burglars?"

"No, I'm not. The chief said they hadn't confessed. In fact, they were denying everything."

"All the evidence pointed to them, right?"

"It wouldn't be the first time circumstantial evidence kept the law from getting the real criminal."

Damn it, why hadn't he trusted his instincts? They'd never been wrong before. "But I'm going to find out exactly what is going on."

He turned and hurried out of the room.

"What are you going to do?" Jessica stayed right on his heels.

"Follow them. See if they're up to mischief."

"Do you think they are?"

"I don't have a good feeling. Let's leave it at that until I get something a little more concrete." He took the stairs two at a time and hurried into the bedroom.

He rummaged in a drawer and pulled out his knife. After strapping it to his calf, he grabbed his gun and holster. If something was going down, he'd know soon enough. He scooped up his socks and shoes before going back downstairs to the window so he could watch the activity next door.

What *did* he have to go on? Nothing but a gut feeling, but sometimes that was all anyone ever had. At some point a person had to forget logic and go with what they believed.

He sat in the chair and slipped on his socks, then his shoes. He heard Jessica coming down the stairs as he finished tying his shoes and looked up. The foyer light cast a soft light on her as she rushed down the stairs. She was dressed all in black, like a cat burglar. The clothes hugged each delicious curve. For a moment, the Merediths didn't exist.

Damn it, she was doing it to him again. Making him forget what he was supposed to be concentrating on.

"Where the hell do you think you're going?"

Her eyes widened. "With you, of course." Before he could say a word, she hurried on. "Don't worry, I'll stay out of your way."

"You're right—you will stay out of my way because you're not going anywhere." It was bad enough being in the house with her. Following behind possible criminals? Not while he had breath in his body. It wasn't going to happen.

"That's not fair," she argued.

"Yeah, well, life isn't always fair." He turned back to the window, hating the way his words sounded, but he didn't want her putting any crazy notions in his head.

George came out of the house and hurried to the car, stumbling once, but quickly regaining his footing. He opened the back car door and climbed in. If the moon hadn't been so bright, George's dark clothes would've blended well. For the first time since meeting him, the flashy young man wore very dark, subdued clothes.

Just like Barry had been wearing.

"Jessica, I don't have time for this. Barry is in the car. George just joined him. I'm going to follow them and see what's happening. I'll feel a lot better if you're safe."

"I told you that I could take care of myself."

"I'm sure you can."

She crossed her arms in front of her. He was doing it again. Patting her on top of the head. Maybe not literally, but in his mind that's exactly what he'd done. Treating her as if she had no experience. Hell, he was barely paying attention to her. It was as if he'd already dismissed her.

How could one man be so blasted obstinate? She only

wanted to go with him when he followed the Merediths. If they did attempt a burglary tonight, he might need her help. "I don't see what the harm would be."

"No, you're to stay here, Jessica." For a second she had his full attention. "No arguments. And I refuse to talk about it anymore."

"It's my father's job that's on the line."

He turned and smiled. The kind of smile that made her want to . . . want to . . . scream! It reminded her of the first time they'd met. She felt a moment's urge to wipe the condescending look off his face just as she had then.

"You'll stay here at the house or I'll call a halt to the whole operation right now."

"You wouldn't dare. Not when they might be the real criminals." Would he?

"Agree to my terms or find out exactly what lengths I'll go to." He stepped forward and took her in his arms. "I don't want you to get hurt. Don't you know how much I care about you?"

But she didn't want him just to care about her. She wanted him to love her. She stepped from his embrace. Oh hell, had their relationship gone that far?

"Okay," she choked out. "I'll stay out of your way."

Conor opened his mouth to speak, then closed it. His attention returned to the window.

She'd fallen in love with him. Damn, that wasn't supposed to happen. Wouldn't her father have a field day with this? She'd fallen in love with a man who didn't want to make a lasting commitment. Sure, he'd enjoyed the sex. His idea of a long-term relationship was maybe a few weeks. This was just fucking great.

She squared her shoulders. This wasn't the time to worry about her love life. She would have to put it on hold a while. At least until they discovered what the Merediths were up to. Right now, she had other things to worry about. Like getting around Conor's stubbornness. What if he needed help? There was only one way to assist him, but if she got caught he'd kill her.

Sure, she'd stay out of his way, but Conor wouldn't be alone. At least not when he trailed them. Unlike the time when Barry caught her, she'd be more careful. A sudden chill swept over her—a foreboding. Just for a second, she wanted to rush into his arms.

She was being ridiculous. What could go wrong tonight?

Now who was she kidding? Anything could happen.

"You'll call for backup as soon as possible, won't you? I mean, if they're up to something illegal?" She didn't want him taking any chances.

"I have my radio and cell phone. I want to make sure they're not leading me on a wild-goose chase before I alert anyone." He suddenly grinned. "Don't worry, I'll be fine. As far as we know, they're only going out for junk food."

All she could do was nod and watch him leave—then sneak out the back. She didn't have a good feeling about this. Maybe she should alert her father. But what if they *were* going for junk food or actually to move something? They were supposed to be movers. But this late? Stranger things had happened, and they were pretty strange.

Maybe it would be better to wait before she alerted her father. Just until she knew what was going down.

Taking a deep breath, she went around the side of the house opposite the Merediths. She and Mike had camouflaged his motorcycle at the side of the garage behind some tall bushes, covering it with a green blanket so it wouldn't get scratched. All she had to do now was wait.

Ten minutes later, and she was still waiting. Had she and Conor been wrong? Maybe they weren't going out after all. Maybe they liked sitting in the car? It would be just her luck if he caught her on Mike's bike. He'd probably dump her on her father's doorstep and never speak to her again.

It still hadn't clicked with Conor that she really could take care of herself. Trying to convince him of that fact had been impossible. He reminded her of her father, brother, and male cousins—he was a typical bullheaded man.

The car inside the garage roared to life. She jumped, heart pounding inside her chest. Good lord, if she was this jumpy, what would she do if this actually turned out to be a robbery in progress?

No, except for the goat incident, and a couple of minor problems during this stakeout, she'd been a pretty decent cop. She could handle herself in a tough situation.

With some of her confidence returning, she plastered herself against the wall on the other side and waited. She didn't have long.

When Conor pulled out, she strapped her helmet in place, rolled the bike from its hiding place, and climbed on. The motorcycle started the first time. Her cousin's dire warnings echoed in her mind. If anything happened to his toy, he'd never forgive her.

No, she grinned, and for a moment forgot the seriousness of what was happening. He hadn't liked it when she'd called his bike a toy. This was his baby, and she'd better remember that or he'd be the one skinning her alive rather than Conor.

She flipped on the headlight switch. A single beam of light lit the way.

The first few wobbles effectively removed any humor she'd felt. Had it been that long since she'd driven a motorcycle? Her heart beat frantically as she tried to regain her sense of balance. By the time she was down the driveway and onto the street, her confidence had returned, and the bike kept to a steady course.

Biting her lip, she glanced down the residential street. No cars in sight. Had she already lost them? They must've turned the corner. She drove to the stop sign. Relief washed over her when she saw the back of Conor's car. She turned, keeping a safe distance. *Please be more concerned with the car in front of you*, she prayed.

She shivered. The night air had a distinct chill to it. Why

hadn't she thought to wear a jacket? She frowned. In July? There wasn't a chill in the air. Nerves? Maybe . . . more than likely. If Conor guessed she was behind him . . .

Surely he wouldn't suspect she was on the motorcycle. And she'd be careful to stay out of the way. If the Merediths were about to commit a crime, she would at least be ready to call for backup.

She played out the scenario in her head.

Conor would catch the burglars in the act and signal for backup. The Merediths would be arrested, the missing tape found and returned to the mayor. Her father's job would be secure and everyone would go home happy. She would hurry back to the house without him knowing she'd even gone out.

Unless, of course, her father did have the real burglars locked up. If the Merediths stopped at one of the all-night stores, she and Conor might feel extremely foolish and end up with nothing to show for the time they'd spent in the house.

A delicious shiver ran down her spine. That wasn't exactly true. She would be taking a lot of yummy memories back to her apartment.

But memories won't keep you warm on a cold winter night.

She really hated it when the voice of reason popped into her head. Especially when it was right. She tightened her hand on the grips and forced herself to keep her mind on what was happening.

Conor turned on Main Street, where there was a little more traffic. Jessica kept two vehicles behind him and wondered why she had such a feeling of dread. Like something *would* happen tonight that could possibly change the rest of her life. And no matter how she tried, she couldn't shake a feeling of impending doom.

Conor turned twice more, and again the traffic thinned. She dropped back, putting more space between them. He turned another corner. She frowned. Duncan Road? Surely they weren't going to pull a heist tonight. The only buildings in this area were warehouses.

There wasn't another car on the road, and Conor was driving at a snail's pace. She copied his speed, slowing at turns in the road so her headlight wouldn't be detected, then hurrying to the next bend in the road.

Suddenly, Conor's brake lights flashed bright red. She stopped at the top of a hill under an overhanging tree limb and shut off her headlight. His interior light came on as he opened his door.

Hiding the motorcycle behind a tree, she began to hoof it. Nothing like a jog down a narrow road late at night. It was right at the top of her list of things to do in this lifetime. Right along with getting mugged while jogging on a quiet country road in the middle of the night.

She guesstimated it was only a quarter of the distance she usually ran. No big deal, if she didn't step into a pothole and twist her ankle. She kept to a slow but steady pace to avoid just that.

After a couple of minutes of jogging, Conor's car seemed to be farther than when she'd started. A film of perspiration dotted her forehead, and her heart boomed worse than a base drum at a high school football game.

She stopped, leaning against a mesquite tree and drawing a deep breath. Damn it, she wasn't a couch potato. Just the opposite. She was in damn good shape. So what was happening? Why couldn't she get her act together?

Too much adrenaline? Fear? No, she didn't think it was that. Excitement? She had a feeling that was closer to the mark. That and not focusing. That had to be it.

Get control.

She stretched her neck toward one shoulder, then the other. Slowly, she raised her hands above her head in a deep circle before bringing her palms together. The spiritualist said it would bring cosmic energy to the center of her body. She hadn't tried that one yet, figuring her belly button didn't really need energy.

Hell, she'd try anything once.

Focus! Deep breath. Her pulse slowed as she thought about a cool mountain stream on a warm summer day.

"Yom-da-da-da-da."

She opened her eyes. Calmness and serenity surrounded her. Maybe this shit really worked. Clamping her lips together, she narrowed her eyes and mentally placed a great, big target on Conor's car.

Right now she felt as if she could tackle just about anything. Maybe her father was right when he'd told her that being a cop was more in her blood than she realized. It still didn't change the fact that she'd let an arsonist get away while she freed an ungrateful goat or that she'd felt like one of the guys all the time. The goat incident might just have been the catalyst that pushed her to spread her wings and fly in another direction.

Yeah, she was really trying something new here. Okay, she had to admit that going undercover had been intoxicating. Conor thrown into the bargain hadn't hurt, either. Damn it, she didn't want to be a cop any more than she wanted to have a relationship with one.

Almost there, she slowed to a walk and finally admitted to herself she didn't know what she wanted anymore. She looked up. "Would you please tell me what the hel . . . heck I'm supposed to be doing?"

Silence.

Figured.

As she approached Conor's car, she crouched down, surveying the area. She didn't see him. He'd parked beside a small metal outbuilding. A long row of warehouses loomed ahead. She slipped to the corner for a better view. Taking a deep breath and holding it, she peered around the side.

The full moon gave barely enough light to make out the metal buildings. Conor, holding his gun, looked inside one of them. The Merediths' car was nearby. Before she could take another breath, she spotted a man sneaking up behind Conor. She didn't have time to give a warning as he raised a metal object and hit Conor over the head. Conor slumped to the ground.

She slapped a hand to her mouth and swallowed her cry. Oh my God! Oh my God! He'd killed Conor. She bit her bottom lip.

No, she refused to think like that. Conor might not be dead. It could've been a glancing blow, or something.

She had to know for sure. Cautiously, she moved closer, keeping to the sides of the other warehouses until she was only a few feet away.

Her whole body began to tremble. Her legs had as much strength as cooked noodles. Unable to do anything else, she sank to the ground.

The man threw down his weapon and began pacing in front of the warehouse. She glanced toward Conor, afraid there'd be a pool of blood under his head.

Had his arm moved?

She strained to see, pushing to her knees. Yes! She was almost certain he'd moved. She breathed a deep sigh of relief, then turned a narrowed gaze on the man who dared harm her lover.

There was something familiar about him. Her brow knit as she scanned the area. In fact, she'd been to this warehouse. If she wasn't mistaken, it was listed through the agency she worked for. Her gaze returned to the stranger. Realization dawned. No, it couldn't be.

Slowly she came to her feet. Now she was pissed.

Chapter 20

Al? That's who stood over Conor? She clenched her fists, then unclenched them. No, it couldn't be gentle Al.

But . . .

The man had the same walk—the same build. She was almost positive it was him.

But, her Al?

He was her friend . . . sort of. Not . . . not some criminal off the street.

Good lord, he lived with his mother. A frown drew her lips downward. At least, she thought he did. He said he did, but she'd never once met the woman. She'd only heard how much his mother loved to garden, and how she'd been so utterly lost since the death of her husband, Al's father, and how she depended so much on her son to care for her.

But she'd never met this saint of a woman.

Still, wouldn't she have suspected something? Been a little suspicious? When he turned toward her, she took a step back, even though she knew he couldn't see her. In that brief moment she got a good look at his face and all speculation vanished. It was Al.

Son of a bitch, he'd scammed her. He'd probably been laughing at her the whole time. She clamped her lips together to keep from screaming. Why hadn't she guessed his true nature?

She wracked her brain, trying to come up with clues that might have warned her. He'd shown an interest in her family and the wave of burglaries. Her stomach flip-flopped. Had she unwittingly given him information? Had she handed it to him on a silver platter? Conor and her father had suspected there might be another person involved. They'd been right.

Her. Albeit unknowingly. Guilt washed over her. Now Conor was hurt. And it was her fault.

Her gaze fixed on his still form. Al better hope the most Conor suffered was a bump on the head.

"George! Barry! Get out here!" Al's high-pitched, maniacal laughter bounced off the metal building and echoed through the darkness. This wasn't the same man she'd known and trusted. How could she have even thought he was a sweet, gentle friend?

She gritted her teeth, as anger like she'd never before experienced ripped through her. "That son of a bitch," she ground out. He'd used her. No one used her like this and got away with it.

She slipped her cell phone from her back pocket and flipped it open, punching in her father's number.

"Why are you calling this late?" he answered without a hello, but then, she never called this late unless she needed him.

"Dad, something is going down and we need backup," she whispered.

"Where are you?"

She moved to the other side of the building in case the light breeze decided to shift, sending her voice down the hill and alerting Al and the Merediths that there was someone else around.

"I'm just west of town. Remember those warehouses just off Duncan Road?"

"Yeah, I know them."

"Good. We'll need assistance, but I want you to hang back so I can see what's up. I don't want to put Conor in any more jeopardy than he's in." She paused for half a second. "The Merediths are here. Al knocked Conor over the head."

"Al!"

She cringed. "Yeah, Al. They don't know I'm here. I don't know how he's connected with the Merediths, but they're involved in something illegal. Before you storm the warehouse, though, I want to make sure Conor is out of the line of fire."

He didn't say anything for a few minutes. "We'll play it your way. Be careful."

Her smile held no humor. "I'm a cop and you trained me well. I'll call to tell you when to make your move."

She closed the phone and clipped it back on her pocket before going around the building to take up her vigil.

"Hurry up," Al said. "We've got company."

"Company?" Barry growled as he opened the side door to the large metal building. He and George stepped outside. Light spilled over Conor. "Who is it?" He pushed Conor with his boot until he rolled faceup.

Barry smacked George. With a pained expression, George grabbed his arm.

"I told you we couldn't trust him." Barry glared at his younger brother. "*Now* look what's happened."

Al's head jerked up. "You've had contact with him?"

Barry shuffled his feet when he turned back to Al. "He's just our neighbor. Probably wants a cut of the loot. Trudy invited him over for supper." He glared at George. "I told you he was trouble."

"You idiots!" Al stomped his foot.

Barry and George took a step back.

"What's all the commotion? Y'all talking loud enough to wake the dead." Winston Meredith ambled out of the warehouse, hitching up his pants and spitting out of the side of his mouth.

"Your neighbor here happens to be a cop, you fools!"

Winston lumbered over to Conor's still form and nudged

him none too gently with the toe of his boot. Conor groaned. Winston spat again, then wiped tobacco juice off his chin.

"I know'd he was up to no good." He turned a menacing glare in George's direction. "Ain't nobody stupid enough to want you as a friend. Always was dumb and always will be. Hell, your ma couldn't stomach you no more than me. That's why she dumped you on my doorstep and took off."

"The problem is, what are we to do with him?" Al squatted beside Conor.

"Kill him." Winston spat on the ground again.

Jessica's stomach lurched. She fumbled for her cell phone, slipping it out of the holder, ready to call her father.

"No, not just yet. Put him where he'll be out of the way while we finish loading the truck. I met the bastard once and he acted like I wasn't good enough to lick his boots. Drag him inside and tie him up. I want to have a little fun with him before I kill him."

"It'd be a sight easier if I shoot him right now." Winston spoke casually enough to make Jessica wonder if he'd killed in the past. He made it sound like it was something he did every day.

"No." Al stood, prancing in front of Conor. "I want him to know who's ending his life. He needs to be taught a lesson. Maybe then he'll see that brains win over brawn any day."

"What-a you mean?" George sidled up close to the other men. "Conor is-a not bad person. Maybe if-a he promises not to talk . . ."

"Drop that phony accent." Al spun around and took a menacing step toward the smaller man.

George ran backwards and slammed against the side of the warehouse.

"Do you really think anyone buys that you're Dutch?"

"It's Italian-o," George mumbled.

"Around me, you'd better be American. Now drag him inside and tie him up before he comes to."

Relieved that she had a little more time, Jessica put her

phone away and rested her head against the metal siding. Surely if Conor was badly injured, they wouldn't worry if he were bound or not. Would they?

"Reckon he's got help on the way?" Barry's gaze darted left, then right

"If he did, they'd have swarmed all over us by now. Besides, if you'd listened to the news today, you'd have heard the cops think they have the burglars in custody." Al looked down at Conor. A malicious grin spread across his face. "No, cops stick together. He was only checking us out. Just got a little too close. Probably thought he was invincible. I'll show him just how invincible he is."

Al might have fooled her once, but she'd have the last laugh. The Merediths were too stupid to realize she wasn't a harmless housewife. They hadn't seen anger like what she was about to unleash. She was about to become their worst nightmare.

Okay, stay focused! Take a deep breath. She breathed in, then exhaled as determination stole over her. A low growl came from somewhere deep inside her as she stealthily made her way down the hill, keeping close to the warehouses. She was ready to tackle anyone or anything that got in her way.

At the bottom of the hill, she glanced around. All clear. She crept to the door and tested the knob. Unlocked. Fools. She eased the door open a crack and surveyed the room.

Winston, Barry, and George loaded a large truck with what were probably stolen goods while Al directed their moves. Of course, he wouldn't want to get his hands dirty.

She and Conor had been wrong about one thing. They weren't pulling a heist tonight. It looked more like they were getting rid of the merchandise. She'd told Al the cops were getting close. Coward that he was, Al wouldn't take a chance robbing anyone else. Better to cash in and lie low.

Her gaze swept the room. Boxes stacked three-high made two short rows down the center of the warehouse. TVs, VCRs, and furniture were scattered about the building. Slowly, she looked around. Her breath caught in her throat. Conor was slumped forward in a high-back wooden chair, his wrists tied to the arms.

They didn't even bother keeping an eye on him. But then, why should they? Conor was obviously out cold and bound to a chair. What trouble could he possible cause them? On the other hand, she'd let them see just how angry she could get.

Wait. His head moved. Only a little, but if she wasn't mistaken, Conor only pretended to be unconscious.

Relief flooded through her. She wanted to hug him around the neck, but first she had to set him free.

She slipped inside, quickly hiding herself behind a row of boxes. Crouching low, she'd almost reached the chair before running out of cover.

"Pssssst."

Conor's head jerked around. He squeezed his eyes closed as if the sudden movement had caused him pain. Another reason to make Al pay dearly. She didn't forgive or forget when someone hurt those she cared about.

This close, he looked better than all right, though. He looked pretty damn fantastic. She waved, smiling at him.

Then frowned.

He didn't look at all pleased that she'd come to rescue him. In fact, he looked very displeased. Her eyebrows drew together. Of all the ungrateful people—he actually glared at her! She should turn around and leave. Let them dump his carcass in the dirtiest, stinkiest river . . .

Okay, so maybe she'd go ahead and save his hide, but she expected a thank-you when all this was over. Damn, he really needed to learn that she could handle herself, unless maybe animals were involved, goats in particular. Right now, the only animals she saw were the two-legged kind, and those she could handle a lot better.

As soon as the coast was clear, Jessica scurried to the back of the chair and crouched down, carefully sliding a nearby

box closer for more concealment. Now she had ample cover-
age from the crooks.

"You could at least look relieved."

"Get out of here," he snarled under his breath.

Conor quickly lowered his head and continued to watch
the burglars from half-closed eyes. At least they hadn't seen
her slip behind his chair.

His head began pounding like drums at a bongo festival.
He'd just thought it hurt before. If they spotted her, she'd be
killed right alongside him. His insides spit and hissed like fat
on a grill. He tried to blot out the vision of Jessica's lifeless
body, a bullet hole . . .

That wouldn't happen. They'd escape. Then she'd be safe.
And *he'd* kill her!

"The least you can say is thanks. I *am* risking my life to
save your ungrateful butt. By the way, how's your head? I
saw Al whack you."

"Your friend's aim was off. I'll live." At least he hoped so.
He wanted to kill Jessica himself, and he couldn't do that if
he were dead. "Please, get out of here while you still have the
chance."

"Nope. And Al's no longer my friend. He used me to get
information on who to burglarize. I owe him one."

"Jessica, leave. Now. Go get help."

"I'm not stupid, Conor." The man gave her absolutely no
credit. If they were going to have a relationship, things would
have to change. "I called Dad. They should be on the way
and as soon as I give the word, they'll storm the building."

"Good, now get the hell out of here."

"Not without you."

Why would he think she'd listen to him now when she
hadn't in the past? She wouldn't leave after George caught
them kissing that first day. He should've called a halt to the
operation then.

"Don't go to sleep on me, Conor."

"I'm not asleep." Aggravating woman.

"Call for backup then."

"Can't. I just tried my phone. No signal. Too much metal. I don't suppose you have a radio handy?"

"It's clipped to my belt."

"They didn't search you?" Surprise laced her words.

"Remember who we're dealing with."

"You have a point there."

"They found my gun and didn't look any further. They missed the radio. Get it and call for help."

"Gotcha."

Her hand slid between the back of the chair and the seat. To his way of thinking, she took an extra long time feeling around until she had the radio unclipped. Surely he was imagining things. This was serious. They could both end up dead. Jessica must understand the danger. At least he hoped she did.

"Okay, got it, but I'm not calling until we're both out of the way of flying bullets."

He didn't have time to argue the point. "Then cut me loose, but hurry." If they became aware someone else had joined him, he might at least be able to put himself between her and danger.

"Uh, I don't suppose you have a knife on you?"

She didn't have a weapon? What had she planned on doing? Throwing the stolen loot at the bad guys? He let out his breath, telling himself to calm down. They might get out of this yet.

"Strapped to my right calf. Try not to cut my leg off when you bring it out of the sheath."

"Don't tempt me, or I'll cut a little higher," she mumbled.

"What?" He wasn't sure he'd understood her.

"Nothing. I'll slide under the chair. See if you can bring your leg back so I can reach it."

"Wait," he whispered as Al started to turn around.

Barry said something, drawing the other man's attention

long enough for Jessica to scramble back to her position behind the chair, and for him to feign unconsciousness again.

Conor tried to make his breathing slower than normal, but
it wasn't easy when his heart raced ninety miles an hour.
After a few moments, he glanced through partially lowered
lashes.

"Okay. All clear. Jessica?"

"What?"

"If they see you, make a run for it. Don't look back. Promise me." When she didn't say anything, he added, "Please."

"Sure thing."

A couple of grunts and Jessica's hand snaked inside his
pant leg. His muscles tensed as her silky softness caressed
him. He bit back a groan. Damn it, this was no time to get
sexually aroused. But if she didn't hurry, that's exactly what
would happen.

All thoughts of making love to her disappeared as she slid
the knife from its holder. He kept the blade razor-sharp. He
only hoped she realized that one wrong move and she could
cut either one of them.

"You can breathe again," she whispered.

How did she know? She was going to drive him crazy. "Be
careful. It's sharp."

"Ugh, I hate knives."

"Tell me again why you became a cop?"

"Very funny, Conor."

The ropes binding his left arm loosened. He kept still. If
they happened to glance his way, it would appear as if he
were still bound. A few seconds later and one arm was free.

"I have-a to take a . . ." George cleared his throat. "I
mean, I gotta take a leak. I'll check on the prisoner."

"Yeah, yeah." Al waved him away with a look of disgust
on his face.

Sweat beaded Conor's brow. He hoped Jessica would have
the sense to get the hell out of there if George spotted her.

With one arm unbound, he'd be able to hold them off long enough for her to escape. He hoped.

"You are not-a so smart as you think-a, eh?" George spoke in a loud voice. In a whisper, he continued. "I will-a not let them kill-a you, *mio amico*. You helped me with-a Trudy and I do not-a forget my friends."

Good old George.

"Are you awake-a, Conor?"

"Yes, I'm awake-a . . . awake."

"I will slip-a you the knife to cut-a the rope." Turning sideways, he glanced back toward Al and his family, then spoke in a louder voice, "Everything is fine. He's still unconscious."

"Just do your business and get back to work. I want to leave in the next thirty minutes." Al looked disgusted that he'd gotten a smudge on his suit and seemed more worried about brushing it clean.

"Yes, sir."

George slid his hand inside his pocket and pulled out a switchblade. Keeping it close to his side, he pushed the release button. The blade jumped out, gleaming as it caught the overhead lights.

"Run like-a the wind, *mio amico*. Do not look back." Keeping his gaze on the truck being loaded, George dropped the knife.

Conor inhaled sharply and jerked his legs apart. The point imbedded itself in the wooden seat of the chair, landing a hairsbreadth from making him a soprano. Like a tight wire that'd been twanged, the knife quivered for a few seconds before coming to a halt. A bead of sweat trickled down his face.

George sauntered away without looking back.

Snickers came from behind his chair.

Damn it, this wasn't funny. He eased his hand away and cut the other rope before closing the knife and slipping it in his pocket.

"Do you realize what will happen if you're caught?" His words came out harsher than he'd intended.

"You worry too much."

"Will you please call for backup?"

"If you'll quit interrupting me. What do you think I'm doing back here? Twiddling my thumbs?"

He opened his mouth, then snapped it closed. Arguing with her would only make matters worse. Besides, he didn't think he'd win.

"Five-twenty-five to five hundred, give us five minutes, then join the party."

As soon as she let off the mic, he realized her mistake. Static from the radio echoed across the cavernous room.

Al whirled around.

Chapter 21

"Run!" Conor breathed as Al slipped his hand inside his coat. "For God's sake, Jessica! Get the hell out of here while you have the chance!"

"I'm not leaving you."

Too late. Al brought out his revolver. Glancing from side to side, he made his way across the room. Conor kept still so he wouldn't realize the ropes were cut.

"Who's there?" Al yelled.

Barry, George, and their father all looked toward Conor. Barry set a box down and picked up a crowbar that leaned against the side of the truck. As he approached Conor, he slapped it against the palm of his hand.

"Now what?" the old man asked.

"I heard something." Al never took his eyes from Conor's face. "I see our guest is awake."

"You probably just heard him," George supplied.

Al shook his head. "No, it was a scratchy noise."

"I knew from the start there was something sleazy about you," Conor spoke loudly, hoping to distract him. "I'm surprised Jessica didn't pick up on how worthless a human being you are."

"Not exactly worthless." Al preened. "I've made quite a haul from my export business. And how much easier can it be to case a joint when Jessica's the one showing the property? Of course, we robbed other houses so there wouldn't be a pattern." He laughed gleefully. "But she was nice enough to supply me with plenty of information. Even told me Daddy was getting close. I didn't realize he was *this* close, though. But then, you apparently haven't informed him we're closing shop, either, or they'd be all over us by now." He frowned as he dusted a speck of dirt from his white suit.

Stall them. Keep them talking until backup arrived, and he and Jessica might just make it out of this in one piece.

"Why would the chief's daughter tell you anything?"

"Oh, she didn't know she was giving away family secrets. But she was proud of her papa and the work he does. It only took a little nudging for her to ramble on about the burglars and the problems they were causing him. A little info here—" he shrugged "—a little there."

The box behind Conor's chair tumbled over. He froze.

Al stepped to the side of the chair. His eyes narrowed as his grip tightened on the gun. "Come out from behind there!"

Conor's guts twisted into knots. "You hurt her, and I'll make sure you die a slow and painful death."

Jessica stood. "You really should pick up a little around here. It's very dangerous having all these boxes in the way. Not to mention the dust."

How could she act so calm? Didn't she know what could happen? Even if backup arrived in the next few minutes, bullets were bound to fly. "I told you to run. Why didn't you?"

She shrugged. "It's only Al." Her gaze raked over the other man as if he were an ugly little bug she was about to squash. "Besides, when I run at night my heart rate speeds up and it's hours before I can fall asleep."

"Well, you'll probably sleep good tonight—at the bottom of a river." Of all the females, how the hell had he gotten stuck with her?

"Oh, Conor, don't be so dramatic."

Him—dramatic! He clenched his jaw. He'd show her *dramatic* if they got out of this alive. "Jessica . . ."

"Shut up!" Al screamed waving his gun between them. His right hand began to twitch. Conor took a deep breath, hoping Al's condition wouldn't spread to his trigger finger.

"Al, you don't look so good." Jessica clicked her tongue in feigned concern. "Your face is blotchy."

"She's right," Winston pointed out unnecessarily. "You ain't gonna throw up or nothin', are you?"

"No!" Al's voice hit a note high enough to shatter crystal. "Just shut up! I want everyone to shut up!"

"Hey, what's that?" Barry bent and picked up the radio Jessica had kicked under the chair.

Al's eyes bulged. "A police radio, you idiot." His body began to shake so hard Conor expected him to break into small pieces any second. Oh jeez, and Jessica looked like she was ready to take them all on by herself. When she opened her mouth, he knew instinctively nothing good would come out.

"You're going down, Al." Jessica planted her hands on her hips and glared at the quivering leader. "You might as well give up."

"It's all your fault! My mother warned me about girls like you."

"Too bad you didn't listen." Jessica smirked.

Al growled as he raised his gun. Conor jumped to his feet just as Jessica twisted her body and kicked. The gun flew out of Al's hand at the same time Conor landed a thudding punch to the surprised man's jaw.

"Look out!" Jessica cried.

Barry raised his arm, ready to bring the crowbar down on Conor's head, but Jessica's warning gave him enough time to jump and roll out of the way.

In a flash of movement, Jessica brought her arm down in a perfectly executed karate chop. Then, with well-placed aim, she kicked him in the balls. Barry doubled over, gasping for breath.

The old man grabbed her from behind. She bent and

dropped to one knee. The elder of the Meredith clan flew over her shoulder, landing with a thud and a grunt.

"I'm your friend!" George's high-pitched scream echoed through the warehouse. "I gave him a knife."

"Chill out, George," Jessica said.

Conor looked around him. Barry's hands were between his legs and he was coughing. The old man looked dazed. And Al wasn't moving. Okay, so maybe he'd done that one. At least he'd been good for something.

She could've at least told him she knew some defense . . . Visions flooded his mind. The chief had mentioned Jessica could handle herself. Angie had told him the same thing. Even Jessica had tried to tell him. He looked at her now.

She shrugged. "I tried to tell you, but you didn't seem terribly interested."

"But . . . but . . . this?" He waved his arm around the room.

"I had to protect myself. Growing up in a nearly all-male family can be hard on a girl. I took a few karate classes."

"A few?"

She rolled her eyes toward the roof. "Okay, I'm a black belt."

He planted his fists on his hips. "This is information I think would've been nice to share with me."

Al staggered to his feet. With barely a glance, Conor turned and punched him in the face. With an expulsion of air, Al wobbled back to the floor. Damn, that felt good.

He faced Jessica again. "I might not have worried quite so much if I'd known that little fact."

"You were worried? About me? Why?"

"I think you know why." He pulled her into his arms and gazed down into her face. He loved Jessica with all his heart, and he wanted her for his wife, but did she feel the same way? He hesitated.

The warehouse doors banged open. Officers spilled into the room. Jessica stepped out of his embrace. A cold chill swept over him. Was she rejecting him?

"Jessica, are you okay?" The chief rushed to his daughter's side.

She turned. "Sure, Dad, never better."

"Good job, both of you." Her father beamed, slapping Conor on the back and hugging Jessica to him. "I knew you could do it." He sneered at the burglars. "Get these maggots in handcuffs and loaded in the cars."

Conor willed Jessica to look at him, but she refused to meet his eyes. He couldn't let her go. He wouldn't. He took a step toward her.

"Conor! Tell-a them I helped you to escape. I am-a your friend." George's voice raised an octave with each word.

Conor glanced over his shoulder. Two officers were handcuffing George. "Hey," he nodded toward the little guy. "Could you take it easy on him?"

They didn't have to know it was Jessica who cut the ropes. George's heart had been in the right place. The poor guy looked scared out of his wits. He'd make sure the courts went easy on him. He might even get probation. He'd be in enough trouble when Trudy got hold of him.

Something occurred to Conor. "Hey, George, do you know anything about the items that were taken from the mayor's house?"

"The jewels, they were-a fenced."

So they *were* the burglars. "What about a tape?" Maybe if the video was returned, the chief's job wouldn't be on the line.

"The only tape we have-a . . ." He shot a glance toward Jessica. "Excus-a, it is not-a so nice a tape. If-a you know what I mean. It was-a in the mayor's vault with-a the jewels. We shoved everything-a into the sack and it-a went, too." He stood a little straighter. "I know a little about-a filmmaking. I've been in the movies myself-a. This one is very, very poor quality."

"Where would that tape be?" the chief asked.

"In-a the glove compartment of the truck."

"You don't think the mayor has a secret life? You know, that he might have made a dirty . . . uh . . . ." her words trailed as she glanced at both men. "That would explain its importance, since this is an election year."

"My job was on the line because the mayor was caught with his pants down?"

"Literally, I believe," Conor commented.

"But you can't be sure it's the mayor," Jessica put in.

"There's only one way to find out." With purposeful strides her father strode to the truck and yanked the door open. After rummaging around inside, he slammed the door and joined them, tape in hand.

"We'll take it back to the office and see exactly what's so important it almost cost me my job." His expression was grim.

"There is-a VCR and TV in-a the room at-a the back," George supplied.

They looked at each other. Without speaking a word, all three moved to the rear of the warehouse. Once inside the small office, Conor turned the TV on while the chief slipped the tape into the machine.

The screen went from dark to light. A man and two women were in bed together, but they weren't sleeping.

"I'd say that's the mayor, but neither of the women resembles his wife." Jessica stated the obvious. "This tape is a little more upscale than the last one I watched, though."

Frowning, the chief reached across and snapped the TV off. "And since when did my daughter make a habit of watching porno films?"

"All in the line of duty, Dad."

"Humph!"

"What are you going to do now?" Conor asked.

"I'm not giving the tape to the mayor, if that's what you're asking. He's been a thorn in the city's side for some time. Changing the zoning laws so his friends could open their sleazy businesses. Always been too wily to get caught. I think this should put a stop to him."

"Good for you, Dad."

"Well, that about wraps this case up. I guess you'll be glad to get back to your own homes." His eyes filled with warmth when he glanced at his daughter. "I know you've never wanted to work as a cop. I appreciate what you did for me."

Here it comes, Conor thought. She'd tell her father just how much she hates law enforcement. His gut wrenched with pain. He didn't want to lose her.

"Actually, Dad, I enjoyed it. In fact, I was thinking maybe I didn't give it a chance. Like everyone has told me, what I did could've happened to anyone. Maybe wearing a skirt isn't all it's cracked up to be, either." She looped her arm through her father's and started toward the door. "What do you think about me becoming an undercover cop? I have the skills . . ."

"No."

They both turned and stared at Conor.

"It's too dangerous. No wife of mine is going to put her life in jeopardy. I'm not going to sit at home and worry about where the hell you are."

She slipped her arm from her father's and walked the few feet to stand in front of Conor. "That's about the most unromantic proposal I've ever heard."

He looked everywhere but at her. "Well, will you?"

"Will I what?"

He'd jumped into it with both feet this time. Taking a deep breath, he met her gaze head-on. "Marry me."

"Of course I'll marry you. I love you."

She'd said yes. His heart pounded. She loved him. They'd be a family. He wanted to laugh and shout at the same time. Grinning, he tried to pay attention to what she was saying.

"We could be partners, you know, undercover. Like Marty and Angie. After all, I have redeemed myself by helping catch the Meredith gang. Unless another goat comes along." She began to pace in front of him as she thought out loud. "We need more than just burglars, though. Something with a little more substance."

"No wife of mine is going undercover." What the hell was she thinking? Going undercover . . . no way.

She snapped her fingers. "I know. I could pretend I'm a hooker." She struck a seductive pose and tossed her hair over her shoulders. "You know, a woman of the night . . ."

There was only one way to get her mind off this ridiculous notion. He pulled her into his arms and brought his mouth down on hers. A couple of seconds passed before she softly moaned and began to kiss back. If he had to kiss her the rest of their married life, he would. Anything to keep her from harm.

He pulled away and gazed into her eyes. "No more foolish talk?"

"Kiss me again."

"You won't ever mention this crazy scheme about wanting to be an undercover cop?"

She shook her head. "No, Conor. Now kiss me."

He happily obliged.

She sighed, tangling her fingers into his hair. She really was going to hell for lying.

Here's a sneak peek at
MaryJanice Davidson's next Brava novel,
THE ROYAL PAIN,
available in November 2005 . . .

Shel Rivers looked down at the small foot wedged in his doorway, then up at the ridiculously good-looking woman attached to said foot. She didn't look mad or pissed or haughty. Just had a patient look on her face, like, *You're gonna get this thing off my foot, right?*

Finally, he said, "That's a good way to break something," after a moment that felt longer than it was.

"Not before you get shot," she replied, and shouldered her way past him. A good trick, since he had, at best estimation, four inches and thirty pounds on her. He got a whiff of lilacs as she brushed by, and he almost reached out to see if her black, shoulder-length hair was as silky as it looked. "Dr. Rivers and I will be right out," she added, and closed the door on the protests of everyone else in the party.

The princess (princess! in his lab!) looked around the small, cluttered room for a moment, her small hands on shapely hips. Then she glanced back at him. He actually forgot to breathe when those crystal blue eyes fixed on his.

"I don't think we've been properly introduced," she said pleasantly.

"And I don't think your security team is going to like this at all."

"I'm Alexandria Baranov—"

"I know."

"I'm talking now, please. And you're Dr. Rivers. You're also rude and annoying, which is fine, but *nobody* slams a door on me."

"Especially when your family built half the aquarium," he snapped, trying not to look at her breasts.

"Irrelevant. I wouldn't tolerate that behavior if *you* were funding *my* work. What a disaster area," she continued, turning in a circle to take in the whole room. "How do you find anything in here?"

"None of your business."

"I think we could find some paperwork to prove that isn't true. What's so important? What are you working on?"

"Is playing twenty questions part of the tour?"

"No, it's part of being relatively pleasant. And why did you dodge the tour? You don't even know me."

Because she was rich. Because he was busy. Because she was a princess and he was a lowly army brat. Because she was too beautiful. Because she was trouble with a capital T, and he'd had enough of that to last five lifetimes.

She was waving a hand in front of his eyes. "Dr. Rivers? Hellooooo? Is anyone in there? Is it lunchtime already?"

He jerked his head back and gave her a good glare. "I've got more important things to do than play tour guide for a stuck-up VIP."

He was sure she'd get pissed, but instead, those amazing blue eyes crinkled at the corners and she grinned. "I bet you don't," she said, and turned to reach for the door handle.

"Okay, okay," he said, grasping her elbow. She took his wrist and pulled it away, almost absently, and in the bottom of his brain a small red flag popped up. "I'll give you the damned tour. But no annoying questions."

"You're a fine one to talk about annoying," she retorted.

"And no potty breaks."

"I went on the plane."

"And I'm not going to be doing this all day, either."

"You can't," she pointed out. "I'm having lunch with Dr. Tomlin in three hours."

And here's a hilarious look
at Gemma Bruce's
WHO LOVES YA, BABY?
coming in November 2005 from Brava . . .

The night was suddenly still. Cas peered into the woods again. He would swear someone was standing just inside the ring of trees, out of the moonlight. He rolled tight shoulders and cracked his neck. What the hell was he doing in Ex Falls, chasing burglars through the woods?

He snorted. His just deserts. He'd chased Julie through these woods more times than he could remember. And caught her. He smiled, forgetting where he was for a moment. He'd been pretty damn good at Cops and Robbers in those days. He'd been even better at Pirates.

A rustle in the trees. *Wind? No wind tonight.* Another rustle. Not a nocturnal animal, but a glimmer of white. All right, time to act, or he might still be standing here when the sun rose, and someone was bound to see him and by tomorrow night, it would be all over town that he had spent the night hiding behind a bush with an empty gun while the thieves got away.

Cas said a quick prayer that he was out of range and stepped away from the bush. He braced his feet in the standard two-handed shooting stance he learned from *NYPD Blue,* and aimed into the darkness. He sucked in his breath.

A figure stepped out to the edge of the trees. There was just enough light for Cas to see the really big handgun that was aimed at him.

The "freeze" he'd been about to yell froze on his lips.

"Freeze," said a deep voice from the darkness.

Hey, that was his line. He froze anyway, then yelped, "Police."

"Yeah. So drop the weapon and put your hands in the air. Slowly."

Cas dropped his gun. "No. I mean. Me. I'm the police."

"You're the sheriff? A sound like strangling. "Why didn't you say so?"

"I did. I was going to, but you—Who are you?"

"I'm the one who called you." The figure stepped into the moonlight. Not a thief, but an angel. Not an angel, but a vision that was the answer to every man's wet dream. A waterfall of long dark hair fell past slim shoulders and over a shimmering white shift that clung to every curve of a curvaceous body. His eyes followed the curves down to a pair of long, dynamite legs, lovely knees, tapering to . . . a pair of huge, untied work boots. He recognized the boots, they were his, but not the apparition that was wearing them.

He must be dreaming. That was it. It wouldn't be the first time he'd dreamed of Julie coming back to him. Her hair long and soft like this, hair a man could wrap his body in. A body that he could wrap his soul in. Mesmerized, Cas took a step toward her. She stepped back into the cover of the trees, disappearing into the darkness like a wraith. He took another step toward her and was stopped by a warning growl. His testicles climbed up to his rib cage. *Stay calm. It's just a dream.* Strange. He'd imagined Julie as many things—but never as a werewolf.

He barely registered the beast as it leapt through the air, flying toward him as if it had wings. *Time to wake up,* he told himself. *Now.*

He hit the ground and was pinned there by a ton of black fur and bad breath. The animal bared its teeth. Cas squeezed his eyes shut and felt a rough, wet tongue rasp over his face.

"Off, Smitty."

Cas heard the words, felt the beast being hauled off him. He slowly opened his eyes to find himself looking up at six legs: four muscular and furry; two, muscular and sleek—and definitely female. He had to stop himself from reaching out to caress them.

Her companion growled and Cas yanked his eyes away to stare warily at the dog. He was pretty sure it was a dog. A really big dog.

"Never lower your firearm on a perp who might be armed." She waved the muzzle of her weapon in Cas's direction, then leaned over and picked up his .38 from the ground. She looked at it. "And maybe, next time, you should try loading this." She dropped it into his lap and heaved a sigh that lifted her shoulders and stretched the fabric of her shirt across her breasts. And Cas forgot about the dog, as he imagined sucking on the hard nipples that showed through the silk.

She stomped past him, shaking her head. The dog trotted after her.

Cas watched them—watched her—walk away, her hair trailing behind her, the work boots adding a hitch to her walk that swung her butt from side to side and set the fabric, shifting and sliding against her body. And he wanted to touch her, slide his fingers inside the shift, and feel warm, firm flesh beneath his fingers. But mostly he wanted to touch her hair.

Halfway to the house, she paused and looked over her shoulder. "They're getting away," she said and continued toward the house.

After a stupefied second, he pushed himself off the ground. What was happening to him? He never thought about groping strange women, even magical ones like this one. He licked his lips, stuck his .38 in his jacket pocket and followed after her.

When he reached the porch, she was at the front door. So was the dog.

"Uh, miss . . . ma'am? If you'd call off the dog, I could take down some information."

He saw a flick of her hand and he had to keep himself from diving for the bushes, but the dog merely padded past her into the house.

"Well, if you're not going to chase the thieves, you may as well come in," she said and turned to go inside.

"Wait," he cried.

She stopped midstep.

"You might want to leave those boots on the porch."

She looked down at the work boots, sniffed, then wrinkled her nose. "Oh." She leaned over to pull them off.

Her ass tightened beneath the soft nightshirt, and Cas had a tightening response of his own. He shifted uncomfortably and stared at the mailbox until he got himself under control.

This was ridiculous. He should be used to this. For three months, women called him in all sorts of getups at all hours of the night. He was, after all, the town's most eligible bachelor. Actually he was the town's only eligible bachelor. None of them had the least affect on him. But this one knocked him right out of his socks. Made his dick throb, just looking at her. She might not be Julie, but she looked pretty damn good. He might as well find out who she was and what she was doing here—and how long she planned to stay.

"Coming?" she asked and let the screen door slam behind her.

Oh yeah, thought Cas, *I'm coming*.

And here's a first look at Erin McCarthy's
THE PREGNANCY TEST
available now from Brava . . .

She covered her face with her hand. "God, I think I'm blushing. This is just so unbelievable."

"But in such a good way." Damien put his hand on the small of Mandy's back and herded her in the direction of the hotel shop.

Good thing it was a short walk, because now that he had been given the green light by Mandy, he was more than a little eager. He was on fucking fire.

Mandy hung back in the store, hovering over by the imported magazines displayed both in English and Spanish, her cheeks a charming pink. Damien didn't feel any embarrassment whatsoever. He strode over to the counter and asked the clerk, "Where are the condoms?"

Why waste even five minutes looking for them?

The man, in his late twenties, grinned at Damien and pointed behind him. "Individual or a box?"

"Box." No sense in having to repeat this shopping expedition if things went according to plan.

The clerk slapped the box down on the counter, and Damien studied the busty Hispanic woman in a bikini on the front. The carton was bright yellow, the bikini a violent orange, and while the label was in English, the small script was in Spanish. He hoped like hell these weren't novelty condoms. He wasn't wearing anything with parrots on it.

"Would you like some Mamajuana, too? Good stuff." The man pointed to a bottle of what looked like alcohol, shelved next to the rum.

"What is it?" Not that he had any intention of getting drunk. He wanted to remember every second of this.

"You drink it. We call it Dominican Viagra." The clerk winked. "Helps you last, if you know what I mean. If this doesn't work, they say you should just go and kill yourself."

Did he look like he needed Viagra? What the hell. He was so hard he could moonlight as a woodpecker. Damien shook his head. "I don't need any help, thanks." He handed over the six hundred pesos for the condoms, which he shoved in his pocket, and turned to find Mandy. She was biting her lip, arms over her chest, staring vacantly at a display of T-shirts.

"Have fun!" the clerk yelled with a knowing grin.

And people thought New Yorkers were rude.

Fortunately, he'd forgotten how to blush. But Mandy looked like she'd spent too long in the sun, so he took her hand and hustled her outside to the quiet walkway that led to the main lobby.

And kissed her eagerly.

"Damien," she protested, trying to pull back. "There are people around."

"No, there aren't. Not a single one." The path was deserted, everyone still down at the buffet, and it was lush with foliage, and thick with humidity in the glow of faux gas lamps.

But she was still darting her eyes around, hands pressed on his chest to hold him at bay. So Damien dropped his mouth to her forehead and gave her a soft kiss. "My room is in the first building on the right."

"Then it's closer than mine. I'm by the adults-only pool." But she didn't move in the direction he had pointed to. She worried her lip, and Damien watched her, waited for her to say what was on her mind. "I just want you to understand that I don't usually . . . I don't sleep around. I thought Ben really cared about me, and well, I've never really fancied one-night stands. But that's all this can be, because I can't get in-volved with anyone until I've sorted out my own life."

Damien brushed a hair back that had caught on her lip. "This isn't a one-night stand. It's not just about sex. It's about being together, enjoying each other, if only for a few hours." It was about loosening the suffocating chains of loneliness and reaching out for something simple and uncompli-cated. "But I'm not looking for a relationship, either."

He couldn't believe he was about to admit this, but he wanted her to understand, wanted her to know what this—she—meant to him. "I haven't been with a woman in three years."

"You haven't been in a relationship in three years?"

"Yes, but I also haven't had sex in three years."

Understanding dawned in her eyes. "Oh. Oh, my." She stroked his forearm. "Since Jess?"

He nodded, not willing to say any more. "That's been a conscious choice I've made, and now I'm making the conscious choice to change that. Let me have you tonight, Mandy."

There was no way she was going to say no. He could read the acquiescence in her eyes, the way she leaned toward him, stroked his arms and opened her mouth. Her breasts pressed against him as she tilted her head to the side and gave a small, sweet sigh.

"Oh, I'm not a bloody idiot, Damien. I have every inten-tion of doing this—I just needed to make sure we were clear on what it was, and that you don't think I'm some sort of swinger who sleeps with her boss in the Caribbean on every job she takes."

He raised an eyebrow. "That definitely wasn't on your ré-sumé."

She gave a soft laugh and wet her lips, making him want to suck on both her lip and her tongue, taking turns. "What if I don't meet your expectations? Three years is a long time to wait. I'd hate to be a disappointment."

That was a joke. He'd be lucky if he got a full five seconds in her before he exploded. "As long as you don't have some sort of objection to oral sex, we'll be fine. I have it in my head that I'd really like to taste you."

Her breathing quickened. "Funny, that. I had a dream you were doing that very thing to me, and I was really quite enjoying it."

Damien's groin tightened. What the hell were they doing standing here then?

"You know, you're usually much more efficient than this. Move it, Mandy. Before I drop your sundress here on the sidewalk." And he reached for her zipper.

Mandy had taken Damien's threat seriously, and a quick two minutes later they were in his room, her beach bag tumbling to the floor as she reached for the buttons on his linen shirt.

She'd seen the way he looked in his swim trunks that afternoon and she wanted to touch that broad chest. She wanted to explore his hard flesh, make him tremble with want. She wanted to draw this all out and enjoy every blasted second of it since she was facing a future of celibacy.

Damien's own hands were busy unzipping the back of her dress. But whereas she was fumbling, overeager, nervous, he was quiet, studied, intent. Goose bumps rose on her flesh as his fingers trailed over her back. His room was at the end of the hall, remote, the sounds of the resort buffered by palm trees and flowering plants. The whirr of the ceiling fan and the uneven tempo of their breathing were the only sounds in the room.

All her doubts, all her concerns, fear about how she should behave and how he might react to her pregnancy, her body the way it was now, had all evaporated when Damien told her he hadn't been with a woman in three years. She'd seen it then, what he had been telling her. That they both needed each other, just here, just now, to touch and taste and push on each other in uncomplicated pleasure.

She wanted that. She wanted him.

Buttons free, she spread his shirt and sighed as the palms of her hands caressed hard, warm muscle. "You have a lovely chest."

His lips quirked up. "What a coincidence. I was thinking the same thing about you."

Mandy glanced down and saw that with the zipper undone, her dress had slipped a bit, only to come to a crashing halt at her cleavage. Nothing could get past her newly blossoming breasts, and her plump flesh was bursting out of the top of her strapless bra.

"This isn't my natural state, you know," she told him, pushing his shirtsleeves down to his wrists. "Every day I wake up to find they're a bit bigger, like I've taken an air pump to them."

Damien's thumb ran over the swell above the bra. "I like the end result."

"Yes, well, easy for you to say." Mandy gripped his wrist as his thumb brushed lower and lower, skirting her nipple. She gave a sound of disappointment. "But at this rate, I fully expect one day to roll over and have them clap."

He laughed, expression relaxed and amused. "I love your sense of humor."

She was about to tell him that back in England, at the Wycombe Abbey School for Girls, she'd been quite the comedic thespian, but she only had time to open her mouth before he ripped her dress down to her waist, and she promptly forgot how to speak.

Or breathe, when his head descended to her chest and his tongue traced above the rim of her overburdened bra. Back and forth it went, as if it was on a leisurely stroll in the park, and Mandy shivered, appreciating fully how much more sensitive her breasts were now. Torn between wanting to just enjoy his teasing tongue and urging him to dispense with her bra and head south to her nipple, Mandy gripped his wrists and squeezed.

Damien lifted his head, and Mandy expected him to shove her dress down, strip himself, and slide right into her standing up.

Or maybe that was just wishful thinking.

But she had expected Damien to be urgent, to take charge, to rush through to the release they were both seeking.

He was taking charge, yes, but he wasn't interested in rushing. Which had its pros and cons.

As she tugged his shirt off and dropped it to the floor, Damien pulled the clip out of her hair. He stroked in it and smiled. "I love your hair. It's just like you. Sort of free, with a mind of its own, but always in control."

Was that the way he saw her? Mandy thought that was just a lovely way to describe her, even if she felt control was the last thing she possessed. Unable to resist touching him, she smoothed out his dark eyebrows, traced his cheeks, brushed along his lips in a caress that was too intimate, but felt so, so right here with Damien. His lips pressed in a kiss over her fingers and she smiled, knowing she felt as raw and vulnerable as she looked.